OA___

A LORDS OF ACTION NOVEL, VOLUME 3

K.J. JACKSON

First Edition: January 2017
ISBN: 978-1-940149-21-9
http://www.kjjackson.com

K.J. Jackson Books
Historical Romance:
Stone Devil Duke, *A Hold Your Breath Novel*
Unmasking the Marquess, *A Hold Your Breath Novel*
My Captain, My Earl, *A Hold Your Breath Novel*
Worth of a Duke, *A Lords of Fate Novel*
Earl of Destiny, *A Lords of Fate Novel*
Marquess of Fortune, *A Lords of Fate Novel*
Vow, *A Lords of Action Novel*
Promise, *A Lords of Action Novel*
Oath, *A Lords of Action Novel*

Paranormal Romance:
Flame Moon
Triple Infinity, *Flame Moon #2*
Flux Flame, *Flame Moon #3*

Be sure to sign up for news of my next releases at
www.KJJackson.com

DEDICATION

– As Always,
For my favorite Ks

{ CHAPTER 1 }

The tapping of boot heels coming down the marble stairs made Miss Livia Somerson lean tight against the cool stone. She knew she needed to hide, and she hoped the darkness of the slight shadow casting downward from the stone staircase was enough—at least until the source of the clomping boots disappeared into the night.

Breath held, her head crooked at an odd angle, she watched from the dark corner where the staircase met Baron Swenhall's manor. The back of her cerulean blue skirts ground into the wall, surely getting impossibly dirty. But that, she would just have to suffer.

Concealing herself from the descending lone man was far more important.

His boots crunching onto the granite gravel of the pathway, the man paused at the bottom of the staircase, looking both to the right and left.

Please to the left. Please to the left. Please.

He stepped to the right, moving from the direct light spilling down from the ballroom and along the path to the outer perimeter of the neat boxwood-lined gardens. Stopping, he surveyed the gardens, or the fields and forest beyond them, or the half-moon night sky—she wasn't sure which, and didn't care, just so long as his attention stayed in the exact opposite direction of the house.

Liv stared at the backside of the man. He was tall—very tall, with black boots and breeches, and a crisp dark jacket that sat tightly on his shoulders, making his form blend into the massive darkness beyond. Only his hair, dark blond and unruly enough to be rakish, but cut longer than fashion dictated, reflected the scant light from the ballroom.

The smooth stone behind her chilled the flush on her neck—the whole reason she had dived into the shadows—and she prayed the sheep she could hear bleating past the gardens kept up their racket, as it was the only thing that could drown out the pounding of her heart.

It started just below her ribs. The air bubble she could not control.

Drat that punch. Drat that her mother had never let her taste something so deliciously wonderful as that drink until tonight.

If only she had known.

Blast it. Even if she had known, she still would have sipped her way through six glasses of the concoction in the last hour. Probably more.

She swallowed against the air. It fought back.

Hiccup.

Her gloved hand slammed against her mouth, mortification setting in at the sound. It had been as loud as the great bell of Bow. She hadn't fathomed that uncontrollable body sounds would be part of the delicious dizziness in her head.

The figure in front of her spun around and took a step toward her.

Heaven help her. Wrong. She had been very wrong. He wasn't just tall. He was huge. Huge and looking straight through the shadows at her face.

Her hand dropping to her side, Liv dug the heels of her slippers into the ground, pressing herself flatter against the stone. Not that it would do any good.

He took another step toward her. "Are you spying?" His voice was a low rumble. From any other man, the deep baritone would sound odd, but the voice perfectly matched the size of him. He looked at her with suspicion, the hard lines of his face culminating in a frown that looked permanent.

"Spying?" *Hiccup.* Her humiliation reached a new height of ridiculousness. Her hand clamped over her mouth again as she glanced upward, trying to see past the French glass doors that led to the ballroom at the top of the stairs. "Far from it."

"What are you doing out here…Miss…?"

Her gaze dropped to him, her voice just above a whisper. "I apologize. I have no nefarious intentions here in the shadows. I just did not expect anyone to remove themselves to the Baron's gardens just yet. It is still early in the eve."

"Yes, it is early." He looked up at the ballroom doors. "But I am out here to escape an inordinately ambitious title-hungry mama that cornered me direct and was entirely too forward about her daughter that recently came out and…" His sentence rambled before he realized the inherent rudeness, and his words faded.

Liv sighed with a groan, tucking a dark strand of hair that had escaped her upsweep with the last hiccup behind her ear. "My mother? Mrs. Somerson?"

"I did not hear her name, as she interrupted introductions to rush on so." His look dropped to her. "So you are the pup she was glowing about?"

"I imagine, yes." Liv nodded. "Of the eligible women inside, I am the only one present that has an ambitious matchmaking mama. She was dressed in silver, crown to toe?"

His lips drew back into a tight line with a nod. Almost apologetic, but not quite.

He looked over his shoulder awkwardly—searching for escape once more, Liv imagined.

"I take no offense, sir." Liv couldn't hold him at fault for his lack of contrition. Her mother had one goal in mind that evening, and that was to gain an introduction between her and Lord Reggard—or any other eligible bachelor at hand, as this poor gentleman had just experienced. "My mother is an enthusiastic bulldog when it comes to making a proper match for me. I fear for Lord Reggard when he appears. She will latch onto him, teeth bared, and refuse to let go."

His look snapped back to her. "Lord Reggard?"

"Yes. Do you know the man? As the highest ranking gentleman to be in attendance tonight, he does not know what is coming for him when he arrives. My mother is determined to achieve introductions with the man and then serve me up to him. A stuffed pig on a platter, so to speak. She has been planning this for weeks—months." She stopped, sighing. "No. If I am adamantly honest, the last six years."

His eyes squinted, searching her out in the shadows as he took another step closer. "How old are you, Miss Somerson?"

"Sixteen."

"That seems a bit young to be served up."

"Not according to my mama. She has been in a flurry the last two years, waiting for me to come out. Ever since Papa's business has done well. She can only think of marrying me upward. This is her first ball with me to parade about, so you must forgive the hysteria she is in." *Hiccup.* Her mouth clamped shut. Blast it. Her tongue rambled and she had hoped she was done with the bubbles creating havoc in her lungs.

She craned her neck to look fully up at him.

Had he moved closer? Or had she shrunk?

Granted, she had been trying to make herself small against the wall of the building, but now she suddenly felt downright tiny. Foreign to her, for she had never felt tiny in her life—she was always a full head and a half taller than every other girl her age—courtesy of the blood from her father's Norse ancestors, he would always tell her proudly. Pride for him, awkward for her, as she had looked downward upon every boy she had ever known.

Liv's chin dropped, her look going to the lapel of his jacket. Her tongue suddenly felt huge, a great wad of fat stuck in her mouth. She mumbled words out anyway. "I have said far too much. The punch inside. I did not know it would do this to my head. Or my mouth. It is running wild without any regard to proper decorum."

His head tilted to the left, his right brow arching. "Is that why you are hiding in shadows?"

Hiccup. Liv swallowed again. The mortification of being discovered cowering in the shadows was wearing thin, and even with the fog in her head, she already recognized there would be no recourse back from the disjointed ninny she had just presented herself as.

She nodded. "Yes. You can plainly see I am in no position to be introduced to even the fifth, illegitimate son of an earl, much less an earl himself. I very well recognize that fact, even if my mother does not."

He nodded, a slight smirk lifting the side of his face. "I *can* see that."

The indiscreet smirk rankled Liv, sending ire in her belly brewing. She *knew* she was foxed. She *knew* she was acting like a dolt. But for him to agree? To smirk about it?

"The smugness lacing your assessment of my current state is not appreciated, sir." Her arms flew up, folding in front of her, the blue silk reticule dangling from her wrist swinging wild. "I may be soused, but I can still recognize eyes that reek of arrogant condemnation."

His head bowed, slightly awkward at the scolding. The whole of him, suddenly slightly awkward in his size. Awkward in his height, in his mass. "I did not intend to judge."

"I would think not." Her finger flung out from her belly, pointing at him. "Especially as I now know you are out here to hide, just the same as me."

His cheeks lifted into a smile. The smile was not awkward. The smile he wore well. Even in the dim light, she could see the smile took away all the hardness in his face.

He inclined his head to her. "There, you have me. I am a fully grown man, hiding from your wee mama. You know my secret as I know yours."

She laughed. "Exactly. I will withhold my judgment if you withhold yours."

"Deal." His head lifted as a new set of music started from beyond the French doors above them.

A swath of light from the ballroom cut across his face, lighting his eyes. Free from the shadows, they looked gentle, a light color Liv could only barely make out—maybe it was the smile that unleashed it. Not a trace of hardness remained on his face—none at all. A rather handsome face, in fact.

Staying within the line of the shadow from the staircase, she chanced a small step forward. "I cannot tell in this light—are your eyes truly blue?"

"My eyes?"

She shifted her head back and forth as she looked upward at him, trying to catch sight of his eyes in different light. "Yes, they are an interesting shade—blue when the light catches them—almost a deep violet in the shadows."

He chuckled. A low, warm sound that cut through the night air.

"What is so funny?"

He looked down at her, his eyes curious. "I believe you are the first person, other than my mother, to ever have commented on the color of my eyes."

"Well goodness, why not? They are most unusual. Even in the dim light I can see that."

He shrugged. "People usually don't bother looking up high enough to see my eyes."

"They talk to your chest?"

"Or my neck. That seems to be the tolerance for most people on how far they would like to stretch their necks backward."

Liv laughed, almost a chortle. She slapped her gloved hand over her mouth for a moment to strangle the awkward pitch. Fingers slipping from her lips, she shook her head at him. "That is terrible. I don't think I believe you."

"You will notice my cravat is impeccable. I fully well know what people will be staring at."

Liv guffawed—a true and obnoxious sound that she had never heard from her lips before. She did like this man. She liked him quite a bit. Even if he did make all manners of disturbing sounds spill from her lips.

He chuckled at the sound, the smile widening on his face. "I would presume your mama has never heard you laugh like that? I daresay she wouldn't let you out of the house if she knew you were capable of it."

Her hand thumped onto her chest, her belly still clenching in silent laughter, now at herself. "*I* have never heard me laugh like that. You, sir, never should have turned around when you heard that first hiccup. Your ears have surely been ruined for all of time. And let that be a lesson for you."

"Which is?"

"To walk away the next time you hear hiccupping in a shadowy corner. Nothing good can come of it. There is no treasure to discover wherein hiccupping exists."

His eyes met hers. "Treasures come in all shapes and sizes, Miss Sorenson."

"And sounds?"

He laughed. "Yes, and in sounds. Ear of the beholder, and all."

She grinned. "I do enjoy you, sir. Or maybe it is the punch. But I now fear what a disappointment the droll Lord Reggard will be."

"Droll?"

"How can he be anything but? Especially after the time I have had chatting with you, Mister…Mister…?"

His head tilted to the side, his right eye scrunching up as though he was bracing himself. "Lord Reggard."

"No, sir. Your name."

He sighed. "Tieran Vistel, thirteenth Earl of Reggard."

Her jaw dropped, air rushing into her throat.

He nodded, reaching out, the knuckle of his forefinger slipping under her chin and gently closing her mouth.

She slapped his hand away. "You? You are Lord Reggard? And you didn't think to advise me of that fact earlier?"

"There was not a spare moment." He shrugged. "Not between your…chatter."

"My chatter?" Her hand thumped flat onto her chest, instant indignation narrowing her eyes at him.

The natural frown returned to his lips. "Is there a better word for it?"

She exhaled, her annoyance deflating from her chest. She had been chattering. A tongue out of control. And in front of Lord Reggard, of all people. An earl. What he must think of her boorish behavior. Her mother would be mortified—all her dreams dashed.

Her eyes went wide and her gaze snapped up to him. "Please, my lord. My mother…"

"Miss Sorenson, I can see by the thousand emotions flashing across your face that you seem to be under the impression that I have not enjoyed our conversation." He took one step closer, looking down upon her. "That could not be further from the truth. I have enjoyed your company. Enjoyed it very much."

Her jaw slipped downward again. "Oh. I would have thought…"

"That as a droll earl I could not laugh—could not enjoy the amusement in the situation?"

"Possibly."

"But you are now disabused of that notion?"

A small smile, apologetic, found its way to her lips. "Yes."

"Do not worry. Your mother will only hear glowing tidbits of how I enjoyed your company. To that purpose, we will need to spend a few moments together inside the ballroom so the gossips are not forced to conjure imaginations on where our paths intersected."

She nodded, her practiced, formal debutante smile masking her face the moment he mentioned the ballroom. "Of course."

In that moment, Liv realized how very close the earl was to her, and how very petite his mass made her feel. Her eyes dropped from his face, stopping at the cut where his dark vest closed.

"The joy left your face."

Her look jumped upward. "What? I am smiling."

His frown deepened. "I never want to see a fake smile on your lips again, Miss Somerson. Pass them out at will to others. But not me. Can you do that?"

She nodded, suddenly aware at how very adept this man was at reading her every thought. While she had no inclination as to what was in his mind or even what he wanted of her—if anything at all.

"And you do not need to feed the worry that has invaded your eyes." His blue eyes raked down and then up her body. "You are far too young for the platter that I would want you presented upon. While I imagine you would be delectable, I enjoy my meat slightly seasoned."

Liv swallowed hard, not sure if it was an insult or a compliment.

He smiled, banishing the frown from his face once again. "But someday. Someday I may very well come for that platter."

"You are assuming it will not have already been eaten by another." Good heavens, her tongue had gone more wicked than she could have ever imagined it to be. If this was how she acted soused, then she needed to never touch a laced punch again.

Or touch it often. She hadn't quite decided yet which was a more enjoyable state.

Lord Reggard chuckled. "Maybe. But I don't think so. I think the meat will age properly, patiently, and be quite ready for me when I come for it."

She gave him a wicked smile. "Or it will go rancid out of sheer boredom waiting to be devoured. Especially when there is no proof of intention."

His mouth quirked into a partial smile. "No proof of intention?"

The giddiness in her head commandeering all good sense, Liv nodded.

He leaned forward, the air around him swallowing her, wrapping her, becoming her whole world. He paused for only a moment before his lips found hers.

For as large as he was, she recognized instantly his lips fit perfectly against hers—soft, slightly tangy from the punch he must have also sipped. It warmed her body down to her toes—in a way the punch could never hope to do.

The kiss so quick and so very new upon her, she kept her eyes open, taking in every specific, individual sense—smell, sight, touch, sound, flutter in her belly—and locking it into her memory.

His mouth opened against hers, his tongue slipping past her teeth, tasting her. Liv's eyes closed, surrendering to his mastery. A kiss that reached so deeply into her soul, she could feel it mark her, for all of time, as his.

He drew away slowly, that same smile that transformed his face playing along his lips. His eyebrow cocked in question. "Proof?"

The edges of her lips curled up as her mouth opened, breathless. She opened her eyes to meet his and offered one nod to his question. "Proof."

{ CHAPTER 2 }

"Is that the woman?"

Tieran's look swung to his late wife's great aunt. Aunt Penelope sat in the center of a settee upholstered with embroidered rosebuds, jabbing her cane in the air, her wrinkled hand clutching the gold gilded pigeon that topped the stick of wood.

He blinked the bleariness from his eyes. "What woman?"

Her eyes didn't veer from the crowd across the room in Lady Desmond's gambling house. "The one you were engaged to before leaving for the war."

Tieran swiveled on his side chair, his eyes jerking through the crowd, searching.

The cane cracked against his shins, instant pain running up his legs.

Damn her. She was uncannily strong for her advanced age.

"Keep your head on straight, Reggard. You look the ostrich. And those are gruesome birds—nothing to recommend them."

"I understand their meat is tasty," he said out of the side of his mouth, his eyes still mining through the crowd.

There.

Dark hair, pinned high to perfection and wrapped with a simple black braided band, bobbed above the heads of several men.

His breath held, he followed the dark hair.

The woman turned, her profile in view. Perfectly proportioned nose. High cheekbones. Full lips. Dark eyes.

Hell.

It was her. Liv.

And Aunt Penelope knew exactly who she was.

"You spotted her—I can see it in your eyes, Reggard."

Taking care to set his face to neutral, Tieran looked back to Aunt Penelope. "What do you know of her?"

"I know who she is." Aunt Penelope settled both of her hands atop her cane as she looked into the far crowd. "Rachel told me."

Tieran's eyes flew to the ceiling, his words muttered. "Did my wife not keep any of our marriage private from you?"

"Do not toss your eyeballs to the sky at me, Reggard. Rachel was nervous, that is all. What wife wouldn't be with that beauty in the room?"

He shook his head, refusing to turn and look into the crowd once more. "I never once spoke of her beauty to Rachel. I never would have disrespected my wife so. I didn't even want to tell Rachel who the woman was."

"But you did. And my Rachel had eyes, dear boy. That is all it took to recognize the woman her husband once loved was Aphrodite reborn."

Tieran grunted. "Aphrodite with the heart of Judas."

Aunt Penelope cackled, pounding the tip of her cane on the wood floor. "Beauty can conceal much, Reggard. That was what I told Rachel."

He nodded, taking a long swallow of port, and then balanced the glass on the arm of the chair, two fingers holding it upright. He looked over to Aunt Penelope. "Did she believe you?"

Dammit. Why had he even asked? Rachel was dead. Had been for two years. What did it matter if he had inadvertently hurt her feelings when they were first married? He loved her. She knew that. She knew it until her last breath.

But still.

That he had ever made her wonder or doubt that he adored her—the thought sent a bolt of guilt into his chest, making it tighten. He could not stomach the thought that he had ever made Rachel feel like less than the beloved wife she was.

"She did." Aunt Penelope tapped the toe of his boot with her cane to pull his attention back to her. "You know as well as I that, for as gentle as Rachel was, she was built with a stern backbone. But that is neither here nor there, God rest my dear niece's soul."

Tieran lifted his glass again, tipping it back and draining the contents. He needed another.

He hadn't wanted to come to the blasted event with Aunt Penelope, but she had insisted. It fit his purpose for the evening, but he had hoped to find a dark corner where he could scowl away all but the densest acquaintances.

But Aunt Penelope had been persistent. Lady Desmond only opened her gambling house once a fortnight, and Aunt

Penelope insisted this was the night she was going to win so much coin at the tables that she would need an escort home, for fear of being robbed.

As it was, she lost all her stash of money within the first hour.

And now Tieran was stuck with her in the middle of the crush, moored in memories of the past.

One more drink—maybe three—and then he could send Aunt Penelope home, no guard needed.

Her cane lifted in front of him, pointing to the crowd gathered around gambling tables on the far side of Lady Desmond's ballroom. "A shame about her husband passing. Lord Canton was a fine gentleman. And I am still waiting for the trollop to shed her widow's weeds—I won't get paid that enormous pot until she does."

Just as he was about to excuse himself to gather another drink, Aunt Penelope's words stopped him. Tieran sank back into the chair, looking to her, his eyebrows high. "You bet on when Lady Canton would stop wearing black with the dragons?"

"Do not look so incredulous, Reggard. It is common fodder amongst my friends—innocent entertainment to pass the time."

Tieran rubbed his eyes, clamping down on his tongue. Aunt Penelope was always going to do exactly as she pleased. "So why have you not won?"

"I had Lady Canton pegged at one year and nine months to shed the black—I gave the tart the longest margin by far. Why Doreen, for heaven's sake, had placed her coin on three months for her to move on to half-mourning—ridiculous. Lady Canton is keen on flaunting her disregard of society's expectations, but even she would not stoop so low as to shed widow's weeds at three months."

"Yet it has been three years since Lord Canton died, so why have you not collected?" Tieran asked, his voice dry.

Her cane swung in a wide arc before hitting the floorboards. "Exactly, Reggard. Why haven't I collected? We surpassed my bet long ago—so I have every right to collect—no?"

Tieran shrugged, attempting to dismiss the sour taste settling into his mouth. He didn't exactly want to be privy to the morbid fact that Aunt Penelope and her dragons were now betting upon lengths of grieving.

"Yet Edith insists I do not officially win until Lady Canton sheds the widow's weeds and officially moves to color—the old bat thinks to keep her coin by dragging this out—that I will die and be buried before Lady Canton appears in anything but black."

He rubbed his eyes again, looking up at a passing couple, the woman clinking coins in her hand as they scoured the room for their next game of chance. His eyes trailed after them—the woman's hand tight to the crook of her husband's arm as she looked up at him. Rachel used to look at him like that.

His mouth opened. "Pray tell me you did not bet on the longevity of my grief as well, Aunt Penelope."

"Of course not, Reggard—and I would not allow the dragons to do so either. It is not amusing entertainment if you actually know the person." She waved her hand in the air, the jostle shifting the orange turban on her head askew. "Besides, you have always worn black, and only black, so it would have been impossible to determine a winner."

His look snapped to her.

"And I know you loved, Rachel, my boy. I would not cheapen that." Her voice went gruff as she straightened her turban. "I am aware you would have gladly given your life for hers."

Her words as close to an apology as she would ever come, Tieran nodded. "You can tell that same fact to your nephew."

"Fletcher is still holding to his grudge? That boy is stubborn beyond belief."

"You raised him."

"Yes, and I apparently gave him far too wide a margin when he was young. But the curse limits his time on this earth, so what is the harm?"

Tieran grit his teeth, holding back his response. *What harm?* Only a brother-in-law that wanted to kill him at every turn.

"There is a woman Fletcher wants me to meet," Aunt Penelope said.

That got Tieran's attention. "Who is she?"

"I do not know yet. He is being very mysterious about her. The very first one he has ever brought to me. You should meet her as well when the time comes."

"I don't see why. Lockston hates me."

"He doesn't hate you, Reggard."

"I killed his sister."

Her cane slammed onto the ground. "You need to stop saying that out loud. Think it—fine. But never say it. It is a stupid sentiment. You say it enough times, it becomes truth. Truth for you. Truth for Fletcher." She lifted the cane, poking his thigh with it. "Stupid is not truth. Stupid is stupid. What happened to Rachel is nature, boy—it happens hundreds of times over every day in this world. You think you are the first? The first to feel the pain of losing a wife? Losing a babe?"

Tieran glared at her. Aunt Penelope had never held her tongue with him, and he had always admired her for it—until this very moment. She had no right to dismiss his grief. To dismiss his guilt with the flip of her cane. It was his unborn babe that had been too large for Rachel's body. He had killed her just as sure as he had stuck a knife in her gut.

"Forgive me for actually feeling the loss of my wife."

"Do not dare to pin me as callous, Reggard. I loved Rachel as my own."

"I think it is time we take our leave." His voice growled, barely in control. "We have stayed for too long."

"And you have grieved for too long, Reggard."

His look pierced her. "Be very careful how you proceed at this moment, Aunt Penelope."

Her weathered cane flipped in an arc, dismissing his snarl. "I proceed as I see fit." She smiled, spotting someone over Tieran's shoulder. "And there is my auxiliary plan—the dowager duchess has finally arrived with reinforcements."

"Reinforcements?" Tieran glanced over his shoulder to see one of Aunt Penelope's friends making her way through the crowd, carrying a swinging fat reticule that looked swollen with jingling coins.

"Coin enough to last the night." Aunt Penelope wobbled, her frail bones lifting her onto her feet, her cane digging into the floor in front of her. "Make yourself comfortable, Reggard, you cannot escape this torture quite yet."

She shuffled off, meeting the dowager duchess with a smile, pushing her turban into place.

~ ~ ~

Liv stared at the dice on the purple velvet of the hazard table before her.

She had gotten good at this.

Making sure her fingers didn't quiver when they picked up the small cubes of wood. Her face a mask of indifference. Her breath even, never a gasp of delight or disappointment passing her lips.

She glanced up at Lord Fodler, the only other one left at the table. He masked nothing.

Red splotches had exploded on his brow, magnified by the strains of sweat he kept rubbing at with the butt of his palm. His thin lips drew in again and again, smacking, impatient.

His reaction alone told her he had no business betting off the last shreds of his estate against a woman. Yet there he was, the scraps of a five-hundred-year-old fortune sitting on the table in front of him.

Her eyes demurely downcast, Liv elongated the moment as long as she dared. Let him writhe in his torture. The man deserved it. Deserved every piece of destruction she would deliver to him. Tonight, or the next night, or the next night. However long it would take. She would deliver it to him.

She could afford to lose a fortune twenty times over. Lord Fodler could not.

Liv's fingers slid over the purple velvet—purple, because Lady Desmond liked to be different and thoroughly embraced with flair the running of a fortnightly gaming hall in her home. Liv wasn't sure if, being a widow, Lady Desmond needed the extra income, or if she just enjoyed the drama, but either way, she was the fairest of hostesses. Members of both sexes were welcome at her tables equally, and Liv had waited a long time for Lord Fodler to come to gamble at one of Lady Desmond's events.

Liv picked up the dice, shaking them. They clinked effortlessly in her palm, slipping along the exquisite silk of her gloves.

The murmurs of the crowd surrounding the table hushed, every breath held, waiting for the dice to roll.

Liv flung open her fingers, freeing the dice to fly. The first landed solidly onto the six side.

She swallowed the gasp in her throat. Odds against her, she had set on six only to draw Lord Fodler into his last bet. But now she was halfway there.

The second die tumbled—three—one—five—and then fell into a spin on its corner until it wavered, slowly dropping.

Six.

Twelve combined.

The table was hers.

And with it, the entire destruction of Lord Fodler's estate.

The crowd, now six people deep in spots, erupted. Laughter, jeers, hisses. A cacophony of reactions, if ever there was one. Liv didn't offer the slightest glance at the crowd.

Her chest expanded with giddiness, yet Liv simply leaned over the table, her eyes still downward, her stoic face unfaltering, and she began to collect the notes and coins off the purple velvet. The board partially cleared, she did afford herself the tiniest peek upward at Lord Fodler.

The red splotches had disappeared, not a speck of color left in his ashen face. His jaw had dropped, quivering. He was either overwhelmed with shock, or was attempting very hard not to fall into tears.

Not only had he lost every last bit of his fortune—he had lost it to a woman.

Ruin like no other.

"Well played, Lady Canton. Most impressive." The creamy bust of Lady Desmond dipped into Liv's downcast view as she helped Liv to collect the far markers.

With Lady Desmond between them, Liv stole another glance at Lord Fodler. His shock was quickly morphing into rage. She gave quick thanks that it was here in Lady Desmond's establishment that she finally bested Lord Fodler. The widow's gaming house was not only fair, it was also one of the safest places Liv had gambled in.

Yet she knew she might be in trouble tonight. Fury had already mottled Lord Fodler's face, and he had little regard for life—that she knew too well. She would do well to exit Lady Desmond's townhouse with haste, before Fodler found a way to act upon his rage.

"You have given the crowd quite a show, Lady Canton," Lady Desmond said, setting a pile of coins and notes in front of Liv. "And I do have to thank you for that. My coffers will be more than brimming over the next months. Scandal does breed good business, I have found."

Liv smiled up at Lady Desmond. "Then we have both been fortunate tonight."

Lady Desmond motioned to the pile in front of Liv. "Shall I gather these and secure them for you?"

"Yes, please, that would be a help."

The whirlwind of chatter created a din in the enormous drawing room adjacent to the ballroom as the crowd began dispersing throughout the floor. Liv glanced up, noting the flush in the cheeks of the patrons, the animation of their hands. Gossip abounding. Lord Fodler's humiliation building.

Then she noticed it—one head high above the height of most of the crowd. A head, a body that did not move. Eyes. Eyes of blue that matched the deep, dark crevices of a sweet violet in springtime. Eyes that questioned her. Beseeched her. Judged her.

Eyes she hadn't seen in years.

Tieran.

She had spotted him several times throughout the years. Passing on the far ends of the same ballroom. A glimpse once, on Bond Street. In opposite boxes at His Majesty's Theatre.

But every time Liv had spied him, it was his back or the side of his face—and he was always turning away. Turning away as though he had already seen her and was well on his way to remove her from his sight.

And Liv had never allowed herself to be disrespectful to Tieran's wife by approaching him. She had married. He had followed suit. Both of them had taken oaths. Plus, she had seen Tieran with his wife—he was a happy, doting husband—and Liv refused to complicate his life or his marriage just to assuage her own regrets.

But now, in that very moment—across the table and far above Lord Fodler's shaking head—was the first time Tieran's unmistakable blue eyes were pinned on her since he had left for the war. And they did not even begin to flicker away once she met his gaze.

The harsh condemnation, thick in his look, twisted her belly. Ravaged it more viciously than the game of hazard she had just played.

Lady Desmond leaned down, her voice low in Liv's ear. "Lady Canton, would you like an escort to your residence? I can lend you several of my guards."

Liv's look dropped to Lady Desmond for only a second before bouncing back upward. But when she searched above the crowd once more, she could find no blue eyes.

Tieran was gone.

How had he gotten his massive form through the crowd so quickly? Stealth had apparently become his friend throughout the years.

"Lady Canton?"

Liv gave herself a shake, focusing on Lady Desmond. "It is so very kind of you to offer, Lady Desmond. But I do not need assistance on the way home. I have both a footman and my driver with me tonight, and they should be sufficient. There are no precarious roads between your residence and mine."

Lady Desmond responded with a quick nod, and then a pointed tilt of her head toward Lord Fodler as he was being yanked away from the table by several acquaintances taking pity upon him. "It is not nefarious streets I am concerned with, Lady Canton."

Liv's look swung to Lord Fodler as he disappeared into the crowd. A slight frown set upon her lips, but then she shook her head. "I should be quite safe, Lady Desmond. Charles and Mr. Niles are overly adept at my protection. I hired them for this very reason. But I do thank you for your concern."

"Of course, Lady Canton. As widows in this madcap world, we need to stick together. Again, it was a fine show you put forth tonight." A twinkle set into the woman's eyes, a mischievous smile lining her lips as she leaned near to Liv's ear once more. "I have said this before to you, but I am not always genuine in my words, so I will repeat them with honesty—you are welcome anytime here at my establishment, Lady Canton."

With a warm smile and a slight hum, Lady Desmond stepped away toward the back room attached to the drawing room.

Liv watched her until she disappeared behind the door, amazed at the woman's poise. Lady Desmond was not but a year older than Liv, but she held herself with such regal, independent elegance that Liv had to admit she was thoroughly envious of the widow. Lady Desmond had forged forth into a new life without a husband with nothing but grace.

Something Liv hoped to someday emulate.

Someday.

After, of course, she first took care of the list.

{ CHAPTER 3 }

Her look fixated on the passing streetlamps, Liv rearranged the blanket on her lap. Her enclosed carriage kept her out of the nip of the wind, but she had been chilled since seeing Tieran in the crowd at Lady Desmond's.

Once she had left the gaming table, she had circled the drawing room, the ballroom, and the side rooms three times before accepting the fact that Tieran had been standing in front of her, near enough to touch, to talk to, and then he had disappeared.

As much as she had attempted to push him from her mind in the past six years, the instant surge in her gut at his presence forced her to acknowledge how very little success she had managed in forgetting him.

He had been a widower for two years now. And from what Liv understood of the gossip on the matter, Tieran had never recovered from the loss of his wife in childbirth, and was now entirely partial to spending his time with the 1811 cognac at White's.

Not that she could judge him for how he grieved.

Her own husband had been dying since the day she met him, so while a profound bond had been forged—Lord Canton had saved her and Liv had, in return, saved him from his own family numerous times—their marriage had never been more than a deep, respectful friendship, with the love born from that.

But now. Now there were no spouses to be respectful of, and Liv had desperately wanted to corner Tieran at Lady Desmond's townhouse.

She had hoped to—at the very least—angle herself near to him, listen to him talk, or possibly brush against the side of his jacket. But most of all, she had hoped for another chance to meet his eyes without the cloud of judgment marring his blue irises.

The carriage hit a dip in the cobblestones, jarring her thoughts, and Liv looked out the coach's window just as they passed her solicitor's building. She would have to remember to visit him first thing in the morning to make sure all of Lord Fodler's assets were transferred to the trust that helped the girls. For as much wealth as Lord Canton had left her, Liv had no need for more, and she knew Lord Fodler's assets would be better spent on the girls.

The back springs of the carriage suddenly jumped upward—a heavy load seeming to fall off the back—and Liv flew forward. She caught herself in a partial crouch, her hands jammed onto the edge of the opposite bench.

A muffled grunt cut through the carriage walls as a body in a black coat fell past the coach's window.

Thud.

Liv heard the body hit the ground. No. Not her driver.

Flipping around, she pushed off the bench and scrambled to the side of the coach. She jerked down the flap of the box on the side of the carriage next to her bench. For most of the gentry, the side box held a small selection of spirits. For Liv, it held only one thing—a pistol, always at the ready, powdered and loaded.

Grabbing the pistol, she instantly damned the slipperiness of her gloves and set it down on the bench to rip off the silk.

The carriage slowed.

Not allowing time to think on her actions and grow cowardice, Liv took a deep breath and twisted the handle of the door, shoving it open as she sprang down onto the cobblestones.

Stumbling a few steps, she looked behind the carriage only to see two dark lumps in the empty street. Both her driver and her footman. She prayed Mr. Niles and Charles weren't dead. A frantic search around, and Liv realized it had stretched late into the night, and there was no other traffic on the street.

Her gaze whipped to the front of her carriage, to the horses, and she saw a man, burly, that she did not recognize yanking on the bit of the left horse to stop the coach. The left horse reared, knowing it was stopping when it shouldn't—Mr. Niles had exacting standards when it came to training his horses.

Liv squinted at the man struggling with the horses. A mere robbery? She breathed a slight sigh of relief. A bumbling robber she could handle—or at least escape from.

Lifting the pistol and cocking it to the ready, Liv started to shuffle backward next to the carriage. If she could skirt along the rear of it, she could make her way back to her solicitor's establishment and then disappear down the alley to the door that led up to the apartment where his articled clerk lived. She would be safe there, at least for the moment.

Her heel caught on a raised cobblestone, and she scampered backward to catch her balance. Her shoulders hit a mass, stopping her fall. A mass of man, not building, along her backside.

Before she could twist around, fingers dug into the back of her upsweep, tearing at her hair before shoving her forward.

She slammed into the back right corner of the carriage, the edge of it digging into her belly. In a spin, she managed to catch the footboard with her free hand before she fell to the ground.

"You thought it would be that easy—ruining me, you vicious whore?"

Liv looked up, her hand tightening on her pistol along her skirt.

Lord Fodler. Not a simple robbery at all.

She had to get the barrel of her pistol between herself and Lord Fodler. She pushed upward off the footboard, pulling herself to her full height—taller than him—as she lifted her pistol.

Aimed at his chest, the pistol stopped his movement.

"You think to steal back what you have lost?" Liv attempted to hide the shake in her voice.

"No." The one word was cold, chilling. "No, I don't mean to rob you."

At that moment, Liv saw silver flash in Lord Fodler's hand as he lifted it.

His own pistol was aimed right at her belly.

"You think it will be that easy to kill me, Lord Fodler?" Liv met his eyes, ignoring the panic swirling rampant in her chest. "There were too many witnesses tonight—everyone knows of your downfall. There is no recovery for you."

Lord Fodler shrugged, his gleaming silver pistol reflecting the low light from the streetlamps. "Then I guess I am only left with revenge, since I don't have anything left to lose."

For the first time, Liv recognized the crazed look in his eyes. There would be no common sense, no scheming her way out of this. Lord Fodler meant to kill her.

And she wasn't sure she could pull her own trigger.

"Your own life—you will lose that, Lord Fodler—you will hang for this."

He snickered. "Silly whore. What I have left is not worth living for. A noose does not bother me."

Lord Fodler's arm lifted slightly, his finger twitching.

And then he was flying through the air. Flying sideways.

Bang.

The sound of a pistol shot boomed down the empty street, radiating into adjacent blocks.

Lord Fodler smashed into the brick wall next to the carriage. He fell, slumping into a heap on the ground.

Before she could even comprehend how Lord Fodler had just been crushed into a brick wall—or that she had been the one to pull her trigger—Tieran ran past her, giving one monstrous kick to the inert head of Lord Fodler.

Eyes wide, her body finally reacted to her brain and Liv jumped away from the carriage into the street, searching for the brute by the horses. Gone.

She turned back to Tieran. He was heaving—his fists so tight his knuckles were near to bursting—and looking down at Lord Fodler as though he wanted to kick him a hundred times over and it still wouldn't be enough.

Liv took a wobbly step toward him. "Tieran?"

He leaned down, picking up the pistol still snagged in Lord Fodler's forefinger. Uncocking the gun, he slid it into his dark jacket before looking at Liv.

He didn't say a word, only stared at her, rage pulsating along his jawline.

Her head swiveled, her eyes searching the street as she took another step forward. "What about the other man—he was by the horses?"

Tieran's left hand unfurled, and he shook it, dissipating the rage. "I merely asked him if this was worth dying for."

"And?"

"He took one look at me and ran."

She nodded, the frown deepening on her face. Of course the man ran. Who wouldn't when looking up at the wrath of Tieran?

Her look landed on the lump of Lord Fodler. "Is he… is he dead?"

"Does it matter?"

She glanced up at Tieran's face, then looked again at the body.

"Do you honestly want to help him after what he was just about to do to you, Lady Canton?"

Her look jerked back up to him. *Lady Canton*? That was how he was addressing her now?

Tieran shifted, impatient. "Do you want to help him?"

Liv shook her head. Of course she didn't want to help the man. She wanted Lord Fodler to rot in the hell he deserved.

With a quick nod, Tieran stepped past her. "I thought not. You do not have that magnanimity within you."

He moved down the street to her driver and kneeled next to him, his hands running along the man's neck.

Liv followed, stopping behind Tieran. "Mr. Niles, is he alive? Please say he is alive."

"He is alive. Unconscious, but alive." Tieran didn't look up to her.

Liv exhaled, nodding. Her gaze moved on to Charles, hoping for the very same thing.

Without another word, Tieran picked up Mr. Niles and brought him to the carriage, settling him on the floor of the interior. He went back to Liv's footman—also alive—but with a deep gash along his temple that oozed fresh blood.

Grabbing the bottom hem of her black gown, Liv dabbed at the wound as Tieran carried him, hopping fast sideways steps to keep up with Tieran's long strides. Settling Charles on the floor next to Mr. Niles, Tieran bent their legs to tuck them into the tight space, then snapped the carriage door closed.

Without glancing her way, Tieran moved to the front of the carriage. "Come, I am delivering you and your men home."

Liv sighed, following Tieran. Before she could grab the handle to hoist herself into the driver's perch, Tieran snatched her about the waist and lifted her, plopping her down on the high bench.

He retrieved the reins from the front of the horses, and walking back, he stumbled, almost dropping to his knees. Slowly, he righted himself.

Liv jumped to her feet, going to the edge of the perch. "Tieran, are you hurt?"

"No."

She stared down at him for a long moment. He lifted his foot onto the step below the perch, the ball of his foot missing the step two times before landing squarely in the middle of the metal rung.

"Are you drunk?"

He shrugged, not looking up at her.

"You did all of this while you were soused?" Her voice pitched into a shrill whisper. "You could have gotten killed—you could have gotten me killed."

He looked up at her, his eyes piercing. "You were already a breath away from that, had I not intervened."

"Well, yes, but—"

"Do not be dramatic about it, Lady Canton." He shifted the reins to his opposite hand. "You would be amazed at the things I am capable of doing while inebriated."

"Would I?" She nudged the side of his shoulder with the toe of her slipper, the pistol still in her fingers tapping along her thigh. "Move please. Maybe I should ride down below."

He stared up at her, unmoving. "Sit."

For as much as she bristled at his command—and it was an unflinching order, there was no denying that—Liv recalled how extremely stubborn Tieran had always been. Whereas years ago, she used to delight in confronting his stubbornness directly, she wasn't sure at all what this man in front of her would do if defied.

And she was suddenly very aware that she didn't know who Tieran had become in the years since he left for the war.

The thought struck her, not letting go. She had always thought of Tieran as she had known him six years ago. Those years when they had fallen in love, and everything was right, and the world was glorious.

She had given no imaginations to what had happened to him in that time. No imaginations to the possibility that he had changed just as irrevocably as she had.

"There is no room for you to sit inside the coach, Lady Canton." The constant frown on his face hardened. "Not with your two buffoons knocked to darkness. So you can ride up there, or balance yourself on one of the footman stands in back. Your choice."

Liv took a small step backward. "This will do." She sat.

Tieran heaved himself upward, sitting next to her on the perch. The bench was narrow, and Liv was instantly overcome by his body next to hers. He had always made her feel small. Delicate. Protected in the bubble his sheer size created—a safe shadow to hide within.

A shadow that carried the stench of brandy wafting from his person with every movement.

He flicked the horses forward. "Where did you hire those fools? They were worthless when Lord Fodler and his henchman jumped and attacked."

Her spine straightened, her hands settling in her lap over the cold pistol. "They are usually very adept and they both came highly recommended by my solicitor."

"Maybe you need a new solicitor as well."

"Do not disparage them. They are beyond loyal and they have gotten me out of several scrapes that I very much needed their assistance to escape."

"If they are so adept, why do you have that handy?" He pointed at the barrel tip of the pistol sitting snug in her lap.

"I am not stupid, Tieran. I know the precarious positions that I sometimes put myself in, and I must be ready to protect myself."

"Somebody should teach you to properly shoot it, then."

Her spine already straight, her shoulders snapped back. "I know how to shoot."

"And that is why a bullet nearly grazed my ear?"

"What—no." She jerked away from him, twisting herself to gain angle to see his head properly. The streetlamps only offered dim light, so she reached up to touch his ear, searching for a nick.

He yanked his head from her touch as though fire seeped from her fingertips.

Liv's hand dropped to her lap.

Realizing his extreme reaction, he awkwardly cleared his throat. "It was the other ear. And there is no blood. You needn't feel the urge to tend to it."

Liv nodded, her eyes downcast as she fingered the lines of the pistol. "Forgive me for the rogue bullet. I was in a moral dilemma in that moment."

"A moral dilemma?"

"On whether or not I could take a life."

He nodded, glancing down at her. "So you had apparently decided on yes since you pulled the trigger?"

She shrugged. "Apparently."

"Would it have been worth what it would have cost you?"

She stayed silent for long seconds, staring at the pistol. Yes, it would have been worth it, she wanted to scream. The man deserved to die. Deserved to die for his sins. Ruining him had been gratifying, but mere ruin never seemed enough. Ruin was not utter destruction. Ruin was not death. Not hell.

And Lord Fodler deserved hell.

But she couldn't tell Tieran that. Couldn't have him think even less of her than he currently did. The way he kept his body still, leaning away from her, told her volumes—everything she had ever wondered about the moment when they would meet again, talk again.

She exhaled, ignoring his question as she forced a smile onto her lips. "I did not thank you for your assistance, Tieran. How did you find me?"

"I followed you."

"You did? But I searched for you at Lady Desmond's. You were gone."

"I was behind you, Lady Canton. I have been since you began stalking my new business acquaintance, Lord Shepton, weeks ago."

Lord Shepton? Liv started. Shepton was on the list. She *had* been stalking him. So much so that she had already begun to hone in on the man's vices.

Holding her body still, she dared a sideways glance up at Tieran. He couldn't possibly know of Lord Shepton's sins, could he? And if he did, how could he possibly sink to doing business with the man?

Liv swallowed hard, her gaze shifting nonchalantly to the rumps of the horses before them. "Lord Shepton?"

"Yes, Lord Shepton. And you can stop trying to pretend you don't know the man, Lady Canton." His head turned to her, but Liv refused to meet the judgmental stare she could feel bearing down upon her. "I make it my business to know everything I can about those I do business with. And I do business with Lord Shepton. At first I thought it was a coincidence, your presence around him during the past month. But now I can see quite clearly you have been stalking him, just as you did Lord Fodler."

"You are mad." Her words were hollow, not truly battling his accusation.

"Am I?" His focus went back to the street as he turned a corner. "But I have yet to determine what game it is you seek to play with Lord Shepton. Unlike your motives with Lord Fodler, which were to obviously crush the man so completely at the tables that his entire world crumbled."

Tieran tugged on the reins, slowing the horses to a crawl.

He clearly intended to get some answers from her. And Liv intended to not give him any.

He stared down at her again, no longer judging, but now with a look she thought long lost to the past. It was how he studied her when they first met, like she was a labyrinth he was determined to reach the middle of, no matter how many false turns and dead ends he ran into.

"But your game with Lord Shepton I have not discerned," he said. "I have watched you flirt and disappear into dark corners with the man. You have already managed to create a healthy rift in his marriage. Yet that does not seem to be enough. You continue to make yourself available, enticing him. He is not the most attractive man, spits when he talks, and has a certain odor about him. He is not rich, has no holdings that you could not buy yourself ten times over. I cannot think of a single thing he has that you could possible want."

Liv manifested a careful smile on her face, lifting her voice to pleasant airiness. "Well then, your first instinct must have been right. It is a coincidence. I have no motive with Lord Shepton. As for a rift between him and his wife, I do not see how I can be blamed. I have only chatted about the most inane topics with the man, and I do find him quite witty."

"Witty?" Tieran spewed a chortle. "I have never known a drier personality than his."

"Maybe then, Tieran, you should spend less time following me about and more time talking with Lord Shepton." She conjured her sweetest voice. "It does seem as though you do not know nearly as much about him as you think you do."

Tieran's mouth went tight. "Do not attempt to conceal under your innocent eyelashes the fact that you have turned into a widow coquette. The flutter of them never did work upon me, if you recall."

She recoiled, the words an invisible slap. "That is what you think of me? I am a trollop?"

He stared at her, both eyebrows arching. "I think what I know."

She exhaled, the breath turning into a slight hiss. "And you know so very much, don't you, Tieran."

"I know you married for your precious title the first chance you got. I know that now as a widow—out of boredom or sheer wantonness—you have decided to immerse yourself into the indecent shadows of society."

"You couldn't be further from the truth of it, Tieran."

"No? How many nights in the past month have you spent gambling?"

Her mouth clamped shut, her arms wrapping around her belly as she stared straight ahead.

"Not willing to answer that one?" His voice dropped to a dangerous whisper. "How about this one—how many nights in the past month have you seduced your way into a random gentleman's bed? Your wake of destruction has begun to precede you in rumors, Lady Canton."

The poised smile long since vanished from her face, Liv tried to clamp down on the indignation boiling in her gut. She stared at the empty street, wishing for anything that would make him spur the horses onward. Anything that would give her leave of his company. "I have heard that too many times from your mouth now, Tieran."

"What?"

"Lady Canton. That is the extent of what I am to you now?"

"That is what you became the second you married that decrepit fossil."

She whipped to him, meeting his stare as physically close as she could. Her, he could vilify—but she would not stand for him speaking ill of her husband. "You will stop, Tieran. Lord Canton was kind, and I will not have you disparage his name."

He growled, the sound vibrating, wrapping around his words. "He was an old lecher that married a woman young enough to be his great-granddaughter."

Liv stiffened.

Slowly, silently, she turned in her seat, her back to him, wedging herself as far away as she could without falling from the perch.

He sent the horses onward.

They rode in silence, and Liv wasn't surprised when he turned the coach into the mews on her block. Of course Tieran knew where she lived.

He stopped the horses.

"This is appreciated." She motioned to the back of her townhouse. "While I thank you for your assistance tonight, Lord Reggard, I realize now that there will be no need for our paths to ever converge again. Which should not be a disappointment, as it is apparent that you already know everything about me and I can see how much I disgust you."

Before he could move, she jumped from the driver's perch. The impact of the hard ground jarred her cold feet, so much so she wondered if her bones had shattered.

One deep breath and she looked up at him, giving him a quick nod, her voice as haughty as she could manage with the pain in her feet. "You may leave the carriage here. I will send someone out to help Charles and Mr. Niles. Good eve, my lord."

Liv yanked her shoulders back and spun from the carriage, walking through the back gate that marked her gardens and disappearing behind the tall evergreen hedge.

Tieran made no parting remark.

{ CHAPTER 4 }

Liv collapsed against the inside of her rear door, her breaths coming in heaves.

That she made it into her townhouse without turning back, without pleading with Tieran, without telling him the truth of her motives, without telling him everything that had happened in the past six years, had been a herculean feat.

She had thought she had put everything Tieran was to her in the past. Locked it away in a box never to be disturbed. Her marriage, his marriage, and the many years apart had forced that.

But sitting next to him. It was as though no time had passed since his fingers had last threaded with hers. Since she had strolled with him on the cliff above Rosewood Brook the night before he left for war.

Her head clunked backward onto the wood panel.

All that she had lost.

She had convinced herself over the years that she had accepted the oddity that her life had veered into. Long ago, her mother had determined Liv's destiny would be to become the pampered wife of a peer. To spend her days making calls, with her needlepoint, creating watercolors, practicing her harp, directing servants, and running the household. She had been destined to spend her nights at gay parties, spinning on the dance floor at grand balls, partaking in lively conversations during intermission at the opera.

A life of ease and fun and charming people.

A destiny that was obliterated long ago by a cruel twist of fate.

Within that fate, the only saving grace had been marrying Lord Canton.

And while she had married into his title, her days bore no resemblance to what she had imagined they would as a lady.

They had consisted of two things. One, outwitting a nefarious cousin—the heir to the title—bent on creating an "accident" that would result in Lord Canton's early demise. And two, walking her husband through the last years of his life.

Loss of strength, loss of body, loss of will. She had watched the deterioration progress slowly, her husband fighting it the whole way. Day after day, she had been humbled by how fragile the human body truly was. But the journey to his death had given her things she never imagined the importance of—perseverance, empathy, kindness.

So those long-ago dreams of what her life should have been—she had long since accepted the loss of those.

But Tieran.

Him she had never accepted losing.

No matter how many pitiful attempts she made to do so over the years. That his words tonight had cut her so deeply, crushing her heart, was only proof of that.

"Why are you not gloriously giddy at the moment?"

Liv lifted her head from the door, watching Viola Halverstein bounce along the main hallway toward her.

"You are here." Liv could conjure no enthusiasm for her best friend. She wanted bed. She wanted to crawl under her covers and hide. Hide away from seeing Tieran. Hide away from what he thought of her.

Viola came to a stop in front of Liv. Her round cheeks were rosy, excitement exaggerating all of her movements. "Of course I am here, Livia, how could I not be?"

"How did you get away from the baron?"

Viola's fingers waved flippantly in the air. "I made sure to top off his brandy glass with every sip tonight. He has been asleep for hours now."

Liv leaned from the door, standing straight and motioning toward the staircase leading to the kitchen from the hallway. Viola spun in front of her, moving to the stairway.

"So you obviously heard the news?" Liv followed her friend down the stairs.

"Of course I did. I could have strangled the baron tonight for not allowing us to go to Lady Desmond's. We have not left the house in weeks and the stench of the baron's decay is wearing upon me." In truth, Viola had been waiting for years for her husband to pass on, but the baron was a stubborn old goat. And while his beatings of Viola had lessened over the years, he still was tyrannical over her time.

Viola looked up over her shoulder at Liv as she rushed down the stairs. "I had the stable boy hover for hours in Lady Desmond's stables, waiting for the news of what happened. You must tell me everything."

In the kitchen, Viola went into the larder and pulled four apples from the pile. She set them on the long wooden table centering the kitchen and then grabbed two knives, handing one to Liv as they sat down.

Settling onto the round stool, Liv attempted to wash all memory of the journey home from her mind.

She should be happy in that moment. She had accomplished what she had set out to do with Lord Fodler. She had destroyed him, and she should be elated. Another one scratched off the list.

Viola flipped one of the apples upside down, reaching high with her knife, and slammed down the point of the blade into the exact center of the fruit. The impaled apple split in two with the force, both sides neatly falling from the silver blade. The knife stayed upright, the tip of it stuck deep into the wood.

Liv smiled. Viola had done that the very first night they had met. Liv had been a crumpled shell, alone, sobbing on the stone floor of the kitchen. Viola had come in, picked her up, set her on a chair, and performed that very same trick with a bright red apple.

The absurdity of it had made Liv laugh, cutting through her tears. From then on, countless hours had been spent in the ensuing years in various kitchens, the two of them cutting up and munching on apples. It was where they talked, where they dreamed, where they planned. All of it over neatly split apples.

"Tell me—tell me of Fodler's face, dove." Viola giggled. "Tell me of the moment he knew he was destroyed."

The image of Tieran sending Lord Fodler flying through the air, his body smashing into the brick wall, flashed in Liv's mind.

Lord Fodler was certainly destroyed, if not dead from that.

Liv blinked away the image. Best to not admit to what had happened—not even to Viola. As odious as Ticran had been to her, she didn't want to cause any untoward inquires to come his way, or gossip to besmirch his reputation—especially after he had saved her.

Aside from the fact that she didn't want to talk about Tieran. Not now. Not tonight. She wasn't ready to revisit the conversation they had on the coach just yet.

Liv picked up one half of the apple, her fingernails digging into the red-yellow skin. She smiled, looking up at Viola. "Fodler's face went white, and then mottled into a splotchy red—almost macabre in how it twisted in fury. He knew full well he was done, nothing left to lose."

Viola laughed, slapping her palm on the table. "Excellent—you have done so well at this, Livia." She bit into her apple. "To be honest, I did not think you could do this, that you possessed the temperament needed for destruction, as you are usually far too sympathetic to others. But this is the fourteenth one—and the hardest one thus far to ruin—and you have shown remarkable spine through it all."

For the insult she could read into it, Liv knew Viola meant every word she said as a compliment to Liv. She shrugged. "I have learned to reserve my compassion for people who deserve it. And Lord Fodler certainly did not deserve it." Liv bit into her apple slice.

"Exactly. I could not be more proud of you, dove. Well, maybe if I had been able to witness it myself, I could be a bit prouder." Viola took a bite of her apple, set it down, and then started fishing into the bodice of her dress. She exhaled, her green eyes sparkling as she pulled free a folded piece of vellum from between her plump breasts. She unfolded the paper on the table, smoothing out the creases as she finished chewing her apple.

The list of thirty-three names sat between them on the table, thirteen names scratched out with one thin line, and a fourteenth to get the same treatment.

Liv glanced at the list. She didn't need to be reminded of the names—she had committed each and every one to memory. But she was reassured of her purpose, as she always was when she saw them.

Viola pointed at a name halfway down the list. "I know you have also been working on Lord Shepton in the last few weeks, since he was at several of the same functions as Fodler." Viola looked up at Liv as she picked up her part of the apple. "How does that progress? Shall we add another target? You do seem to do well managing two of them at once. Possibly one that moves in the same circles as Lord Shepton so you can monitor them at the same time?"

Liv nodded, chewing slowly. To be honest, every man on the list was a target, and Liv filed away every tiny scrap of information or gossip she heard about any of them, jumping upon every opportunity she was presented with to engage them. Patience was the key, though. They would all receive their justice in due time.

Viola's forefinger tapped on the vellum, running down the list of names until she stopped near the bottom of the paper. Liv noticed four more names had been added since the last time she had seen the list. Thirty-seven. Fourteen done.

Liv inhaled, calming panic. *Patience.* Patience was the key.

"There, how about this one?" Viola pointed to a name. "Lord Lockston. He is a recent addition to the list—but I do believe he is an acquaintance of Lord Shepton's. That may make him convenient. We will have to do some more research into him." Viola popped the remainder of her apple into her mouth, chewing slowly as she studied the paper.

Liv stared at the name, burning it into her mind, searching her memory. Lord Lockston. It hit her quite suddenly. Lord Lockston was a childhood friend of Tieran's. A friend that he had gone off to war with. The brother of Tieran's dead wife—what was her name—Rachel?

Lord Lockston. She had not heard the name in many years.

A chill ran down her spine. Could Tieran possibly know about his friend's activities?

"Is something amiss, Livia?"

Liv shook her head. "No. No bother. It is…" She stepped into her words carefully. "Is the list ever wrong, Viola?"

Her friend bristled, her eyes going to slits. "No. The list comes directly from the establishment. And then it is verified by two runners. It is never wrong. Do not tell me you know Lord Lockston?"

"No. I have never met the man." Liv spat the true-enough words out quickly, attempting to soothe Viola's instant ire. She knew her friend wanted nothing more than to be in Liv's position, to be free of the baron and his harsh control over her life. To be the one to ruin these men. Viola wanted to dispense justice on her own terms. But the baron was still alive—and there was no way he was going to allow Viola freedom from his exacting control.

Liv offered a dismissive smile to erase her question about the validity of the list. "Lord Lockston is on the list, and that means he needs to pay."

"Yes, he does." Viola's heart-shaped mouth lifted into a wicked smile as she flipped another apple upside-down and wedged the knife free from the table. With a wild swing that was dead-on, the apple split, slices falling perfectly.

"I am so very glad to have found you those years ago, Livia." Viola smirked, stabbing half of the apple and holding it up to Liv. "We are so like-minded, it is uncanny."

Liv chuckled, grabbing the slice of apple.

Thank goodness she had Viola. Her friend always did know how to make her forget her own woes.

{ CHAPTER 5 }

Tieran stretched out his legs inside the cramped coach—as much as he could do so without crushing Lady Lockston's plum-colored skirt.

His late wife's brother, Lord Lockston, had married the woman weeks ago, and Tieran had been snagged by Aunt Penelope to run the fool's errand of delivering Lady Lockston to her wayward husband outside of London.

If there was one thing he knew about his childhood friend, it was that Fletch floated, skipped randomly through his life depending upon whatever hit his fancy at the moment, and that he would not look kindly upon Tieran delivering his new wife to him. But Aunt Penelope had insisted on Tieran's assistance, and he had never been able to refuse Rachel's aunt.

His knee cracked on wood as he wedged it against the door of the coach. He would have much preferred to ride horses to Wellfork Castle. It would have not only been far more comfortable for him, but they also could have gotten there in an hour and a half from London proper, instead of moving at a slug's pace on the deep-rutted roads. But Tieran didn't know enough about Lady Lockston—just what Aunt Penelope had told him—to know if she could suffer the ride on horseback.

So instead of comfort, he had cramped himself into the coach.

He looked across the coach at Lady Lockston. The plum-colored carriage dress fit her slim body well, a pleasant contrast to her creamy complexion. He couldn't decide if her hair was red or blond—tendrils competing for dominance in her perfunctory upsweep. Her eyes were interesting—not because of the hazel swirling with blue— because of the canniness about them. The woman looked as if she held the knowledge of a thousand, hard-won lessons in those eyes. Far removed from the bubbling naivety he was accustomed to in so many of the *ton's* beauties.

From what he could discern of Lady Lockston, Fletch had made a fine choice in a wife—if he could get out of his own damn way long enough to realize it.

Tieran recognized he set Lady Lockston slightly on edge. She had been self-conscious the entire trip, but he had to admire her spirit. Tracking down a wayward husband was not a pleasant endeavor, and Tieran wondered if she had even the slightest notion about what they were to walk into at Wellfork Castle.

Lord Wellfork was famous for his parties—a constant stream of the *ton's* elite visited Wellfork Castle, and it was well known that adherence to the proprieties of London ballrooms was conspicuously absent in the dark and windy corridors.

One did not go to Wellfork with their spouse. It was, in fact, considered ill form for a husband and wife to accidently appear at Wellfork Castle at the same time.

The ancient castle—heavy upon an open hill with its fat exterior stones greying, yet still noble—appeared out the carriage window, and Tieran glanced at Lady Lockston. She had grown slightly pale, but her back had gone rigid, spiriting her nerve. She was going to hunt down Fletch— there was no doubt about it.

Tieran smiled to himself. It was beyond time a fine young lady reined Lockston in.

Within minutes they were inside, Tieran next to Lady Lockston as they looked down upon the castle's great hall from the minstrel's galley. Her eyes scanning the smattering of people helping themselves to breakfast at the far end of the hall, Lady Lockston gave a slight gasp, her gloved hands tightening on the railing. Tieran followed to where her unwavering gaze had landed.

He spotted Fletch right away. His friend sat at a table of four, laughing his booming roar with his companions. Just to Lockston's right, Tieran saw the slope of a flawless bosom, the top cut of a black dress just barely concealing nipples. The bosom angled forward, tilting perfectly at Lockston while shaking with mirth.

Tieran followed the bosom upward.

Hell.

Liv.

Her black hair piled in perfection, her eyelashes were darkened, making her eyes almost smolder even though it was still in the morning hours. Her full lips pulled wide in a genuine smile, still chuckling at whatever had been said. Tieran recognized it—the specific smile that sent sparkle to her eyes. That drew anyone within sight of her inward, wanting to be closer to the brightness.

And right now, she was drawing his brother-in-law in with full force.

Blast her.

Next to Tieran, Lockston's wife swallowed audibly, almost a gulp. Her hands impossibly tight on the stone railing, she started to sway.

Best to get her down there and drag Lockston away from Liv before Lady Lockston completely collapsed on him. There were limits to what he wanted to deal with—even if it was for Aunt Penelope. Or a one-time friend and brother-in-law that currently hated him.

Tieran nudged Lady Lockston into motion, holding out his elbow. "May I accompany you down?" He pointed in Fletch's general direction.

Lady Lockston gave him a weak smile, her eyes shining gratefulness.

They started downward.

~ ~ ~

Tieran stood at one of the five enormous and intricately carved sideboards lining the end of Wellfork's great hall. Filling his cut glass tumbler to the brim, he nodded, only partially listening to Lord Shepton filling his ear about the falling prices on hog commodities.

If Lord Wellfork was going to set out brandy in the morning in a room with ladies present, then Tieran could only be a willing and proper guest and start imbibing early. The man always did keep exceptional barrels. Besides, Tieran needed a steadying drink after seeing Lockston's face when his wife appeared.

He had fully expected Fletch to punch him when he delivered Lady Lockston to his table. Instead, Fletch had dragged his wife out of the great hall, much to the lady's mortification.

Tieran just hoped he hadn't dodged a fist, only to have it land on Lady Lockston.

He gave a slight shake of his head. Maybe he should have trailed after the pair down the side hallway Fletch dragged his wife into. Tieran had never known Fletch to so much as lift a finger against a woman—or to even have the thought to do so—but he had also never seen Fletch as furious as he had just been.

Lady Lockston certainly made his friend react in ways Tieran had not thought possible. Which was either a good thing. Or a bad thing. A very bad thing.

Tieran leaned out past Lord Shepton, debating, looking once more down the empty hallway where the couple had disappeared. Maybe he should follow, just to make sure all was well.

And if it was, what would he be interrupting? He hid a smile to himself. The corridors in Wellfork Castle were twisty and dark for a reason.

Lord Shepton pointedly cleared his throat.

Tieran looked to his new business associate.

"I asked, Reggard, what you think of the timeline for shipments before the new year?"

Tieran stared at the man, trying to trace back what Shepton had been speaking of. Hogs? Dropping prices?

"Well, as I consider it…" Tieran stalled, taking a long sip of his brandy with his brow furrowed as though he was truly contemplating hogs and prices.

His eye caught sight of Liv over the top of his glass. She still sat at the table Fletch had vacated, chatting animatedly with her remaining table companions.

Her presence made perfect sense now that Tieran knew Lord Shepton was here. Liv was here for Shepton, to continue whatever game it was she was playing with the man.

The game, he guessed, was to ruin Shepton, if her actions weeks ago with Lord Fodler were any indication.

Yet since that night, Tieran had given her a wide berth.

Regret came swift after he left her at her townhouse. He had been sober enough to save her, and drunk enough to sit next to her. To talk to her. To listen to her voice. To brush against her body.

He took a healthy swallow from his glass, emptying his tumbler.

A wide berth indeed. It had been necessity.

As much as he had been curious as to Liv's interest in Lord Shepton, he was not curious enough to entangle himself in her snare again.

Once had been enough. Once had almost destroyed him.

He glanced at the spittle glistening on Lord Shepton's chin as he turned to refill his glass. How Liv had not managed to situate herself at Lord Shepton's table, Tieran could not believe. It would have been easy, and he knew from observing her that Liv was not one to let an easy opportunity flit away. Lord Shepton had a definite lack of acquaintances to chat with here at Wellfork Castle, which was why Tieran had been so quickly cornered by the man.

Maybe she was playing coy with Lord Shepton at the moment. She had always been good at that. Playing coy. Even if Tieran had never let her get away with it.

He had never met a woman more in need of a solid man to keep her in line.

Tieran turned slightly to the tables and watched as Liv nodded at her companions, a full, bright smile filling her face, and then she glanced about the room, only to make eye contact with Tieran.

Dammit. The last thing he wanted was her knowing he was even looking in her direction. He was here for one thing—to deliver Lady Lockston to her husband—and that did not entail getting involved in another one of Liv's machinations.

Her brown eyes flitted away from him, looking to his right, and they instantly turned glassy, almost cold. The sudden change was chilling—and unnerving.

Tieran turned, only to see Lady Lockston stomping into the great hall at his right.

Disheveled, tears streaming, her eyes were frantic as she searched the crowd. Damn Lockston. So the idiot *had* been an arse to her.

Tieran was to her in an instant, leaving Lord Shepton by the sideboard without a word.

It only took a minute to usher Lady Lockston across the great hall and up the far staircase they had descended earlier.

Spotting a footman near the minstrel's galley, Tieran left Lady Lockston by the staircase while he stopped the man to request his carriage be brought around. He would be taking Lady Lockston home immediately.

A blur of dark purple ran past him. Tieran spun around, only to see Lady Lockston sprinting down the stone corridor. As she disappeared around a sharp corner in the hallway, he caught sight of her face, and it was tormented.

Dumbstruck, Tieran looked from the footman, to the minstrel's galley, to the now empty hallway.

"What just happened?" Tieran looked to the footman. "Where is Lady Lockston going?"

The servant looked just as puzzled. "I do not know, m'lord. I just heard the gasp and then she ran. Mayhap she is sick?"

Tieran looked down the empty corridor once more, Lady Lockston long since out of view. She didn't reappear.

He glanced past the balcony down into the great hall, searching for anything that would spur her to run.

He froze.

Just inside the arched stone entrance to the hallway Fletch and Lady Lockston had initially disappeared into, stood Fletch.

Fletch kissing a dark-haired woman. The woman's arms wrapped around his neck. A woman in black, with meticulously coifed hair.

Fletch kissing Liv.

Kissing her in plain view of his wife.

"Bloody hell."

Tieran flew down the stairs three at a time and was to the far end of the great hall in seconds, fury pulsating in every muscle. He wanted to strangle Liv. Wanted to rip her from Fletch and toss her down the hall. Wanted her to feel just as much pain as he had just seen in Lady Lockston's face.

Instead, he settled for Lockston. He yanked Fletch's arm, wrenching him away from Liv. "Bloody blasted hell, you bastard."

Confused, flustered, Fletch twisted his arm free from
Tieran's grasp. "What of you, Reggard?"

"You just did that." Tieran pointed to Liv, who had
stumbled backward, landing against the wall, her arms
going wide, her hands bracing herself against the stone. "In
front of your wife."

Tieran only afforded her the merest glance, instead,
bearing down on Fletch.

"I what?" Fletch met Tieran's glare, wiping his lips
with the back of his hand. "I was just walking into the hall
when…" Fletch's eyes narrowed, swinging to Liv.

"You are a blasted fool, Lockston." His voice
thundering, Tieran's fists ground into his sides. The bastard
had always had it too easy. And he was throwing it all away.
A chance at happiness. A chance at a real marriage with a
woman that obviously adored him. And Fletch didn't give a
damn.

Tieran took another step, closing the gap between
them. "And you are twisted. You cannot have life, so you
want to destroy everyone around you. You bloody well did
it with me—I lost Rachel, and then you made sure to take
everything else from my life—and I was left with no one.
No one. And you have everything—friends, family, a wife—
and arse that you are you're throwing it away."

Fletch blinked hard, almost stunned.

Tieran could see him conjuring excuses. Conjuring
defense. Explanations Tieran had no time for.

Tieran shook his head, a snarl curling his lip. "We were
friends once, Lockston. No more. You have gone too far. I
always thought you would redeem yourself before the end.
Rachel always believed that you had that in you. But now

your bloody selfishness and petty cravings are ensuring you
are to leave this earth a worthless human being."

"Shut your vile mouth, Reggard." Fletch inched toward
his brother-in-law, his grey eyes storming.

"You shut yours, Lockston. Did you not hear me? Do
you not realize what you just did? Talia saw you kissing that
tart from the balcony, you fool."

Fletch paused, and it appeared as though he finally
understood exactly what Tieran was telling him. He looked
past Tieran up to the far balcony of the great hall.

"She saw your repulsive display and she ran," Tieran
said, letting the disgust fly freely in his words. "She is the
best damn thing that has ever happened to you, Lockston,
and you just threw her away."

Fletch couldn't tear his eyes off the empty balcony, his
voice still seething. "Why do you even care, Reggard?"

That gave Tieran sudden pause.

Why did he care? Why had he almost just ripped one
of his best friends in half? Because Fletch was an idiot? He'd
been an idiot plenty of times before, and Tieran hadn't
cared. Because he was ruining the spirit of his wife? Tieran
liked Lady Lockston, but he didn't truly know her.

A warbled breath came from the left.

Tieran didn't even want to admit she was still there.
Still standing. Still watching them. Liv.

No. He certainly wasn't going to entertain the
possibility that he cared because it was Liv that Fletch was
kissing. No. Hell, no.

Rachel. He cared because of Rachel. He cared because
of his wife. Because he loved his wife. Because he still loved
his wife. It was Rachel.

Tieran bit back a blasphemy, attempting to temper his look at Fletch. "I don't care. But I do for Rachel. Your sister would not have wanted to see your despicable arse leave the earth in this way."

"Rachel's dead, Reggard," Fletch said. "So you can leave me the hell alone."

"I should leave. It's what you deserve after the way you dismantled my life after Rachel's death." Reggard rounded Fletch, blocking his view of the balcony where Fletch still stared. "I should leave you in the sniveling shell you are determined to rot in."

"So leave." Fletch's lip curled, the words vicious.

"I will. Do not worry on that, Lockston. There is nothing I would rather do in this moment." Tieran unclenched his fists, heaving a sigh. "But unlike you, I loved my wife. So I care about your life because of her. Because she would have demanded it of me."

"You know nothing of what I feel for Talia."

"No. You're right. I know nothing because I never would have treated my wife—or any woman—like you just did." Tieran's eyes narrowed at Fletch. His voice notched downward. "Do you know, Lockston, that even before your sister, I always believed that if anyone could break the curse, it would be you. But now I am beginning to wonder if the curse is exactly what you are meant for. Had your sister just seen what you did, I think she would think the same."

"Bloody well stop throwing my sister in my face, Reggard. She is dead."

"So you have forgotten Rachel? What she wanted for you?" Tieran shook his head in disgust. "Damn, Fletch, she believed far too much in you."

Fletch shifted on his feet, his mouth twisting. "Yes, well, she always was misguided when it came to the men she loved."

A cut to wound him. A cut he had heard, in one form or another, time and again from Fletch.

Tieran's chest tightened. He had to remember Fletch loved his sister just as much as Tieran had. If he remembered that one thing, he could take the blow. Fletch had lost Rachel just the same as he had.

Tieran's belly clenched as he refused to acknowledge the insult, not allowing so much as a twitch. But he lifted his hand, his finger pointing again at the far balcony. "That woman—Talia. Talia is what Rachel wanted for you. Not this." Tieran's look swung to Liv. He hadn't wanted to look at her, acknowledge her. Her brown eyes were wide, scrutinizing the argument, even as she had tried to make herself small against the stone wall. Tieran looked away. "Not this wretched harlot."

"Watch yourself, Reggard," Fletch said.

"No, you watch yourself, Lockston. You need to make a choice, friend. Life—life with meaning. Or whatever sorry state this is." Tieran looked to Liv again, his eyes raking over every inch of her body in disgust. He crossed his thick arms over his chest, glaring at Fletch. "Now am I going to have to go after your wife, or are you?"

Fletch's mouth dropped opened. For a moment, he fumed. Tieran had pushed far—much too far. But then Fletch abruptly blinked, his lips clamping shut.

With a shake of his head, Fletch pushed past Tieran, sprinting out of the hallway and across the great hall.

Tieran watched him, Fletch's boots clunking on the heavy stones of the great hall. Up the far stairs without pause, Fletch disappeared, the clack of his boots still echoing back along the ancient stone walls.

The black skirts next to Tieran twitched, moving to the arched doorway.

No. She was not about to escape this unscathed.

"Stop." The word was growled, an order not to be refused.

The skirts fell still.

Liv was not blameless in this situation. Not blameless at all. And she was not going to disappear from this hallway without consequence.

"Whatever it is you think to machinate, it will take far more than a sloppy kiss to break those two." His eyes still on the far stairs, Tieran spat the words out before turning to her.

Silence.

He looked over his shoulder at her. Her arms had crossed atop her belly, her lower lip in an angry pout as her cheeks flamed red.

"My kisses are not sloppy."

"No?"

Painstakingly, Liv peeled her arms apart and stepped away from the wall. The gold in her brown eyes flickered as she met his look. Her stare didn't hesitate, didn't veer.

She never had shied away from him.

"No. My kisses work exactly as intended, Tieran. And a man such as yourself could only dream of having mine."

"You forget that I have tasted them."

"Yes. So your dreams are that much better, and that much more tragic." Venom dripped from her voice. "You know exactly what you are missing. What you will never have again. A harlot's lips."

Shit. Had he truly called her a harlot? Arse. Words had been flying from his mouth at Fletch without thought, and he deserved every whit of the bitterness currently oozing from her.

His head tilted, almost apologetic, as words pushed through gritted teeth. "I should not have spoken so… freely…in front of you, Lady Canton."

"I have never been afraid of the truth, Tieran. You know that." The bitterness eased ever so slightly from her voice. "And I much prefer honesty to my face, than to deal with the duplicity of a hypocritical man."

Tieran sighed. He had mangled the apology, not that he was sure he was trying to apologize. He rubbed his eyes with the butts of his palms. "What are you even doing here, Lady Canton? Are you still determined to stalk Lord Shepton?"

Her arms crossed over her belly again. "Why do you insist I am stalking him?"

"Tell me you are not."

Her head cocked, her lips pulling to the side for a long moment. When she opened her mouth, her voice had gone neutral, as though she had not a care in the world. "Since you have respected me enough to tell me the truth of what you honestly now think of me, I can only return the spirit of honesty. Quite simply, Tieran, there is a list."

"A list?"

"Yes, a list. And Lord Shepton is on it."

"What sort of list are you speaking of?"

She looked down, smoothing her dark skirts before looking up at him, her face a mask of indifference. "That part is none of your business, Tieran. Do not ask me about it."

He took a step closer to her, meant to intimidate, but it only brought him close enough to catch a whiff of her scent.

Peaches.

She still smelled of peaches. Damn the smell. He hadn't been able to eat the blasted fruit for years after he'd found out she had married Lord Canton.

He turned his head to drag a breath of air that didn't smell of her. "If you mean to attempt to ruin the man because of some mysterious list, Lady Canton, then you need to rethink your actions."

Her eyes searched his face. "Why do you defend the man? He is a dear friend?"

"No."

Her slippers silent on the stone floor, she shuffled a step closer and lifted her hand, her fingers running along the lapel of his dark jacket, smoothing it to his chest. The movement natural, almost unconscious—the exact path her hand had taken a thousand times over in those first years they knew each other.

Her chin lifted, tilting her head back so she could meet his eyes. "Let me ask you a question, Tieran."

He cocked his right eyebrow in reply.

"Lord Lockston—I have chatted with him several times over the past days here at Wellfork Castle. Yet he did not know who I am. I hinted of our past those many years ago, even mentioned your name, just to learn—" She cut herself off.

"To learn what, Lady Canton?"

Her look dropped, the confidence she had approached him with wavering. "To learn if he knew of me."

Her gaze lifted to him, a glimmer of vulnerability shining in her eyes. "Lord Lockston is—was—a dear friend of yours. That is how you spoke of him years ago. Clearly, the scene with him today tells me you still regard him as a true friend. Yet, years ago, when I was your betrothed, you never told him of me."

Tieran inhaled, his chest rising and pushing into her fingers still lingering on his jacket. "No."

She nodded once, her brown eyes lowering, thoughtful, as her hand dropped to her side. A long breath passed.

Her look snapped up, shrewd, pinning him. "Since we are fonts of honesty this day, tell me, Tieran, did you ever intend to marry me?"

"What?"

"I have come to realize a truth as of late, and I will be honest, it has been jarring to my person." Fingers tapping along the edge of her skirts, she spun, stepping to the side of him, distancing herself before she continued.

"All of this time I had been harboring…hopes…hopes I had no right to entertain, Tieran."

Removed from him, she stared at the scene of cherubs twisted in grape vines on the tapestry warming the stone wall of the hallway. "But you never truly wanted more than a trollop in Cheshire to entertain you. I was nothing more than that, nothing to tell your friends about. Nothing to tell your family about. A fun diversion. You were never going to marry me. Never going to return from the war for me."

The injustice of her words hit him, sending an instant swell of defense he wanted to spew into his chest.

There had been nothing but her—her and her alone—that had carried him through the war years. The thought of her waiting for him, it was all that had mattered. Her face, her laughter—that had been all he could imagine when he closed his eyes, time and again during the war when blood was being splattered before him.

Her brown eyes—the gold strands twisting in the irises. Her uncontrolled smile that turned crooked at the corners, yet only when she smiled at him. Her thick black hair that he adored twisting around his finger.

Had he known she was about to marry Lord Canton six years ago, he would have killed a thousand men to make it back to her. He would have moved the very earth he stood on.

But he had been too late.

He swallowed hard.

No. The past was not something he wanted to revisit with Liv.

Not now. Not ever.

He looked at her, staring at the distinct lines of her profile. Elegant. The years had done nothing but refine her beauty, bringing it to an intelligent, shining peak.

Beauty that she now used for malicious purposes.

His jaw twitched. "So that was why you kissed Lord Lockston? He is my friend and you wanted to make me jealous?"

"The kiss?" Her gaze left the tapestry to land on him as both of her eyebrows arched, sending long wrinkles across her forehead. "You thought that was for your benefit?"

"Was it not?"

Her eyebrows lowered and she shook her head, an odd smile lifting one side of her face. "Do not flatter yourself, Tieran. I don't know when such conceit took over your life, but it is not becoming of you. Assumptions such as the one you just made do nothing but cause embarrassment."

"I am not embarrassed."

Her head tilted to the side, her eyes deftly regarding him. "Then I am embarrassed for you."

"So that kiss had nothing to do with me?"

"No."

"Then why do it?"

She sighed, picking up the side of her black skirts and starting to move past him. She paused for the smallest step, leaning toward him, her voice low. "Quite simply, Tieran, Lord Lockston is on the list as well."

She stepped beyond him and went under the arched doorway, her face serene as she entered the dining hall before he could stop her.

List? What the hell was this bloody list about?

And why was one of his best friends on it?

Tieran's eyes narrowed, watching her black skirts sway with far too much pomposity.

Loyalty, even for an arse like Lockston, reared in his chest.

As much as he wanted to refuse it—deny the need for it—Tieran had to come to terms with what he was about to do. Loyalty demanded it.

It was time to reinsert himself into Liv's affairs.

{ CHAPTER 6 }

Thwap.

A bird thumped into the glass by her head, and Liv sat upright in the window seat, peering out at the snow on the ground.

Her forehead flat against the pane of glass, she spotted the bird, a small, plump sparrow that had landed, stunned, in a deep bank of snow just below the window.

The snow had come down heavy—three days of it—and it had kept her inside, along with the mishmash of characters visiting Mortell Abbey in Yorkshire. Aside from the time in her assigned chambers—and she could only hide in there so long—there had not been the slightest break to escape the lot of them—not even for five minutes.

She needed to get outside. Ride a horse. Walk along the river. Something—anything.

Liv was accustomed to social engagements that ended in a timely fashion—that allowed her to escape at will to the quiet of her house where she could hear her own thoughts in her head. But it had now been a week at Mortell Abbey, and half of that time she had been captive in this drawing room, subject to the strained polite chatter of the dispirited wives, along with the occasional veiled insinuation as to why Liv was even in attendance at the winter house party.

If only they knew she was here for Lord Shepton.

Tapping her forefinger against the pencil in her hand, she glanced down at the sketch paper she had propped against a leather-bound book. Disgust instantly flooded her.

The chest of a giant man, bedecked in the finest of jackets, stared up at her from the paper. She had mindlessly sketched the torso of a man from the waist up. The drawing ended at the neck where she had run out of paper. Thank goodness.

Without the likeness of a face to prove otherwise, she could pretend she was just exacting her proficiency at getting the lines of a torso correct. Yet she knew full well who the chest belonged to. Tieran.

This was the twelfth sketch she had done of him in some form or another—his chest, a hand, the back of his neck, his boots—since she had seen him at Wellfork Castle two weeks ago.

Removing herself to Yorkshire was supposed to be a cure for her wayward thoughts. But her subconscious mind had turned cruel on her, and she was having a blasted time trying to control it. A harlot. She had to remember Tieran's opinion of her—straight from his lips.

Tucking the drawing into the front flap of the book, she slammed the tome onto the window seat. She had thought to sit here and plan, write down every bit of information she had on Lord Shepton, and concoct the best scheme for completing her ruin of him. That was why she was here, of course. To finally trap Lord Shepton. There was no other reason to jail herself for weeks in Yorkshire with a horde of pretentious men and simpering women.

Deliver ruin—she needed to concentrate on that.

Instead, she was fiddling with sketches.

She pressed her forehead on the glass again, watching for movement in the tunnel of snow the bird had created on its way down. She saw feathers, but no twitches. No chirps.

Not that the bird would have an easy time getting out of the pit it had created.

She looked up at the sky. The snow had ceased, but long grey clouds still blanketed the land. The bird needed help, and she needed not to be inside another moment.

After layering on her heaviest wool cloak and pulling up her tallest boots, Liv had just rounded an outside corner of the abbey when she realized the snow was deeper than her boots, and her wool stockings were already soaked around the knees. She also realized why they had been stuck inside the abbey during the storm—moving through snow that deep was exhausting, every step a tiring effort.

It took her another ten minutes of trudging through the drifts, moving along the far north wing of the abbey, before she found the spot in the snow where the bird had landed.

The sparrow was still there, now buried in a tomb of snow. It was moving, fluttering, trying to escape, but only succeeding at knocking more snow on top of itself.

Liv plunged both hands down, elbows deep into the snow. Digging beneath the bird, she lifted it gently from its pit, attempting not to scare it.

The bird stilled. Liv lifted it higher to eye level. Its head swiveled, little black eyes peering at her through the snow covering its head and beak.

It shook, snow splattering in all directions, landing across the bridge of her nose.

She lifted her hands higher, giving it a little jostle. "Go."

Tweet. The bird chirped but made no motion to flap its wings.

She lifted it a touch higher. "Go. Fly away."

The bird sat, head pivoting, looking around.

"Go on." Liv tossed it slightly into the air, expecting that to spur it into motion and fly away.

It didn't.

It fell through the air. A puff of white flew up as it hit the snow, descending into a deep new hole in front of Liv's boots.

"Buggers, little birdy."

She bent, fishing it out of the snowbank again.

Its little black eyes still alert, watching her, it didn't look hurt from the fall, but a mixture of guilt and compassion settled hard on Liv's shoulders. Looking down at the bird cradled in her gloves, she realized the bird wasn't robust at all. Sopping wet, bedraggled, the poor creature was scrawny—the wild tufts of exaggerated feathers earlier had only made it appear much stronger than it truly was.

Liv glanced up at the window into the drawing room. The ladies sat with their needlepoint and their cards, not noticing Liv just outside the room. Her mouth tugged to the side as she contemplated the appropriateness of bringing the bird inside to her room.

If the ladies hadn't even noticed her leaving the drawing room, then they surely wouldn't notice her sneaking along the rear hallways up to her room.

Lifting the edge of her cloak, Liv cradled the bird into a secure spot, wrapping the wool around it to both hide and calm it, and held it to her belly. She lifted her right leg, awkwardly turning around, and followed her deep footprints in the snow back alongside the abbey.

Slipping in through the door at the end of the north wing, Liv had just made it to the second level, moving along an empty hallway to the stairs leading to her room on the third floor, when a shadow appeared in front of her.

She jumped with a yelp, almost dropping the swaddle of cloak.

"What are you doing, Liv?"

Tieran.

The scare sending her heart out of control, her look snapped up to him, irate. He dared to appear without warning, out of the shadows, days away from London—and then decided now was the appropriate time to drop "Lady Canton" and address her as "Liv"? The gall of the man.

Her mouth opened to tell him that exact thing when the bird squirmed under her cloak, its beak poking into her belly. She needed to change course.

"I am attempting to make way to my chambers, my lord." Tamping down on her ire, she barreled forward, attempting to step around him. He stepped to his right, blocking her path. Damn him. He knew he could swallow the width of the whole corridor with his size.

She glared up at him. "What are *you* doing here?"

"I only just arrived, and I have business with Lord Shepton to attend to." His blue eyes settled on her. "I saw you outside, tromping through the snow. What were you doing? Spying?"

Instant indignation sent her cheeks flaming. "Spying? You think I was spying on someone? Outside, in knee-deep snow—that would be the best way to spy upon someone?" Her head shook. "You are mad. And your opinion of me has obviously reached an even lower low."

She lifted her free left hand, pushing the outside of his arm. A weak attempt to get him to move, since she knew she couldn't physically force him to do so. "Let me pass, Lord Reggard."

"No."

"No?" She reeled a step backward at the refusal, her right hand tightening around the bird pouched in her cloak. "Your overbearance has reached an infuriating point, my lord. I will move past you."

His left eyebrow cocked, his arms crossing over his chest. "No. I want to know what you are about, Liv. What you were doing outside. Why it's now so important to get to your room. Are you hiding something?"

Blast it. The arse was not going to let her by. "I am none of your concern, Lord Reggard. None. You will excuse me." She spun, intending to go back down the stairs and make her way to her rooms by way of the main staircase. She would just have to pray no one else intercepted her.

"Stop, Liv."

She made it three steps along the corridor before her right elbow was snatched, jerking her to a stop and ripping her hand from the swaddle around the bird.

Her cloak fell. The sparrow squawked, flittering up to the ceiling to clutch the molding along the uppermost corner of the hallway.

Bugger. *Now* the bird decided it could fly?

Liv shook her arm free from Tieran and ran the few steps to stand under it, her arm stretched upward, trying to reach it, entice it down.

"A bird?"

Her chin whipped over her shoulder as she shot Tieran a withering look. "Yes, a bird. You did this, now help me get it down from there before I am discovered."

"Why not leave it—where could it go?"

"Downstairs, into a room, anywhere."

"So what if it does?"

Her forehead scrunched at him. Was he truly that obtuse? "It is bad for the bird, Tieran. How do you think it will be disposed of? Now help me get it before it flies off."

"You want me to catch your bird?"

"Yes. This borders on insulting—no, it is rude—to bring a scraggly bird into someone's home. And I would rather not be requested to leave the abbey at the moment. Especially when travel is nearly impossible."

She looked back up to the bird, attempting to whistle. It was a weak tweet, at best. She never could whistle.

"Give me your cloak, Liv."

She exhaled a grumble but stepped to the side and removed her black cloak, handing it to him.

Tieran slid both hands under the dark fabric, creating a bowl with his hands. He whistled, a low, pure tone, as he slowly lifted his hands far above his head.

The sparrow's head cocked back and forth, trying to figure the sound out. It didn't even notice the black cloth creeping up at it until Tieran had stretched high, covering the bird with the cloak from below.

"Careful." Liv touched his shoulder.

"I am capturing a bird for you, Liv. I am attempting to be as cautious as I can."

He clasped his hands together along the ceiling, making a pouch for the bird with the cloak. He brought the cloak and the bird down slowly, his heels clicking to the wooden floors as he came down from his toes. "Now what?"

"Up to my room." Liv hurried in front of Tieran, racing up the stairs to make sure the hallway was free of people before she rushed to her chambers. She ushered Tieran in quickly, closing the door behind him.

His hands still clasping the fabric together, trapping the bird in the pouch, Tieran lifted the cloak. The pouch wiggled, the bird clearly agitated. "Why did you have a bird in your cape, Liv?"

"It thumped into a window by my head, fell, and then it couldn't get out of the snow. So I went outside to help it."

"And decided to keep it?"

Her eyes went to the ceiling. "It couldn't fly, Tieran, so I brought it in to warm it."

He lifted the cloak higher. "It just flew without any trouble in the hallway."

"Yes, well, it appears I have already fixed it, then." She pointed at the window. "Here. Let us set it down— carefully—on the sill and it will be able to fly away."

She rushed over to the window, grunting as she pushed upward on the pane with no success. She banged on the windowpane several times to crack the frozen layer holding it closed. Pushing again, the window opened and a blast of cold air whipped into the room.

Tieran waited a step behind her.

She moved to the side. "Careful—set it on the sill, and we will peel open the cloak, and it can fly off." Her hand flew up. "But careful. It's so little. Maybe I should do it."

"I'm not going to crush it, Liv." He gave her a sideways glance as he set the pouch of the cape on the windowsill. "I can manage to control my strength, you realize."

Her mouth clamped shut. She had just been entirely rude to Tieran, and about the very thing that he had always been self-conscious about. People were afraid of him. Afraid of his size.

Had she forgotten that fact?

She settled the bulk of the cloak on the ledge as he held the wrapped bird in place, half of the cloth draping outside the window, the other half draping inside. Slowly, Tieran loosened his hold on the pouch of fabric, letting it slowly fall from around the bird.

They both stepped back from the window. Now free from the cloak, the sparrow righted itself on the ledge, shook, fluffing its brown and white feathers, its head swiveling around at its surroundings.

It looked outside. It looked inside. It didn't move.

Liv waved her fingers at it. It didn't twitch. It just looked at her with its black eyes, its brown and white head crooked.

She leaned toward Tieran. "Why is it not flying away?"

He shrugged. "I don't think it's hurt."

Liv leaned forward, fluttering her fingers at it again. It hopped along the cloak, still looking up at her.

"It is cold out there," Tieran said. "I guess I would choose in here, where it is warm, if I were a bird."

Liv laughed, turning to look up at him. "You are thinking like a bird now?"

He smiled at her, his head slanting to the side. "I do possess an imagination, Liv."

"So did you imagine you were going to be doing this today?"

Tweet.

The bird jumped upon the moment when all eyes were off of it and flew in and across the room, landing on the carved wooden scrolls framing the top of a tall armoire. Both Liv and Tieran turned, staring at the bird.

Tieran was the first to laugh. His body next to hers, vibrating in mirth, made Liv join in within a second.

He looked down at her, the smile wide on his face. "It would seem you have gained yourself a sparrow, Liv."

"It would seem I have. You don't think catching it will be as easy the second time, do you?"

Still chuckling, Tieran looked up at the bird. "I doubt it."

She laughed, waving her hands in the air as she looked to the bird. "Then it can stay. I was going to hide it in here anyway."

His voice soft, warm, he stepped closer, his arm brushing hers. "I had forgotten what a tenderheart you always were for wounded animals, Liv."

She watched the sparrow hop along the top of the armoire as a smile from memories past lined her lips. "And what a tenderheart you always were for helping me help wounded animals."

Her eyes on the bird, she didn't see Tieran descend on her. Didn't see his body align with hers. Didn't see his hand lift, slipping along the back of her neck.

But the force of him hit her before his lips made contact.

Just enough time to part her lips. His mouth was on hers, hot, instantly demanding. He had never eased into his want of her. Never subtle, he charged, volatile. For an instant, his lips on hers were foreign, something she did not recognize.

Then her eyelids slid downward. It rushed at her in a great crashing wave, shoving all conscious thought into blackness as her heart swelled, her body falling into tingling madness. His lips. His breath. All she could feel, all she could think.

The kiss echoed of long ago—how he had always kissed her. Like he was going to devour her, slowly, deliberately, making sure every bit of her body felt pleasure as he was doing so. A promise of ecstasy. A promise of gratification, of worship.

And she wanted more. She had always wanted more. And had never been satisfied.

A rush of cold air hit her, and Liv opened her eyes to find she stood alone in the middle of the room.

Tieran had broken the kiss and now stood by the door, his hand on the knob. Both horror and confusion twisted on his face. "No. I did not mean to do that. It is not why I'm here. You…"

It took her a long moment to draw breath into her lungs. "I what, Tieran?"

He straightened, his hand smoothing the front of his dark jacket as composure returned to his face. "You just looked like you once did. Alive and bold and mischievous like you were getting away with something. Youthful indiscretion. Like you used to be. Like we used to be. And I forgot myself." He gave a slight bow. "You will pardon me, Lady Canton."

Before she could respond, before she could move her body, he was out the door.

She stood rooted in the middle of the room, staring at the thick oak door.

The kiss still sending vibrations through the pounding blood in her veins, she attempted to right her mind—right the facts she knew in her head. Tieran thought she was a trollop—a wretched harlot. He had made no secret of that. And he had not denied he had always thought that.

So why had he appeared here at Mortell Abbey—days away from London and in the middle of a snowstorm?

She doubted it was Lord Shepton that had brought him here.

Did he imagine to finally fulfill what he had wanted eight years ago—to have her in his bed without having to marry her? She *was* a widow now, and as such, the freedom to discreetly move amongst beds was not unheard of. That couldn't possibly be what he was planning. Could it?

Liv drew a deep breath into her lungs, her chest lifting high.

If it was, he was about to be immensely disappointed.

The bird chirped.

Her gaze lifted from the door to look at it.

Exactly, little bird. Agreed.

Tieran had no idea who he was now dealing with. Not the innocent girl he had once left crying in the countryside. That girl was a shadow, a wispy rainbow that had no chance at existing.

And she would be sure to show him exactly who she was now.

Her lips drew tight, bolstering her resolve, but as they pulled, she realized how swollen they were. How raw.

Damn him...

There was one problem. If that kiss was any indication, she was a harlot, just as he believed. For he could have gotten her to do anything he commanded to in that moment.

She needed to harden herself.

But how could she harden against the one thing she had always wanted?

{ CHAPTER 7 }

Liv stared up at the face of the longcase clock in the corner of the music room. She knew her eyes had landed on the creeping minute hand and stubbornly refused to move away when Lady Mortell cleared her throat.

"Lady Canton, did you have an answer?" Lady Mortell asked the question with politeness, as a well-bred hostess ought to, but Liv heard a distinct undertone of crispness in her voice.

Liv had to forcibly close her eyes to break her own stare. "I apologize, Lady Mortell, I did not hear your question. I find myself overly tired tonight. It must be the grey skies of the day."

Grey skies. Humorous. Her weariness had nothing at all to do with dour skies, and everything to do with the dour disposition fixed upon the one gentleman steadily sending shadows over her spirit.

"I asked if you would like to play the harp for us? It would be a pleasant diversion since Oracy and Juilet have gone through their entire selection of sonatas three times now in the past four days." Lady Mortell sounded as weary as Liv imagined her daughters were.

Three times? Liv had apparently stopped paying attention on the second go-through. It wasn't that the girls weren't talented. They were. It was more the perfection that they played with. Precision that bred unremarkable. Not that Liv could condemn them for it—she herself had played with that same meticulousness when she was their age.

If anything, Liv should be at her most attentive in the music room. For once in the past two days, Tieran was not in the same room as her. It was the first time she had been able to breathe properly since he had appeared at Mortell Abbey. Lady Mortell had been conspiring for the past two days to place Liv in close proximity to Tieran, and Liv had been suffocated by his presence because of it.

She understood Lady Mortell's intentions—what better way to pass time when snowbound than to try and create a love match with a widow and handy widower. What better success could come forth from a house party in Yorkshire? Lady Mortell would be able to utilize the tale of it throughout the entire next season.

So Liv had suffered the dinners and the drawing room and the library and the card room all positioned within an arm's length of Tieran. Close enough to hear every comment, every chuckle, every sigh under his breath, every bite of food he took, every sip of port he imbibed. Close enough to catch whiffs of his scent that had not changed in eight years—leather mixed with late summer heath topped with spiced liqueur.

Exhausting.

Liv offered Lady Mortell an apologetic smile. "If I could beg for your understanding, I actually would like to retire. My head has gone to aches, but I do promise to relieve the girls of their duties tomorrow."

Lady Mortell folded her hands in her lap, giving Liv a slight nod. "Of course. Be well, Lady Canton." Not able to fully stifle her sigh, her attention went to her two daughters.

Liv stood and exited the music room before she was intercepted by one of the other five ladies in attendance at the house party. She had chatted for hours with all of them—including Lord Shepton's wife—and each was pleasant, congenial, and only mildly tolerant of Liv's presence.

At the base of the grand staircase, Liv stopped with her foot on the bottom step. She wasn't exactly tired, nor did her head pain her in the slightest since escaping the music room. What she was, was hungry. She hadn't eaten but a bite at dinner, so consumed she had been with trying to ignore the man seated next to her.

Her slippered foot dropped from the step, and she veered to the right, making her way through the many tight corridors and stairs of the abbey to the kitchens. She had already wandered down into the kitchens three times, and Cook nodded at her when she opened the massive larder and nabbed an apple.

Lord Mortell's cook was a simple woman, somewhat worn thin, but she did have an admirable talent with how to serve the local grouse. Outside of Lady Mortell's watch, Liv had made sure to befriend Cook on her first day at Mortell Abbey, as was her habit at any new place she visited for a length of time.

Liv had learned early in her marriage to Lord Canton how valuable staff could be. His staff had become her most important ally in protecting her new husband from his cousin. Their butler, cook, and driver had interceded on numerous occasions when her husband's cousin provoked "accidents" meant for Lord Canton. They had saved her life, even. The staff had become so integral to her life, that she had brought all of them with her when she moved to the dower house after Lord Canton died.

It was a lesson she learned well—to be prepared for anything and to have allies, even if they were in people others generally disregarded.

With a nod to Cook, Liv left the kitchen, green apple in hand, and slipped back up the stairs. She only needed one last thing before retiring to her chambers, and she quietly moved along the shadows to the library.

It was empty, only a small fire lighting the tomes lining the walls, but Liv wasn't particularly picky—she just needed something to draw her mind away from Tieran.

If she could stop thinking about him—at least for an hour—she could reset her priorities. She was here to destroy Lord Shepton, and obsessing on Tieran got her no closer to that goal.

Her head slipped to the side as her fingertips ran along the titles opposite the fire. The sudden click of the library door made her jump, dropping her apple.

The fruit hit her toe and rolled away from her, straight in the direction of the door. Straight in the direction of the intruder.

Tieran stood by the door, watching her. One side of his face was alive with shadows from the fire dancing along his distinct jawline. The other side of his face sank into the shadows, offering no clue as to what he was thinking.

And just what was he thinking? He had gone from dismissing her as a harlot at Wellfork Castle, only to appear directly in front of her in the middle of Yorkshire, in the middle of a snowstorm.

And then he had the gall to kiss her.

She was here for a reason. He was here for a game. It was the only valid conclusion.

The apple rolled to a stop halfway between them. Liv looked up from the fruit to meet Tieran's piercing gaze. He made no motion to move from the door.

"Why are you here, Tieran?"

"In the library? Can I not borrow a book from our host?"

"You may, but I doubt you are in here for literary pursuits." Her hand slid over her belly, unconsciously smoothing the front of her black wool gown. "At Mortell Abbey, Tieran. Why have you come here?"

"As I said, I have business to attend to with Lord Shepton."

"Do not mistake me for daft, Tieran. I have just as much wits about me as I once did. More so now, unfortunately."

"You believe I am here for you?" His face turned slightly away from the fire, sending his look into even deeper shadows. But his eyes stayed riveted on her.

"Yes. But it is the why I seek an answer to. You expressed at Wellfork Castle—in no uncertain words—what you think of me. Harlot." In the last weeks, she had gotten comfortable enough with the word repeating in her head that her voice didn't flinch when she spoke it. "Harlot is what you said. So I should hold no more interest for you. You have conveyed to me all you need to."

His chin dropped, his voice low. "Maybe I am here to understand."

Liv nodded, her eyes lowering to the apple on the floor between them, its stark green a contrast to the dark wooden floors. She knew she had baited him at Wellfork Castle by mentioning the list. By mentioning his friend, Lord

Lockston, was on the list. And now he was here to collect answers.

If only she had kept her mouth closed. If only that moment of leaving him speechless at Wellfork Castle had not been so tempting—and so delicious to deliver.

She was paying for that moment now.

Curiosity had always been Tieran's weakness. And his curiosity could very well mean her own downfall. He wanted to understand what the list was about so he could stop her. For that fact alone she needed to get rid of him.

She took a step toward him, staring at him, searching her mind. When she was young, when he had been her betrothed, what had he respected most about her?

Her honesty. That she didn't pander about topics. That she didn't curb her tongue for politeness or to spare feelings—her own or others. That she didn't have the wherewithal for duplicity.

Such simple days those were. Innocent.

She inhaled an aching breath. Honesty. It had been a long time since that trait was useful. But she had always preferred it.

"There is nothing here that you need to—or are willing to—understand, Tieran. So I would prefer if you would remove yourself from Mortell Abbey."

"Why?"

"This is too hard for me." She leveled her gaze at him. "You. Being near you. Having your eyes on me. Condemning me. Have you not already judged me enough to last your lifetime? Or do you prefer to torture me as well—vengeance in whatever form you can manifest it?"

"Why is my presence torture, Liv?"

She took another step, stopping just before the apple. "You know why. You know exactly how I still look at you, and you have shown very little mercy in how you have treated me in every one of our recent interactions."

His eyes flickered, unprepared for her answer. "How do you look at me, Liv?"

Her mouth opened, almost answering. With love. With love that had never wavered over the past eight years. She knew it. And he damn well knew it as well.

Her jaw clamped shut, her teeth clacking together.

"I judge because I am attempting to understand, Liv."

"Did you kiss me in an attempt to understand as well? Or was that just to explore how much of a harlot you can treat me? To finish what you started eight years ago—to finally bed me and be done with me?"

"Liv, I apologized for calling you a harlot—I was only attempting to make an impression upon Lord Lockston and I never meant—"

"You didn't apologize, Tieran."

"I did."

"No, you said it was unfortunate that I heard you use that word." Her hand came up, palm to him. "I will not quibble on it. You do not need to hide what you think of me, Tieran. I am well aware."

For a reason she couldn't discern, her words spurred him into motion, and he pushed from the door, walking slowly toward her. Almost the stalking of a wild cat on prey in the darkest hour of the night.

The air around him—the force of him that she always felt just before his body brushed hers, enveloped her.

But he stopped, just before the apple. He bent, picking it up from the floor. Pulling a tuft of his shirt sleeve further from the arm of his jacket, he proceeded to rub the apple clean with the white linen.

He stared at her, his hands working the cloth along the apple. "We need to stop this, Liv. A truce. For the moment. I am here, and you cannot leave, so let us call a truce. I will behave. And I will strive to not offend you again."

"You think you have offended me?"

"I haven't?"

"One would have to care to be offended."

He blinked, his blue eyes stung, his hands on the apple stopping.

But before she could take a breath his look seared into her, scrutinizing. She had said the words, brash, to protect the little dignity she had left. No matter that it was a lie only moments after she had decided on honesty.

"You do care, Liv." His hands started rubbing the cloth on the apple again. "And you are right—I am well aware of how you look at me."

Air left her lungs. What had she just been pretending— that she preferred the honesty?

Not honesty like this. Not honesty that left her bared and naked to Tieran, while he remained sheltered, fortified in his cocoon of indifference.

She wanted her feet to stay locked in place. She *needed* her feet to hold her ground. But betrayal came from her own legs, turning her, sliding her across the floor, the urge to distance her body from his overwhelming.

She stopped in front of the windows at the far end of the library, looking out into the dark night. Clouds still blocked the night sky, the blackness beyond making the glass a mirror instead of a window.

She watched his reflection in the window. The size, the strength in his body as he moved to set the apple on a side table at the other end of the library. Even with the distance, his body dwarfed hers in the window's reflection.

She closed her eyes. If he truly desired a truce, he would go. Leave her in peace.

The air around her crackled, and her eyes opened. Tieran was directly behind her. Again, he had moved with a silent stealth, a skill she had never known him to possess.

In the window she saw him lean forward. His breath warmed her ear in the next instant, his right hand sliding along her bare skin into the crook between her neck and shoulder.

"I saw it in your eyes, Liv. I saw the hurt at Wellfork Castle."

She tried to shake off his hand, but her shoulder went weak, the movement only managing to squeeze his hand closer onto her neck. She looked at his reflection. His head was tilted downward, his focus solid on her, his mouth next to her ear. "You saw nothing, Tieran. You saw what you wanted to see. You do have an imagination."

He shook his head. "No. I saw you wonder. I saw the hurt when you asked me about Lord Lockston knowing you. When you landed on the blasphemous conclusion that I never wanted to marry you."

She froze, her eyes closing.

She had just begun to resign herself to the fact that Tieran had never wanted to marry her. He had only wanted to use her for a dalliance those many years ago.

But now this. Not this. Her life was so much simpler without this. Without his breath on her neck. Without his words of the past.

"I never spoke of you, Liv, for the very simple reason that I didn't want them to know of you. I didn't want to chance losing you to one of them. I never wanted my friends to have to meet with my jealousy."

His palm slid slightly up her neck, his fingers spreading along the line of her jaw as he looked down, his lips by her ear. "You are beautiful, Liv, and I was young and unsure of myself and I did not want to have to defend against anyone swooping in and wooing you from me."

With a shake of her head, her eyes opened to stare at his reflection in the window. "You thought so little of me that you did not trust I would not be swayed away?"

"My friends are rogues, Liv. Charming is their natural state."

"You were charming."

He looked up, meeting her eyes in the window's reflection. "Yes, well, you were the only one to ever see that in me, Liv."

She inhaled sharply, her chest contracting.

No. She did not want this. She wanted simple. Wanted vengeance. Wanted to work her way through the list without interference. She didn't want the maelstrom of emotions that Tieran caused. Not the things he would demand of her—he was here to stop her.

She didn't want this battle with Tieran.

Not when she didn't believe for an instant she could win it.

Yet as she exhaled slowly, looking at him in the window, words forged up from her belly, from her soul, that she couldn't quite control. "The only person I ever wanted to tell me I was beautiful was you, Tieran." Her voice, already soft, fell to a mere whisper. "And that is still true."

His head dropped, his lips finding the soft spot just below her ear. His left hand slipped around her side, his palm pressing her belly, pulling her into the length of him. "Then let me take you away from here, Liv. Let us leave before you do irreparable harm. Harm that is not necessary. It is not too late to change course."

His words slashed into her. The very thing she feared.

He only wanted to stop her.

And he was willing to manipulate her feelings for that very purpose. He didn't mean a single word he spoke.

"Damn you." She spun, jumping to the side and out of his reach. "Your cruelty knows no bounds, Tieran. And you are severely mistaken about me. I am not a whore you can manipulate so easily. A few kisses—some breathless words—no. Not me. I am not that stupid."

Turning, she ran across the library floor, slipping out the door and into the shadows of the hallway.

She didn't need her apple and a book anymore.

Her mind would be far too consumed with the bastard that night.

{ CHAPTER 8 }

Heel to toe. Slow, exact, light. Disturb nothing. Silence. Balance.

Tieran scanned the hay strewn on the dirt before him. To move without sound could very well be the most valuable skill he had gained during the war. Possibly the only thing. The war had given him very little beyond the destruction it had caused.

He heard the voices at the far end of the stable. The low monotone of Lord Shepton.

A laugh.

Liv's laugh.

Tieran had to check his step, holding back against speed. He ignored the abrupt urge to run down the center of the barn, growling, ripping Liv away from Lord Shepton. He had to remember she had only been gone for fifteen minutes—twenty at the most. How much trouble could she cause in that amount of time?

His foot went down slowly, continuing the exact pace that kept his movement silent. Surprise would be his ally. The minx had escaped the house without him seeing. Escaped to further whatever her agenda was with Lord Shepton. And she needed to know that he would always be there, lurking, watching, ready to intercede.

She meant to ruin the man, and Tieran was more determined than ever to find out why.

He leaned his head forward, peeking into the last stall of the stables. Liv stood at the front of a white speckled horse, holding an apple to the mare's chomping teeth. Fully clothed, a thick black wool riding habit hid every bit of her skin, not a scandalous touch of her bared to the world.

But she was smiling. Glowing at Lord Shepton as he stood but a step away. And the man was obvious in his ogling of her breasts.

The sight sent a visceral rage burning through his chest. Lord Shepton had no right to Liv's smile—especially when he was blatantly categorizing her assets, imagining what he was going to do with them. And she was allowing it. Tieran had more than once seen Liv cut a man direct in the middle of a ballroom for even glancing downward at the slope of her chest.

Whatever her plan entailed with Lord Shepton, she was more than willing to sink to incredible lows to achieve her goal.

His stomach curdling at the scene, Tieran straightened and casually strode around the wall of the stall. "Lord Shepton, you are here. What a coincidence I found you."

Shepton jumped a step away from Liv, pasting a flat smile on his face as he looked to Tieran. At least the man had the good sense to feign innocence.

"Why is that, Lord Reggard?"

"I was speaking with Lord Mortell about our investment. He had several questions for you that I thought you would be the one better to answer."

Lord Shepton moved toward Tieran, strained curiosity on his face. "There is no need to discuss our affairs with my brother-in-law, Reggard."

"Just passing the time, Shepton." Tieran shrugged. "He was curious. I was bored. Regardless, he would like to speak with you."

Lord Shepton sighed, shaking his head. He turned as he left, offering a slight bow to Liv. "Lady Canton."

She smiled brightly at him. "Lord Shepton, we can continue our conversation later."

He nodded a touch too eagerly, then made his way out of the stall, having to turn sideways at the entrance to slide past Tieran. Tieran wasn't about to move aside for him.

Standing at the stall's opening, Tieran watched the back of Lord Shepton retreat down the long length of the stable. He waited until the man stepped outside before he turned to Liv.

The smile that only a moment before had been shining brightly at Lord Shepton had completely vanished.

A scowl sat on Liv's face now, pinching her full lips inward at the corners, her warm golden eyes narrowed at him. Even with the glower, she was still beautiful. Blast her.

"You are blatant in your interference, Tieran."

He crossed his arms over his chest, attempting to keep his lips from hinting at the smile trying to escape. "Am I?"

Her arms mirrored his, crossing over her belly. "Do not be so smug about it."

"Smugness has nothing to do with it. You are attempting to ruin the man."

Her right hand flew up. "Yes, I know—and you are here to stop me."

His bottom lip jutted upward, a frown taking over his face. "I told you I am here to understand, Liv."

"To understand how to stop me."

"Or to help you. Whatever you need to do." His head cocked to the side at his own words. They had flown out of his mouth without thought. Without him considering what they truly meant.

She went to the side of the stall, pulling her hanging cloak off a wooden peg. "What I need to do is leave Mortell Abbey now that you are here."

"Pity the snow blocking the roads, then."

"Yes. Pity that." She snapped her cloak with a shake and then spun it around her shoulders.

"I see your mare is saddled. You were planning a ride?"

She looked over her shoulder to her horse as she secured the cloak's clasp at her neck. "Yes, Lord Shepton was about to show me to the Roman ruins on the bank of the brook before you interrupted. It is supposed to be fascinating. There were Roman baths there. The roads are not fit for carriages yet, but I understand the horses should have no trouble with the trail."

Tieran glanced down the empty middle walkway of the stable. "Well, now that Shepton is disposed of for the rest of the afternoon, it looks as though you have two choices— one, let me accompany you to the ruins."

"I will take choice number two."

He looked at her, smile playing on his lips. "You are welcome to it. It entails sitting through the fourth go-through of the selection of sonatas by the Mortell girls. They are warming up as we speak."

Liv groaned.

Her head tilted down, she looked up at him through her long dark lashes, suspicion evident. "This is how you imagined us to proceed, Tieran? Light and easy, like we are old friends chatting up the *The Times*?"

The question threw him. How did he wish to proceed with Liv? He had come up to Mortell Abbey to disrupt whatever she was planning with Lord Shepton and to learn what he could about this list she spoke of—a list that apparently threatened one of his best friends.

He had come to Mortell Abbey firmly regarding her as the enemy. But then he had found her with that damn bird. Listened to her try to lie to him in the library. Felt her soft skin under the pads of his fingers.

And he was succumbing to the realization that Liv could never be his adversary.

So why in the hell was he still here?

He shrugged in answer to Liv's question.

Her hands flew up in defeat. "Very well. This, unfortunately, is the more desirable choice." She turned to her horse, running her glove down its nose, muttering to herself. "I can do polite chatter just as well as the next. Inane conversation is the key, since every time I talk with you, you manage to twist conversations and make me expose myself. And then you delight in crushing whatever vulnerability I dare to display."

Her head snapped to the side, looking at him over her shoulder. "Was I just talking out loud?"

Tieran swallowed a guffaw. "Yes."

"Blast it." She sighed and then waved her hand at him. "Get your horse, then. And next time, you would do well to exit the area before a lady starts speaking to herself."

Tieran unthreaded his arms, stepping away from the entrance to the stall. "I will strive to avoid your ramblings in

the future, Liv. A clue that they are coming will be helpful,
though."

"Go."

With a chuckle, Tieran moved down the stable, going
to the stall where his steed stood ready and rested after the
long trek to Mortell Abbey. But his chuckle faded once he
was out of Liv's sight.

Crush her vulnerability? Is that what he had done to
her?

No. He wouldn't have. He was sure of it.

He turned into the stall of his horse, pushing the
question from his mind. Sink away. Sink the thoughts he
didn't want to dwell too long upon. Sink them into the sea
of black in his mind where he buried the questions that
stung, the demons he didn't want to revisit. Sink. Disappear.

Minutes later, under the wispy grey sky, their horses
picked through the snowdrifts in single file until they
arrived at the main path that ran through the thick woods
of the Mortell estate. The snow was less deep on the path
that skirted along the stream, back and forth into the
forest, and wide enough that Tieran could nudge his horse
alongside Liv's mare.

She allowed it, neither prompting her horse forward
nor holding it slow.

His calf brushing her black skirts occasionally, Tieran
looked over at Liv. The cold had sent bright pink into the
normally porcelain skin of her cheeks and nose. It made her
look alive. More so than she ever was in a drawing room.
Much like she looked at Lady Desmond's when she won the
pot against Lord Fodler.

His gaze bored into her. Lord Fodler had to have been on the same list as Fletch.

"How did you even manage an invitation here to Mortell Abbey, Liv?"

"How did *you* manage an invitation?" She asked the question without pause, her look locked into the forest before them.

"I received no invitation," Tieran said. "I am merely here to conduct business with Lord Shepton, as much as you would like to think differently. The snow keeps me here the same as you."

"Pish—you managed to get here in this snow, and you can just as easily leave." She lifted her hand gripping her reins and pointed at his horse. "These drifts are but a mere trifle for that beast you ride."

Tieran subconsciously leaned forward to pat the neck of his horse, soothing the barb that his horse didn't even understand. He looked to Liv. "I answered your question, now I think you can do me the courtesy of answering mine. How did you find yourself here at Mortell Abbey?"

She glanced at him, then set her look back onto the trail. "My late husband owned half of Lord Mortell's foundry. It was one of the assets he left me. So now it is my funds that keep the company on the high side when necessary. Lord Mortell is kind in that he does what I wish of him. And I wished to come north for fresh air."

"At the same time as Lord Shepton?"

She shrugged.

"And Lord Mortell's youngest sister is Lord Shepton's wife?"

"Correct."

"From what I witnessed, Lord Mortell adores his youngest sister."

"Does he?" Liv smiled innocently. "I had not noticed."

His eyes narrowed at her. "And Lord Mortell was particularly interested in Shepton's investment with me. Almost as if it was his own money that was at stake, and not Shepton's."

The side of her mouth lifted. "That is quite observant of you."

"Do you expect less of me?"

She looked to him, the sly smile that had captured half of her face falling away. "The years have changed us both, Tieran. I have no right to expect anything of you. So I cannot assume that just because you were once the observant sort, you still are."

He nodded, his focus not leaving her. However the banter had just turned, it had obviously twanged an unsettling chord with her.

He cleared his throat, staring at the half-frozen stream the trail had sidled next to, searching for something benign, something to return the light mood they had been enjoying.

"How are your parents, Liv? They are well, I assume? Did they move to London with you?"

"Oh." Her eyes snapped to him, her head cocking. "I guess I thought you knew…I don't know why you would have…"

She blinked hard at him, her look swinging forward. He could see her harden herself with a deep breath. "They died four years ago. In the fall. A month apart. Smallpox infested the village, and both of them succumbed to it."

Guilt sliced through Tieran. Both of her parents. He knew how much she had loved them both, even as demanding as they were of her.

And he hadn't even known she had lost them. Gone through that pain. His own parents had died within the same year when he was young and he knew that devastation. "I am sorry, Liv. I would have…"

His voice trailed. He would have what? Shown up at her door? Held her while she cried? Attended their funerals?

They both knew none of that could have happened.

She nodded, her lips drawing inward as tears swelled in her eyes. One tear escaped, rolling down her cheek. It stopped, freezing, its downward momentum halted. She flipped it away with the back of her kidskin glove.

Looking at him, she attempted a sad smile through her frown. "A cruel twist, since they were the very reason I turned my life the way I did, and then they were gone" —the fingers of her free hand slowly flittered into the air above her mare's mane— "just like that."

The trail dodged inward, and in the next steps of the horses, they arrived at the Roman ruins. Or more correctly, the ruins of the castle that was once built around and above the Roman baths. Only the walls of grey stones, much the same ones as Mortell Abbey was built with, stood from the ground, still stacked taller than Tieran in some areas, not even up to his knees in others.

Tieran looked to Liv just as she angled her face to a single thin ray of sunlight that broke through the clouds. The ray lit the tiny flakes of snow blowing from the trees—a thousand diamonds floating in the air around her head.

He had to forcibly turn his head from the sight. From the innocent pleasure on her face.

In front of them, the snow had melted down to the ground in a wide ring around the building. Tieran dismounted his horse and wrapped the reins to a tree along the edge of the melt. Sprigs of green fought up through the brown layer of dead grass, and his horse dipped straight for them.

He turned to Liv, taking her hand to help her alight from her sidesaddle.

"The air, it is warm right here," she said as she gained her footing on the dormant grass.

"I believe it comes up from the baths below. A natural warm spring that they built the baths around. Or so Lord Mortell told me."

Liv nodded, walking toward the ruins. "I did not expect this. Do you think we can still get below to see them?"

Tieran tied off Liv's mare a healthy distance from his horse where another handful of green grass shot up. Falling into step behind Liv as she picked her way around the crumbled blocks of the outer walls, he watched her pull and push at the stones, her curiosity brimming forth. He recalled it quite suddenly—her infectious enthusiasm for the new and interesting. She had always wanted to see and experience so much more than she had in Cheshire.

"There." Tieran pointed past her head to the right. "I think there is an opening through there."

She jumped a step, rushing to where he pointed and then veered inward past the outer wall. "Yes. Stairs going down." She looked over her shoulder at him as he rounded the corner from the outer wall. "The entrance around it is still intact."

Just as Tieran opened his mouth to advise against going down—he had no idea how safe the stairs were, or if the stones could crumble above them—Liv disappeared into the niche along the wall and out of view. No time to even plead caution.

With a sigh, he followed her down the circular stone staircase, its width designed for much smaller men than he.

Ducking under the low opening into the bath chamber, Tieran was engulfed in humid warmth. Once his eyes adjusted to the low light emanating from the small, rectangular slits along the top of the chamber, he found Liv already halfway across the wide room.

Her back to the wide, square recess in the floor partially filled with dark water, she stared at the wall as she stripped off her gloves and removed her cloak. Setting them down on the long stone bench that ran the length of the chamber, her fingertips went to the wall, brushing aside a thick coating of dirt.

It wasn't until Tieran was a step away from her did he realize what held her rapt attention. Where she had brushed away dirt, a mosaic of tiles had begun to appear.

From the area she had cleared, he could recognize the black eyes, nose and mouth of some type of green serpent. A monster from the sea, if his imagination ran free.

She looked up at him, a grin on her face. "This is extraordinary, Tieran. These are Roman?"

"I believe so." He took off his gloves, running his fingers across the ancient tiles she had uncovered. Gritty

dirt stuck to his fingertips, some of the mortar and tiles crumbling under his touch.

Liv spun around, her hand sweeping around them. "And this bath—can you even imagine how glorious it would have been when it was first built? The warmth when just above it is cold?" Her jaw shifted to the side as she looked at the pool of water. "The green water aside, one could swim in the length of that bath, though I do not know if I would enjoy bathing with scores of other people."

Tieran chuckled.

Her look went to an opening at the far end of the chambers, which, presumably, led to more baths. Darkness flickered across her face, stealing the smile from her lips. "Lord Shepton insinuated these were…ruins…above ground ruins, some crumbling buildings. Not these, these hidden chambers…" Her voice drifted to silence.

Tieran recognized exactly what she had just realized. He had no patience for it. "Why else would he want to accompany you out here, Liv?"

Her look snapped to him as she forced a brittle smile. "Of course I should have suspected—simple facts I should have inquired about with Lady Mortell." She shook her head, disgust crossing her face. "I have been thinking of other things."

Her look dropping to the floor, her hands clenched as she rubbed the dirt between her fingers and her palms, flecks of blackness falling along her skirt. "I need to wash the dirt from my hands."

Without waiting for him to reply, Liv moved past him and went to the circular staircase, rushing upward.

Tieran watched as Liv, only a few steps in front of him, gulped fresh air once she had escaped the ruins, hurrying to tromp through the snow to the edge of the nearby stream. The moving water had managed to defy the cold holding hostage to the land, only half of it frozen over.

Liv picked her steps carefully down the bank, the toes of her boots slipping on the icy rocks. At the edge of the stream she went to her knees, bending over the water.

Tieran followed her, his boots crunching across the rocks.

Standing in silence behind Liv as she swished her hands in the open stream, he watched the water bubble along the edge of the shelf of ice covering the stream. He couldn't tell which was winning—the ice, or the warmer water, holding on, refusing to freeze.

"You want to ask me a question. I can see it." Her voice came soft, just above the gurgling of the stream.

His gaze darted to the top of her head, the black wool bonnet she wore shielding her face from his view.

Setting her wet hands on her black wool skirt, she remained on her knees next to the stream. It took several moments before she twisted her body so she could look up at him. Her left eyebrow had lifted in question. "You can just ask it, Tieran. There is no need to lurk about it on my account."

Tieran stared at her, unnerved by the incisive way she looked at him. She always could read him. She could from the start. And she had never shied away from provoking him when he preferred to remain silent.

Maybe she was right. Maybe now was the time.

Tieran took a bracing breath. "Why did you marry Lord Canton, Liv? Why did you not wait for me?"

{ CHAPTER 9 }

"Liv?"

She gave herself a slight shake, dismissing the shock that had seized her. How long had she been staring at Tieran with her jaw askew? Still on her knees, she twisted forward, looking down at the stream, attempting to exhale the breath that sat stubbornly in her chest. "I had thought you were going to ask me about the list."

"Should I ask you about the list?" His low voice came down upon her from behind, heavy. "The other question is more important to me, Liv."

She nodded, but could not turn back to him, her cold hands curling onto her wool skirt. Nor could she manage to gain her feet. Not yet. Not when every bit of strength in her body had just deserted her.

She saw it in his eyes. Hurt from years ago surfacing. Unspeakable pain she recognized because she had felt it herself. Hurt she had never seen Tieran let surface in his blue eyes. Anger, she had seen plenty of. But never the pain. She hadn't believed he had felt it, just the same as her.

"Liv."

"No. It is fine." She held her bare hand up, the back of it to him as she closed her eyes.

She just needed one more moment. One more second to steady herself. She dragged air into her lungs, the cold stinging as it descended deep into her body. "You have never asked the question, Tieran. You have never had the chance to. It would be the one thing I would want to know."

Rocks crunched behind her, an impatient sound.

"You did not wait for me."

Her eyes stayed closed, her head slowly shaking. "I thought you were dead."

"So you married an old man—older than your grandfather—for what?" She heard him take a step toward her back, his space overtaking hers. "The title? The money? Did you turn into your mother while I was at war? Willing to exchange everything for a title—even if it came with a lecherous old fool?"

"No." She sprang to her feet, spinning to him, her hand landing flat on his chest, pushing him. "Do not dare to speak ill of Lord Canton. You do not get to do that. You will respect him, for he saved me. He saved me and I saved him."

Tieran shuffled one step backward. Only one. "Saved you from what, Liv? What could you have possibly needed to be saved from?"

Her hand slid downward from his chest, deflated. "Ruin."

She wasn't ready to have this conversation.

She would never be ready. Not with Tieran. Not with anyone. Aside from Viola, the only people that knew of her past were dead and buried.

Her gaze dropped from his face, unable to witness the questions, the searching in his eyes. How many answers did she owe him? How many truths? What was love owed?

She backed up.

Three steps, and her heel dropped, slipping off the icy bank of the stream. She fell backward, arms flailing.

Tieran caught her arm, yanking her onto solid ground before her skirts touched water.

His hand a vise around her upper arm, he stared down at her, not releasing her.

"Liv, you need to tell me. I am owed an explanation."

She twisted her arm, a final weak attempt to break free, to escape the one thing she swore she would never do. Speak of the past.

He didn't let her go.

Her eyes closed for an elongated breath.

What did it matter now? Her mother was dead. Her father was dead. Every reason she'd had for marrying Lord Canton had disappeared with time, no longer relevant.

If Tieran took what she told him and ruined her in society with it, did it matter? He would just be verifying to the *ton* what half of them already thought of her. *Vulgar, lewd, shameless, trollop.* She knew exactly what words were whispered as she went by. And she had become immune to it long ago. Were it not for the fortune Lord Canton had left her, and the many teats it offered for investments, she would have been ostracized long ago.

The ruin she could live with. The harder thing to contend with was the very real possibility that if she exposed her soul to Tieran, offering herself up bare to him, he could smash her vulnerability into tiny, irreparable pieces.

But he was right. She owed him this. This explanation. No matter what it cost her.

Words gathered, she opened her eyes to stare at the dark lapels of his overcoat, half open in front of her.

"The summer I married Lord Canton."

"Yes?"

"I had been out riding on Thunder—do you remember her?"

His fingers on her arm twitched, but his grip didn't loosen. "Yes. I remember. A fine filly."

Liv nodded. Thunder had been a fine mare. Beautiful and bold and fast. A white streak across the fields. "I had taken her out on the high cliff above the Rosewood Brook. Do you remember that spot? We spent so much time there walking along the cliff. I would go there every time I missed you."

She smiled, soft. "Which was every day. All day long. For more than two years. Mama grew tired of me always disappearing, but she also knew how heartsick I was for you, so she let me be. Papa helped with that, I think, and told her to leave me to my wanderings. Even at the end— when the war had been done for a year, and he knew you were dead, he still let it be. Made Mama let it be."

She gasped a breath, her lips drawing inward. Exhaling, the air, the words came in a rush. "That was where they grabbed me. Stole me. At the cliff. They shoved me in the back of a wagon. Sat on me. Wrapped my head so I couldn't see."

Her eyes closed. She couldn't look at Tieran anymore. Not his chest. Not even his clothes. "It was dark for five days. The rocking. I was sick again and again and again. And I lay there. Lay there in the filth of it. The smell." She shook her head, her nose wrinkling at the memory of putrid stench. "I just wanted it to be done. Over. I wanted death. Prayed for it. When they propped me up, dragged me up some stairs, and yanked the mask off of me, I was in a brothel in London."

Tieran's clamp on her arm pinched, digging into muscle, hurting, but Liv couldn't shake free, couldn't tell him it hurt, couldn't even open her eyes. His hand was the only thing holding her up.

"They cleaned me. Verified I had never been compromised. Set me on a stage, meat to buy. Sold me for my virginity. An auction, bidding on me like I was a cow. But the man that bought me did not touch me. He walked out of the brothel with me, a sack over my head, and put me in a carriage. I never even saw what he looked like. The woman inside brought me to a house where there were other women like me. Others that had been sold in the brothel."

Her words had dropped to a wooden monotone. "My body was unscathed, but I was ruined, through and through. I had been gone for nearly a fortnight. Sold in a brothel. I could never go back to my parents. Never again put myself before you even if a miracle happened and you appeared. And that was when a friend I made at the house, Viola, offered me a way forward. She had gone through the same as me—stolen from her home, sold. But she found a way to move forth without ruin. She married an elderly man—an acquaintance, and he had a friend that needed the same thing—a young, strong wife. Lord Canton was old and feeble and he needed someone he could trust to help protect him against a cousin that was too eager to gain the title with his death. He was feeble, but his mind—his mind was strong."

"Lord Canton's cousin tried to kill him?"

"Yes. I did not believe it at first either—paranoia, I thought. But even after we were married he continued his

attempts to kill Lord Canton. He was devious, and I have
the scars from intervening upon several of the attacks. I had
to run from the house to push my husband out of the way
of a carriage, but I could not clear myself and the carriage
wheel cut my arm open. I had to break Lord Canton's fall
halfway down the stairs, roll with him the rest of the steps,
shielding him the best I could. More bruises. Cuts. But I
protected him. That I did. Time and again."

Liv could feel the pulsating in Tieran's fingers on her
arm, the fury he wanted to unleash. But all she saw behind
her closed eyes were flashes, snippets of those days. The
terror that would not release. The utter loss of who she was
and what she should do.

She rushed on, pushing words from her lips before he
interrupted her, before she could speak no more.

"So I had a choice, Tieran. I could marry Lord Canton.
Tell the world we eloped. People would jeer, yes. But I
would not be scorned, ostracized. No one would know
what happened to me—that I had disappeared without
explanation for that length of a time, alone, would have
ruined me. The marriage meant that my parents would
maintain their status. And Lord Canton would gain an
ally, someone to care for him." She heaved a breath, her
chin dropping. "I was so lost. My heart, my soul, my life.
Everything gone. I married Lord Canton because I saw no
other path."

She shivered, the entire ugly truth escaping her, only
to leave an empty, wicked chill in her body. She wished she
hadn't left her cloak in the baths.

Silence smothering them, the gurgle of the stream was
the only thing that moved, that dared to make a sound.

Minutes passed, and Tieran didn't move, didn't say a word. His hand stayed a frozen clamp around her arm.

When she could finally open her eyes, Liv braved a glance upward.

The exact thing she feared.

Her look dropped to Tieran's boots with a gasp, the disgust on his face too much to bear.

"I am sullied. I know. Everything you have believed of me, verified." She shook her arm, trying to free herself. When that didn't work, she stepped to the side, pulling and turning away whether he was going to release her or not. "You now know, Tieran—the truth was what you needed and now you have it. So be done with me."

His grip clasped harder. The five harsh points of his fingers on her skin dug into her muscle, pulling her arm backward, straining her shoulder.

Her arm high in the air behind her, captive, Liv lunged forward with all her might. Not an inch. Not a step. She stood straight, attempting to ease the pain his grip caused, but could not look back at him. He was near to snapping her arm, but she refused to bow to the pain. "I would like to return to the abbey now, Tieran. You have what you came out here for."

"No. No, I am stunned, Liv."

His fingers spread on her arm, and her body instinctively twisted sideways, trying to escape the pain it caused. He reacted instantly, releasing her.

Freed, she started toward the half-crumbled castle. She moved along the outer wall, passing under the stone archway that still held firm against time, denoting the entrance to the structure.

"Stop." He was on her silently, snatching her wrist and spinning her around, trapping her against the stone wall. He grabbed her chin, forcing her to look up at him. "Hear me now, Liv. I don't think you sullied. Never. I am stunned that you believed I would ever toss you aside. Stunned that you did not wait for me to find you—did not trust me, trust in the love I had for you."

She wedged her head away from his grip on her chin. "I thought you were dead, Tieran. You had not come for me and the war was a year over." Her head shook, but it was nothing compared to the frozen tremble coursing through her body. "You were dead and I was facing utter ruin—a solitary life of expulsion and scathing looks—of losing my family and being cut by all those that I once knew. I did what I had to in order to survive, the best I knew how. I cannot apologize for that."

His palm slammed onto the stones by her head. "Dammit, Liv, I was on my way to you."

She cringed, leaning away, her eyes squinting shut against his ferocity.

He dropped her wrist, stepping back, yet his words remained a low roar, repeating his words. "I was on my way to you."

She opened her eyes only to see revulsion on his face. Revulsion that gutted her. "And I had already given up on you."

He stared at her, unflinching.

She had to gasp a breath just to force it past her cinched throat. "I can see the disgust in your eyes, Tieran. The disgust you have for me. For the taint that still haunts me."

"You were never tainted, Liv." Tieran moved to her, grasping both of her shoulders, his blue eyes intent on hers. His voice still growled, but she could hear him attempt to keep control. "Whatever it is you think you see in me in this moment, Liv, you are wrong."

He exhaled a long breath, looking up at the top of the haphazard stones on the wall, his head shaking. His look dropped to her. "Do you want to know how I truly view you, Liv?"

With a sharp inhale, Liv held her breath, staring up at Tieran. Did she want to know? Would it even be possible to bear to hear how she disgusted him? Did it even matter? If he said the words, said them out loud, then she could be done with him. The air emptied between them, and she could move forth without always wondering, without hoping that someday their paths would entwine again.

She nodded.

His chest rose with a deep breath as he centered his gaze on her, the rawness of his look searing into her soul. "The very first moment I saw you, Liv, hiding along that stone staircase in Cheshire. In that moment, you were innocence. You were tall and beautiful and sparkling in the way only a sixteen-year-old could be. You were soft and gentle and soused and charming and bold—even as you were hiding from the world. There was not a flicker of fear in your eyes when you looked at me—you were only curious."

His palms on her shoulders slid inward, resting along her skin as his fingers wrapped behind her neck. "You glowed, Liv. A present meant for me alone. I knew it the second I saw you. A present to unwrap, layer by layer, with countless surprises. Innocence. That is how I saw you then. And against my own common sense, that is how I see you still."

"Yet the things that have happened—"

"It is how I see you, Liv, as much as I would prefer not to. As much as I have wanted to let the malice I have harbored for you over the years poison everything I felt for you—it could never overcome the fact that at the core of all of my thoughts, I see you and I still think innocence—I feel the innocence."

His eyes on hers terrified her, the depth of what he said, what he believed. Yet she held his gaze, even more afraid of what would happen if she looked away. She was no innocent. He had to know none of what he believed was true, and he was only lying to himself in attempt to make it real—to go back to a past that had long since disappeared.

The frigid shaking of her body started again, clattering her teeth. "It is not real, Tieran—what you think of me. That innocence you see in me vanished years ago."

The corners of his eyes lifted, sparking into a smile that did not make way to his mouth, his lips remaining in a staunch line. "I am not a fool, Liv. And I am not asking you to be a girl of sixteen again. Of course I see the wariness in your eyes, the suspicion of all those around you. But that innocence is still alive in you. I can see it, even if you cannot."

Her hands lifted, wobbly, and she wrapped her fingers around his wrists. "I am a caustic widow—capable only of destruction."

"You don't believe that of yourself, Liv. It may be easier for you to have everyone think that, but it is not you."

"It is what I have become good at."

"Would Lord Canton say that of you, were he alive?"

She looked up at the barren trees, watching snow fall in great clumps as a gust of wind cut above the ruins. "No."

The smile in his eyes reached his lips. "Exactly. I know you are still so much more than what you let the world see, Liv. You always were."

She didn't want to believe him. She couldn't *afford* to believe him.

Her eyes dipping, she shook her head. "I am cold. I need to get my cloak."

Pulling his hands away from her neck, she ducked past him, going into the niche in the wall to the stairs. Down the narrow stone steps she stepped into the large bathing chamber, looking to the left in the dim light for where she had set her cloak. The air was just as thick, just as warm as it had been earlier. Only this time it did nothing to negate the chill in her belly.

Her arms wrapped tight around her middle to hold the shake in her body still, she walked over to her cloak. Tieran's words echoed in her ears, fighting the arguments in her mind, fighting what she knew of the world.

She was a vengeful widow, tainted at her core. Scorned but tolerated by society.

She had to remember that, for she couldn't afford to hope for more.

{ CHAPTER 10 }

She felt him before he stepped into the bathing chamber.

Of course he followed her down. He never did like it when she avoided him.

His footsteps crunched onto the decaying stone, stopping by the entrance.

Liv didn't turn around to him. "You should not believe in what you cannot see, Tieran. You will only be disappointed by what you will eventually discover."

Five steps echoed into the chamber and he stopped behind her. "I do not think so. You are still a present meant for me alone, Liv."

He walked around her to plant himself before her, and her look, wary, lifted to him.

"A gift to unwrap, fold by fold. You need to know the past—what happened to you—does not need to matter in the present. Not in this moment, Liv. It does not for me."

"What does matter in this moment?"

His blue eyes pinned her. "That I have an answer after all these years. An answer that haunts me, because it was I that failed you. But it is an answer I respect."

She nodded. "Then we can return to Mortell Abbey and you can leave for London. Leave me in peace."

"No."

"No?"

"No, because what matters is that I still want you, Liv. That has always been true. It has been denied, but it has always existed."

Her cold belly flipped, the humid heat of the room invading her pores, singeing her cheeks. "Tieran…"

His fingers slipped behind her arms clamped to her belly. Gently, he tugged her wrists from her body. Stepping close until his chest brushed the front of her dress, he looked down at her, his hands at her wrists neither advancing up her arms nor retreating.

"I don't want to deny it any longer." He leaned down, his lips near her ear, his breath hot on her neck. "What would you say if I kissed you, Liv? If I stripped down the sleeves of your dress? Set my lips on your breasts? Your nipples?"

Her knees buckled slightly at his words. What she wouldn't have given a thousand times over to hear those words over the years. "I…I would say I would like that."

His lips slid downward, trailing a path along the line of her neck. Dropping her wrists, his left hand went to the small of her back, pressing her body slowly, fully into his. "You do not worry on what others would say were we to be found?"

The lines he traced with his tongue, the sparks he created along her neck, muddled her thoughts. "I am a rich widow, Tieran. I only need to skirt along the line of propriety."

He chuckled into the crook of her neck. His right hand moved upward, untying and slipping off her bonnet before working the front buttons of her heavy wool riding habit.

She needed this. How desperately she needed this.

She had spent years wondering on this very thing. How Tieran's lips would feel on her breasts, on her nipples, not confined to the skin above her dress as they always had been.

He peeled her jacket away, his fingers quick through the laces of her stays, freeing her skin to the humid air. Picking her up, he walked forward until he reached the stone bench that lined the length of the room. He set her on the long seat, dropping to his knees in front of her as he dragged off his overcoat, jacket and waistcoat.

Achingly slow—far too slow for Liv—he tugged free her stays and stripped down her shift, his eyes locked on hers.

She reached out, her right fingers threading through the side of his blond hair, wrapping around to the back of his head. Her legs spread under her skirts, and she pulled him towards her. He took the invitation with urgency, his lips, his mouth, attacking her skin.

Liv arched backward, the cut of his slight stubble against her skin intoxicating, waking her core, sending it into throbs.

She could not suppress the moan that escaped, coarse, as he clamped fully onto a nipple, his tongue swirling it, teeth grazing against it, turning it raw.

Satisfied he had teased her left nipple to peak, he moved onto the other. The second his teeth ran across the tip, Liv bucked under him, her legs spreading further as she pushed her hips closer to him, her hand deep in his hair, pulling him upward to kiss her.

The kiss stole all her senses until his body pushed forth, the crux of her meeting the bulge straining hard in the front

of his black trousers. Through her skirts she could feel the pulsating. Feel his need for her.

"Hell, Liv, you have always been fire for me," he murmured, his tongue moving downward from her neck to torment a nipple. "I was always afraid if I touched you too long, you would consume me—send me to ashes."

Her left hand joined her right in his hair, holding him tight to her skin, demanding he not stop the onslaught. "And you are willing to take that chance now?"

He pulled away, his look piercing her. "I am a different man, now, Liv. I have touched too much death to still be afraid of fire."

He seized the back of her head, pulling her into a kiss, his lips rough, searing her with wanton need. A kiss of abandon. A kiss weighted with years of unsatisfied hunger.

Her body reacted instantly, her hips grinding on their own accord into him.

"Liv—"

"I want this, Tieran," she said, breathless against his lips. "Since the day I met you, I have wanted this. I have never stopped loving you. I love you still. And eight years is too long."

Savage, his mouth met hers as his hands dove downward, unbuttoning and ripping free the mounds of clothing between them.

Her boots and stockings he left in place. She didn't care. Not when Tieran was in front of her, naked.

Her mouth watering, she stared at the massive size of his shaft, long and sleek and fascinating.

His fingers ran along her bare thighs as he captured her mouth again, his tongue plunging, tasting every moan that rumbled up her throat.

His left hand shifted her forward to the very edge of the bench while his right hand dipped deep between her legs, searching her mound, finding the hard nubbin already throbbing for him, begging for touch. Tieran obliged, every stroke he circled drawing quivers and rasping mewls from the center of her body.

He slid a finger into her, and Liv bowed backward, her hands flying up to the mosaic on the wall behind her head. Fingernails biting into the edges of the tiles, she braced herself as his hand sped, the throbbing in her core building fast, frantic.

"Hold, Liv." He slowed, torturing her at her breaking point.

She screeched, the sound vibrating off the ancient walls as she curled forward, clawing at his back.

He leaned slightly away, searching for her eyes, his words steel vehemence. "No, Liv, I want you coming around me. I need your body to know exactly who you are coming with. Coming in. Your body is mine."

"Yes…yes…" Her words turned into a gargled half plea, nonsensical. But he knew the meaning—she could see it within the fierceness of his eyes as he set the tip of his shaft on her entrance.

His fingers worked fast, drawing her to the brink again, screaming, and then he braced her hips and slid into her.

The barrier jarred him as he hit it—jarred her—but his momentum would not be denied, unable to stop until full hilt.

He jerked his face in front of hers, searching. "You are—"

He went silent, his hands solid around her hipbones as she exploded in spasms, cutting him off. Streaks of pain twisted with the most brutal pleasure, racking her body. Tiles fell around her, shattering on the stone bench as her fingernails flicked them free with every wave hitting her body.

Her legs had wrapped around his waist, holding him solid against her. He waited, and she knew it, but it still took her moments to open her mouth, every word halted with another gasp. "I am meant for you Tieran—I always have been. I have always been yours."

His head dropped, and she could feel the tremors, the immense control over his muscles that he just barely contained. He slid nearly out of her.

It sent fresh spasms tearing across her core.

"Yes. Don't stop, Tieran." She ripped one hand from the wall, gripping his neck, pulling with all her strength. "Don't stop."

He plunged into her slowly, taking care.

She would have none of it. She had waited a lifetime for Tieran. For this moment.

The clasp of her legs tightened, drawing him close, fast, hard. She couldn't control him pulling free, but she could control his thrusts, and she did so every time. Hard. Fast. No quarter given to how his length ravaged her body. Her body that only wanted him deeper, longer.

When his entire body tensed, she took control, pushing herself from the wall and wedging herself on him, her hips swiveling with his shaft fully embedded, forcing him to finish.

A growl, carnal to its core, ravaged her ears, flooded every nook of the chamber as he came. His body emptied up into her, his hands crushing her hips onto him. The muscles along his back, along his arms went into frenzy, flexing with every vibration coursing through his body. But his clamp on her did not falter.

He wasn't going to let her go, nor give her the smallest margin of space. And she didn't want it.

She hung on, Tieran on his knees, her body wrapped around him. Their chests battled with each other for space with each breath that was heaved.

Her eyes cracked open to peek over his shoulder, searching the ancient walls for what was creating the buzzing in her ears. It took her long, dull moments to realize it was her own blood pumping in a frenzy, filling her head.

Tieran's chest lifted with an enormous inhale, shifting her upward.

"Ask me why I came up to Mortell Abbey, Liv."

She had never heard his voice so low, with such a raw crackle in it. Angling her head backwards, her spent body screamed against the movement, but she needed to look at his face. "Why?"

His hand went deep into the back of her hair, fingers digging through the many plaits weaved along her neck for warmth. He took another deep breath, his blue eyes centering on her. "Ever since I saw you at Lady Desmond's, I have been living in fear."

"Why fear?"

"Fear that I will leave you unguarded for a moment in time, and you will marry another and be lost to me again." His voice dipped even lower.

A smile spread across her face. "Well, that is an easy one to assuage. You need not worry on it as it will not happen—I will never marry again."

"What?"

"I have no intention of ever marrying again, Tieran, so you need not fear."

He stiffened, his fingers unthreading from her hair. "Why not?"

Liv glanced at his furrowed brow, perplexed. "I cannot chance it. Lord Canton gave me a life of independence at his death—I would lose all of that if I married again."

He lifted her off his body, setting her on her skirts that had bunched on the long stone bench. "And independence is the most important thing to you?"

His words punctuated the chamber, strained and slow, and a chill invaded her body. The room was warm, but she no longer had Tieran's heat enveloping her.

"Oh." Understanding sank into her chest and she grabbed his forearm as he picked up his linen shirt. "I did not assume this meant anything more than this moment, Tieran. It was what you said and I did not imagine—"

"That I might actually want you in my life?" He shrugged his shirt on, getting to his feet and giving a crisp snap to his jacket as he picked it up.

A puff of an exhale, and her head tilted to the side as she watched the jerk in his movements. "You are upset with me."

"I am not sure what I am with you, Liv. Not at the moment." His arm jabbed into the jacket sleeve. "I took your virginity, Liv. Something I should have been well advised of before doing so. And then you are suddenly proclaiming your intention to never wed again. So at the moment—do not ask my thoughts—do not assume my thoughts—as I am not ready to explore either with you."

She nodded, her head dropping as she wedged her shift out from the pile of her clothing. She had thought she recognized this for exactly what it was—what Tieran wanted—unattached pleasure, a culmination of what should have been eight years ago.

They had both needed this to happen—her probably more so than him—and it had.

She hadn't dared to hope on the thought that Tieran would want her for anything more. Not with their past, and especially not with him now knowing the truth of what happened to her.

She hadn't dared, even though her heart had yearned for hope, begged for it—even started to turn her mind to it—whether she wanted to admit to it or not.

Her shift on, she settled her stays around her chest. She stood, silently turning her back to Tieran. He picked up the ends of the ribbon, yanking her stays tight without a word.

At a loss, she woodenly said the only words that came to mind. "I do have to get back to Mortell Abbey before I am missed and Lady Mortell takes offense. I still have business to conclude there."

A slight grunt escaped her as Tieran yanked the ribbons tight. She inhaled, inflating her chest to make sure she had room to breathe.

"No." His fingers jerked as he tied off the ribbon. "Absolutely not, Liv. I will not allow it."

"What?" She whipped around, her temper flaring, burning away any hopes that had started to brew. "You thought you would bed me and then I would scurry under your control—that you would be able to dictate my every move?"

He stared at her, his jaw twitching, fury creasing his brow as his mouth pulled tight.

He was holding back. Holding back anger he had no right to.

"What is it you truly want of me, Tieran? I have already bared my heart to you because I know no other way to be with you. Only honest. And I could not be near you—with you—without you knowing that."

She snatched her wool skirt from the pile on the bench, pulling it on and securing it in place. "But I never asked you if you love me, because I also, honestly, don't want to know the answer."

Picking up her wool jacket, she paused, her look meeting the brewing storm in his eyes. "But we need to end any association we have, and you need to leave me alone if you intend to try and control me. I have a life, Tieran. A life I was quite happy to lead on my own terms before you appeared back in my life."

"Someone needs to control you, Liv."

"Tell me you did not just mean to speak those words."

"No. I meant them exactly as they sounded." His hand ran through his hair. "Someone needs to control you, Liv—stop you from the path of destruction you are on. Do you truly want a life where your sole purpose is to mete out revenge according to some bizarre list you have? A life where no solace exists for you in the darkest hours of the night?"

"That is what you think my life consists of?"

"Tell me otherwise."

Her eyebrows drew together and she turned from him, buttoning her jacket and picking up her cloak, gloves and bonnet on her way to the stairs. "Do not judge what you know nothing of, Tieran."

She ran up the stairs, going to her horse.

Damn him.

Damn him for always judging her.

Silent minutes later, they were on their way on the trail, Liv nudging her mare for speed every few steps.

She needed to be out of Tieran's presence. Out of the shadow of his animosity, of his judgment, of his need to control her.

It wasn't until Mortell Abbey was in sight, and the horses were trudging through the deep snow, that she could admit to herself the real reason she wanted to escape him.

His words had stung. Words that were far too close to the truth.

Her life did consist of meting out punishment. Punishment that was due.

She wasn't about to stop that now.

If anything, Tieran's condemnation steeled her resolve to that end. He didn't understand that the men on the list needed to be stopped.

And she was the one to do it.

Even if that meant a life lived without solace.

{ CHAPTER 11 }

It was perfect.

She just had to stomach Lord Shepton's putrid breath infesting her pores, his hands pawing her body for another few minutes.

A few minutes and she would be done.

Done with this place.

Viola's idea of Liv traveling to Mortell Abbey had been genius. Viola had correctly predicted Lord Shepton could not go very long without access to his proclivities of his London brothels, and that the last thing he would want to do to relieve the strain in his groin was bed his own wife. Much better to relieve himself with a lonely widow.

It had only taken a few more smoldering looks and some promiscuous words from Liv and he pounced on the opportunity.

The man was ready, salivating at the possibility of gaining access to Liv's skirts. But producing the encounter—and the scene that needed to accompany it—had proved harder than Liv had anticipated.

She could have been done with Mortell Abbey a day ago had she not been forced to play a ridiculous cat and mouse game with Tieran. Whenever she had positioned herself in proximity to Lord Shepton—in the nook below the stairs, along a deserted path in the conservatory, deep in the vaulted undercroft of the abbey—Tieran had appeared. It didn't help that the snow had started again, trapping all the guests to the interior of the abbey.

No matter where she had attempted to compromise Lord Shepton, Tieran had sniffed them out, interrupting Liv before she even started. And then Lady Shepton would appear minutes later—as Liv intended—but all Lady Shepton would witness were strained, but innocent, conversations between the two men and Liv.

Maddening to no end.

And Tieran was enjoying the game far too much.

She wanted to be done with this place. With these people. And most certainly with Tieran.

She had let her guard down with him. And had been rewarded for her own stupidity.

He had enticed her into hope—into believing in the possibility of something more with him. But he didn't want her—he only wanted to *control* her. He wanted to stop her from her plans—the exact adversary she knew he was.

"Be scared, Livia."

Jarred, Liv looked at the spittle on Lord Shepton's chin, not sure she heard correctly.

"Scream for me. Just a little. Scared, so I can hear the fear." Lord Shepton found her left nipple through her stays and shift, twisting it.

Pain. But even more so, disgust welled up from her stomach, reaching her throat. She swallowed back a retch. Of course the bastard would want that. A terrified girl he could abuse.

She grabbed the edge of the copper tub behind her, steadying herself as he mauled her, shoving her back against the wall next to the tub.

Blast it. She had set this scene, offered the hot bath that was ready for her to his wife, and then quickly enticed Lord

Shepton into the bathing room. But she had grown careless, desperate. She had sworn to herself she would position herself where she could easily escape from Shepton should she need to. But this bathing room was at the end of the wing that housed the guest suites, which were empty at this time of day, and far from the common areas of the home.

And the door was closed.

Lady Shepton needed to show soon. Where the hell was she?

Lord Shepton twisted her nipple again, this time hard, brutal. "I said scream, dammit. You offered this, bitch, now deliver it." His fingers started to claw down her shift, exposing her.

Biting a whimper she couldn't let him hear, Liv tried to slide along the wall, only to be shoved into the corner behind the tub.

Her look went wild, searching for something close by to hit him with. She needed to stop the bastard before he went too far.

A click.

The door opened, a maid stepping into the room with Lady Shepton right behind her.

Liv saw his wife's shock. Time slowed. She watched as the shock turned into devastation playing across her face. Every line, every twist of the woman's features.

The sight curdled Liv's stomach, more so than Lord Shepton's hands on her. A torment in her soul that she had to force this upon this innocent woman. Liv had to remind herself that Lady Shepton would be better off knowing exactly what sort of monster she had married.

Regrettable. But necessary.

The maid spun and scurried past Lady Shepton and out the door.

"Robert." Lady Shepton's voice bit through the air.

Unaware the door had opened, Lord Shepton turned his head to look over his shoulder, his hand still on Liv's breasts, still clutching the fabric of her shift downward.

It took him a painfully long second to realize what his wife had just walked in on. He straightened himself.

But his hands didn't drop away from Liv.

Not quick enough.

And not before Tieran walked into the room.

Tieran stopped right behind Lady Shepton, his eyes shrewd, taking in the scene.

The explosion was instant.

"Liv, what the blasted hell are you doing? Get your bastard hands off her, Shepton." Tieran tried to step around Lady Shepton, but she flung out her arm, stopping him.

"No, Lord Reggard. Robert is mine. I will deal with him, and then be done with him. And then my brother will deal with him." She turned and walked out the door.

The ice in her voice told Liv everything she needed to know.

Success.

Liv swiped her arm in front of her, breaking Lord Shepton's contact with her body. It spurred him into motion, and he scrambled from the corner he had trapped her into and ran out the door after his wife.

Liv was surprised he made it past Tieran without Tieran's fist denting his cheek.

She pulled up the straps on her shift, yanking both the front fabric and her stays back into place. She looked to her dress draped on a chair next to Tieran, wanting to hide under the cover of it, but afraid to move an inch in his direction.

Tieran stood by the door, heaving, fury exploding with every breath. The fists his hands had curled into were jammed into his thighs, the skin on his knuckles a taut white.

No. She could not move. Not give him a reason to move.

"Why?" The word hissed from his mouth through clenched teeth. "Why, Liv?"

She straightened, unable to do anything but bolster feigned nonchalance to his look, to his anger. Her chin lifted slightly. "If all goes as planned, Lady Shepton is about to disavow her husband and have her brother cut his finances completely. Lord Mortell will ensure Shepton is penniless, leaving him destitute with his mountainous debt. With luck, Shepton will reach utter ruin within a month."

"With luck?"

She nodded, her lips tight against the incredulous look on his face. "Yes. With luck."

"But why, Liv? Dammit." His fists slammed into his thighs. "Why is this so bloody important to you?"

She steeled herself. Tieran would never understand this—his honor would never allow it. All he wanted was to control her. To take away what she needed to do. And she could talk from here to the moon, and he would not hear her. Her words turned cold. "Lord Shepton is a man that does not deserve to live, Tieran. I cannot kill him, so this is the next best option."

"Kill him?" Tieran's left fist opened, his arm swinging wide. "What? Who are you, Liv? This makes no sense to me. No sense at all—who you are now—what you will do. You are not the person I knew—not the one with nothing but kindness in her heart."

"Kindness in my heart?" Her head flung back, a strained laugh escaping. "You are right, Tieran. You don't know me at all. Kindness was killed in me long ago."

His eyes narrowed to slits. "No. No, I don't think it has been killed in you, Liv. You're lying to yourself on that accord. There is still the woman—somewhere in you—that would pull a bird out of a snowbank to save it. Kindness that stems from your soul and cannot be killed. But you work extremely hard to deny it. That is what I don't understand, Liv."

She could no longer stand her bare arms, her half-naked body in front of him. If it made him move, made him attack, she would just have to chance it. She jumped to the chair with her black muslin dress, grabbing it and stepping into the folds of fabric as she set it about her body.

When she looked up, Tieran still stood rooted to the same spot. His chest still contracted and expanded in heavy breaths.

Her stoic indifference was waning. Even after witnessing the scene he just had, Tieran still saw the good in her—or at least he tried to.

And damned if she didn't want him to see that.

She wanted him to look at her as he had in the Roman bath chamber—with wonderment. Not like she was the devil on earth, not like he was right now.

Tieran lived by a very different code then her. Honor guided him. Vengeance guided her.

And she didn't even want to consider what she was thinking, but there it was.

She wanted him to understand. Wanted him to love her again.

Damn her heart.

She awkwardly fixed the top button on the back of her dress. "What do you want of me, Tieran?"

"I don't know, Liv. I don't know why I didn't leave here days ago." His hand ran over his face. "Maybe I want to know what happened to the woman I loved once. To the woman I almost married."

She took a hesitant step toward him. "Then stay. Understand."

"Understand what?"

"That I am that woman. I do have that kindness. It is just that I am that, and more, Tieran. More that cannot be denied."

He shook his head, his jaw shifting to the side. "You think you are on the side of righteousness."

"I know it."

"Yet look at what you did, Liv. Whatever this blasted list of yours that Shepton is on—whatever wrong you think you are righting. None of that was Lady Shepton's to suffer. Did you not see her face? What you did to that woman?"

"I…" Liv's voice trailed. She had seen. And she had no words to defend herself.

"Exactly." His head shook, his blue eyes going to the ceiling. "I thought this could be different, that you would reconsider your actions—I thought you loved me, Liv."

She rushed forward, her fingers wrapping around his upper arm. "I do. I do love you, Tieran. But that has nothing to do with this—with Lord Shepton. These are very separate things."

His fury exploded and he spun away from her, his fist slamming into the wall next to the door, his knuckles cutting through the plaster. He stopped with a growl, his fist lowering to his side as he scoffed, his head shaking anew. "Dammit, Liv. They are not separate. Everything is intertwined. Everything. You cannot be the extraordinary woman I once knew, and also the vengeful, spiteful woman I just saw. You cannot let a man paw you in one minute and then tell me you love me in the next. No, Liv. No."

"Oh." Her hand snapped flat across her belly, holding in the rock her gut had become. "So this isn't about my love for you. This is about the fact that you cannot love me if I am…like this."

He shrugged, refusing to look at her, his gaze staying locked toward the hallway.

She dared a step to him, reaching up, her fingers on his cheek to turn his face to her. "Don't go, Tieran. Not yet."

His eyes met hers, and they were blank. No anger. No desire. No wonderment. Blank. His voice matched his eyes. "I can't be near you right now, Liv. You—what you did today—it is reprehensible."

"But—"

"There is no defense of it. If you want me to stay, then this—this is where I draw a line, Liv. You cannot do this. Not ever again. No list. No vengeance. Not even a thought on it. No matter what drives you."

With a sharp intake of breath, her hand fell from his face. "You know I cannot promise that."

"Then I leave."

"No." All air left her chest. "Don't, Tieran. Please. Don't leave me."

He paused for the merest moment, her faint, choked words crushing the air between them.

With a slight shake of his head, he turned and walked away.

She stared at the empty doorway for minutes, expecting him to reappear.

He did not.

Heaven's hell. What had she just done?

"Lady Canton."

Liv jumped as Lady Mortell walked through the door and stood, fury shaking her limbs.

"Yes?"

"I am requesting you leave Mortell Abbey at once, Lady Canton."

"Of course, I understand." Liv had expected no less. She had wrought this unpleasant turmoil, and now she had to leave. She glanced to the sliver of the window she could see between the draperies. Snow still whipped at the glass. "I will pack and be on my way as soon as the storm clears."

"No, Lady Canton." Lady Mortell's hands clasped in front of her. Tight, like she was holding back from slapping Liv. "You do not understand. You are to leave. Now. Your maid may remain and pack your belongings."

Liv pointed to the window. "But the drifts…" Her voice petered out as she looked at Lady Mortell. The woman looked like she was about to lunge at her. Liv considered for a brief moment to force Lady Mortell to let her remain until the storm cleared—civility would demand it—but the thought evaporated before fully implanting in her mind. She had already created enough damage in this household.

Liv nodded. "I will be gone within the half hour."

Lady Mortell gave a curt nod. "Lord Shepton will also be exiting the property within the half hour. Perhaps you can share your coach."

Liv looked at the woman blankly, refusing to acknowledge the suggestion as a real possibility. Share her coach for days on end with the man she had just ruined? Not likely.

Lady Mortell spun on her heel and exited the room.

Liv waited until the clicks of her boots faded down the hall before exhaling a sigh.

Vengeance was brutal business.

But she had never realized until that moment, how very much it would cost her.

{ CHAPTER 12 }

Coming down from his room, Tieran saw the lump on a bench—a lump huddled under a heavy plaid blanket by the fire—the second he stepped into the large dining area of the coaching inn.

A lump with several tangles of dark, wavy hair hanging down along the back of the blanket.

Blast it.

Not here.

Tieran looked around the wide room, scanning the faces scattered about the tables and booths at the inn. Her driver, her maid, her footman—not one of them was in the room.

She would not be so stupid.

He looked back to the strands of dark hair, matted flat with wetness.

Fury sped through his veins, thickening with every step he took toward the massive fireplace—stacked Yorkstone from a nearby quarry.

He rounded her, placing himself between her and the fire.

"God's teeth, Liv, tell me you have not lost all sense of intelligence and are not here alone."

She looked up at him. Aside from the rogue strands of hair escaping, only her face was visible in the shroud of the red plaid blanket.

Shock registered in her brown eyes, the gold flecks sparking, but in the next breath, her gaze went weary, dropping to look through his legs at the fire.

"I did not expect you to be here, Tieran." The weariness wasn't just in her eyes, it laced her words.

The ire rattling his bones quelled. He sank down, resting on his heels so he was eye level with her. "What are you doing here, Liv? Alone?"

Her gaze slowly left the tall blazes in the hearth, landing on his face for only a second before flickering back to the fire. "Lady Mortell requested I leave, and I abided by her wishes."

"In this storm?"

"I was not about to fight her on it, Tieran." She tightened the blanket around her face. "My maid stayed behind to gather my belongings and to get the bird outside, and we left Charles to accompany her home. The carriage only made it to the Leeds crossroads before the drifts became too thick. We were closer to this coaching inn than to Mortell Abbey, so I moved onward with one of the horses, and Mr. Niles stayed behind with the carriage and other horses.

"Your driver let you travel here alone?"

She shook her head, and the blanket fell down about her shoulders as her head swiveled to take in the room. Whatever she was looking for, she did not see, and her look landed on Tieran. "Lord Shepton came upon my carriage a few minutes after we were stranded. He stopped and told Mr. Niles he would accompany me. Once we were halfway here, Shepton took off, pushing his horse as hard as he could through the snow. My mare could not keep up, and

he disappeared out of sight—I have not seen him since."
She glanced around again. "You have not seen him here?"

"No, the bastard."

Her look snapped back to him.

"Do you think you have a monopoly on discarding me,
Tieran?"

He winced. The words were meant to bite, and they
pricked as intended.

His head dropped, his hands clasping together as he
rested his forearms on his knees. He looked up at her. "Still,
I cannot believe you would trust Shepton."

"Of course I did not. But what was he going to do to
me in the middle of a storm, Tieran? Accost me in some
fashion from atop his horse? I knew here at the coaching
inn there would be plenty of people about to set between
him and me."

"But for your man to let you leave   "

"For heaven's sake, Tieran, I insisted. Mr. Niles had
three more horses to deal with, a stuck carriage, and
darkness was looming."

"He could have left them and accompanied you."

"Mr. Niles would never leave his horses, and I would
never ask him to. He is making camp with them right now."

Tieran pushed upright on his knees, pulling himself
to his full height. "I should go find him right now and cuff
him."

Liv glared up at him through her dark lashes. "I do not
know why you insist on finding a recipient for your anger,
Tieran."

"Your man deserves it for letting you go. You may not
want to hear it, Liv, but you need taking care of."

She straightened, the blanket dropping further down her body as fire flashed in her eyes. "I realize you are predisposed to not recognize it, but I have been taking care of myself for a long while now, Tieran."

The fire in her eyes flashed for only a moment, dissipating almost as quickly as it had appeared. She sighed, pulling the blanket up around her slumping shoulders as she looked past his thighs to the flames. "Please, Tieran. It was hard to make my way here and I am tired. And you have no right to judge Mr. Niles. My man is as loyal as they come. And he respects that I can well enough take care of my own person."

"It is not right."

"You get no say. Not now. I cannot be drawn in by you again." Her words dropped to a weary whisper, her focus staying on the flames. "You left me, Tieran. All I needed was for you to stay—for even a minute."

Her head shook, her mouth twisting into a frown as the whisper grew softer. "I lose all my intelligence when it comes to you. I cannot believe I offered myself vulnerable to you again…when every single time you have crushed me. And I do not seem to be able to stop myself from making that mistake again and again and again. But now…" She paused, tightening the blanket below her chin. "Now I think I am done."

Tieran stared down at the top of her head. Her wet dark hair glistened in the light from the fire. Even with the mound of blanket wrapping her, he could see her shake, see the shivers.

Panic started to twist around his chest.

This was not Liv. She did not know defeat. Did not know how to surrender to him.

Yet he heard the wound in her voice. Saw how she sat, bowed to the world.

Done. She was done with him.

He didn't want to see it—didn't want to acknowledge the possibility.

"Liv—"

"Please, Tieran. No more. I am soaked to the bone and frozen and I just want the barkeep to tell me the landlady has the tub ready."

"You are waiting for a bath?"

"Yes."

"Then I am standing watch by the door."

She looked over her shoulder to the man standing behind the short bar at the edge of the room. "It is not necessary."

"Look around you, Liv. You are the only woman in this place."

"There is the landlady. And I imagine there are a few women in the rooms above."

"You imagine?"

She nodded, her glare landing directly on him.

"I am standing at the door. I am not about to leave you unprotected in a place such as this."

"No, Tieran." She jumped to her feet, her hands balling in the edges of the blanket. She jabbed at his chest with her blanket-fist. "You do not get to do this. You do not get to swoop in and take care of me. You do not get to be jealous. You do not want me, remember? You left. So you do not get to flit and fly in and out of my life when it suits you or when you are struck with random pangs of protectiveness. I am not yours."

"Lady Canton." The landlady, a thin, wiry woman, appeared next to them, wiping her hands on her apron.

Liv turned from Tieran, looking to the landlady. "Yes?"

"Yer tub be ready, m'lady. Steaming, it be."

Liv nodded, a grateful smile crossing her face. "Thank you. Nothing could be more necessary at the moment."

"And the fire be high in the room," the landlady said. "I left chairs and a rope so ye cin hang 'n dry yer dress by morn, m'lady."

Bundling up the blanket draped around her so it didn't drag, Liv stepped away from Tieran, following the landlady to the stairs on the far end of the room.

Tieran waited until they disappeared up the stairs before following, waiting in the hallway for the landlady to leave Liv's room.

He nodded to her as she walked past him and then went to his room at the end of the corridor to grab a chair.

Carrying it into the hallway, he banged it onto the floor outside of Liv's door. The chair legs scraped against the wooden planks as he adjusted it and sat, banging the back of it onto the door.

Loud enough so Liv would hear. Loud enough so she would understand exactly what he was doing.

He was protecting her, whether she wanted it or not.

~ ~ ~

Tieran leaned his head back against the door, turning it slightly so the tip of his ear hit the wood. His ears perked, straining to hear motion in the room. Water splashing. Wet footsteps padding across the floor. Anything.

But it was silent, as it had been for a while.

His eyes closed not because he was tired, but because he heard footsteps thudding up the stairs at the far end of the hallway. He waited until the person took three steps into the corridor before he opened his eyes. The man jumped, startled, then quickly gave him a nod and disappeared back down the stairs.

That's right, sir, find another room. This is Liv's hallway.

His eyes closed again, and the image of Liv's body, naked, writhing before him flashed in the darkness behind his eyes.

That exact moment in the Roman bath chamber when he had truly believed, to his core, that Liv was finally his. His after all these years. After all the avoidance. After all the longing. After all the pain.

She was his.

He knew it. He felt it when their bodies were joined. It wasn't just flesh. It was her soul merging with his. It was as it had always been meant to be—at long last—because fate had finally decided to overlook his sins.

For that one moment, she had been his.

He adjusted his right ankle slung over his knee, his loins hardening, starting to burn at the image in his mind. If he wasn't careful, Liv would soon need protection from him.

Not that she would allow him anywhere near her.

Not for how fast she had darted away from him in the Roman baths. Not for how hard she had attempted to antagonize him at Mortell Abbey after he took her virginity.

A virgin.

Hell.

He wouldn't have believed it if he hadn't felt it. After what happened to her in the brothel, after years of marriage, after flirting her way through the *ton*. A virgin.

For all Liv wanted to believe she was a canny widow of advanced years, she was, at her core, still the girl he once knew.

But was it enough?

Even if she didn't want to marry him—fine, he could concede that detail—it was unusual, but not unheard of, as some of the grandest love affairs of all time didn't stand upon a license. After Tieran had calmed from the shock of her declaration that she would never marry again—it stung by all measures—he realized he frankly didn't care how he had her, just that he did.

He could allow her that independence.

He had changed in their years apart. So had she. He could accept that she now needed the security of her independence—understandable now that he knew what had happened to her all those years ago.

But then to see her in Shepton's arms. To see the odious man's fingers cutting across her alabaster skin—the same skin he had worshipped not days before.

It was too much.

He could concede much, but another man touching her—with her permission—no.

Not that. Never that.

Anger sliced across his belly. She was destroying herself with every name she crossed off that damn list of hers. Not to mention that one of his dearest friends was on that list.

Destroy them, destroy her. She didn't understand that. Not yet. But he did.

Revenge was about to become who she was, whole and through.

And Tieran didn't know if he was strong enough to stomach watching what it would do to her, because he had experienced the very same thing for himself. He had lived through the hell that revenge manifested, and it was a purgatory he could not bear to witness her descend into.

He tilted his ear back to the door.

It had been far too long. He hadn't heard a sound in the past half hour.

If he had heard the soft splash of water as she got out of the tub, or heard the rustle of her getting into bed, he could relax, just a bit. He had planned to forego sleep and not to move from his chair all night, but he had hoped the tension in his belly would ease once he knew Liv was asleep in her bed.

She was fine. Of course she was. Hadn't she scolded him on that very notion not but an hour ago?

The silence became unbearable.

He stood from the chair without a sound, moving his body in the silent stealth he had mastered during the war. That he could still do so years later was evidence those years would never fully leave him—not truly, as much as he liked to pretend.

He set the chair to the side and turned the doorknob. To his surprise, it wasn't locked. Liv was either continuing her fool actions, or her trust in him was far more ingrained than she would have him believe.

Tieran crept into the room, closing the door and locking it behind him. Sound asleep, Liv sat propped in the tin tub, her head awkward along the side rim of it. Depending upon how long she had been like that, she was destined to have a deep red mark across the side of her face when she awoke.

One tiny jerk in her sleep, and she could slip down into the tub and drown. He couldn't rightly leave her like that.

With a sigh to steel himself, he walked over to the tub. A quick glance at the water, and he shook his head. For whatever peculiar reason, she was still dressed in her stays and shift, fully soaked under the water.

He leaned over, dipping his hands into the bath. Stone cold.

"Liv." His hand went to her shoulder, squeezing gently.

Her long dark eyelashes fluttered, opening to him. A smile was instant to her lips. Innocence looking at him. No memory in her look except for whatever she had been dreaming of—and it looked like the best of dreams.

He kept his fingers on her shoulder, his voice low. "You are soaked, Liv. Your stays, your shift."

Surprise crept into her eyes and she looked downward. It took her a sleepy moment to speak, her voice a husky rasp. "My stays. The ribbons are knotted."

"Why didn't you just open the door and ask me to untie it?"

"I would have had to acknowledge you were outside my door."

Tieran sighed. "Sit up." He moved his fingers behind her shoulder, pulling her upright. "So instead of asking for my help, you ignored the problem completely and got into the tub with half your clothes on?"

Sitting, she leaned forward in the water and her body wavered, swaying in a slow circle as sleep tried to pull her back into its clutches. Her eyelids slipped closed.

Tieran grabbed the towel on a chair next to the tub and stood to quickly lay it down on the bed. Stripping out of his jacket, he caught her behind the shoulders just before she fell backward against the edge of the tub. Dipping his other arm into the bath, he slid his hand under her knees and lifted her from the cold water.

"I don't need your help, Tieran."

"What you need is to be less stubborn." He carried her across the room.

"You would do well to listen to your own words."

He laid her face-down onto the towel on the bed and then sat next to her. He picked at the knot on the back of her stays, the ribbon swollen tight from the water. After several minutes and more patience than he thought he possessed, he had made no headway. His large fingers were no match for the delicate ribbon. He considered for a moment just cutting it, but then he realized a simple knot was about to best him.

He bent over, studying the twisting carefully before picking at the knot again with the tips of his fingernails. Finally, it gave. Quickly unthreading the ribbon from the eyelets, he pulled the stays wide to free them from Liv's body.

He looked to the half of Liv's face he could see, only to find her deep into sleep once more. Her forearm angled to her head, her wrist touched the crown of her forehead as her dark hair formed a wet blanket framing her face.

For a moment, his hand hovered over her shoulder, ready to nudge her awake again so she could take off her soaking shift. Then he thought the better of it.

His hands going to her bare calves, he picked up the bottom edge of her shift and began to shimmy it up her body. As much as he tried to avert his eyes, he could not help but admire the creaminess of her thighs, the soft curve of her backside, the lines of muscle along the small of her back where her waist narrowed.

He paused as the shift reached just below her breasts and inhaled a steadying breath. He was hard, his cock pulsating as he bared Liv inch by inch. She was glorious, every curve, every contour of her body called out to be caressed, worshiped.

But he had little problem reining in his wayward thoughts. Not when she was soft and at peace, her skin glistening in the light of the fire.

It struck him quite abruptly. This was peace he had not seen her carry since their lives had re-twined months ago.

And he was not about to disturb the precious peace that had overcome her body. No matter how much pain was currently pooling in his groin.

His fingers nimble, he quickly slid the shift up over the rest of her body. She didn't rustle, only a soft murmur escaping her as he lifted her head to free the shift.

Leaving the bed, he walked to the fireplace and tied the rope between the two chairs in front of it. He draped her dripping shift and stays in the middle, then went to the haphazard pile of her black clothes on the floor, picking each piece of her riding habit up and shaking it out before hanging it along the rope to dry.

He turned slowly from the fire, his look landing on her. A deep breath lifted her back, her body quivering on the exhale.

He resisted for a long moment. Resisted going over to her. Resisted giving in to the one thought that had sprung into his mind—a tiny bud, opening into a flame.

It didn't take long for him to realize he was powerless against the thought, and he walked over to the bed, grabbing the blanket scrunched by her toes. He pulled the blanket up, covering her long, lean form. She exhaled a soft moan, curling into the warmth of the heavy cover.

Peace.

He sat down next to her hip, the bed bowing under his weight, his mind focused on that one thought that had captivated him.

Peace—he wanted to give that to her.

If she had it in sleep, maybe it wasn't too late. Maybe she could have it once again in consciousness.

He reached up, wrapping a long dark strand of her black hair around his forefinger.

Rachel had given him the gift of peace long ago. Led him back into the world of the living after burning in hell. But his wife had been a rare spirit.

He questioned his own ability to do the same for Liv.

But he needed to try. She needed to be led back from the edge she was about to go over.

And he was the only one to do it.

{ CHAPTER 13 }

Tieran twitched the reins in his hand, and Liv watched as his well-muscled black stallion shifted to the side, dancing in a small circle that set him even with her horse on the road.

The storm had passed, and as they had moved south the snow drifting on the roads had lessened to where their horses could keep an even gait.

She glanced over at Tieran. Having stared at nothing for most of the day but the back of his head and the wide expanse of his dark overcoat stretched across his shoulders, she wasn't sure what exactly Tieran currently thought of her presence.

She had woken in the morning to find him stretched out on the floor next to her bed, his left forearm splayed up behind his head as a pillow. That she was naked under the blanket gave her pause, especially when the last thing she remembered was giving up the fight with the knotted ribbon on her stays, and sinking into the hot water of the tub with her shift and stays still in place.

Liv had thought Tieran asleep on the floor, but the second she turned onto her side, his eyes had popped open to her, the smile carving into his face telling her he knew exactly what she was wondering—how had she been stripped naked and by whom? That same smile had told her the answer as well—Tieran had welcomed himself to assisting her into nudity.

Beyond the wicked smirk, Tieran had been nothing but a gentleman that morning, leaving the room with instructions for her to get ready to depart, as they had much road to cover that day.

No invitation, no request for her to join him. A demand, pure and simple, that they would be travelling together.

At least it lacked ambiguity about how he was going to proceed. He had decided Liv was his responsibility, whether she wanted a say in the matter or not.

Her bones and muscles still aching from the previous night's slow, bitterly cold ride to the coaching inn, Liv wasn't going to call foul on his domineering. She wanted to not only get far, far away from Mortell Abbey, but back to London quickly, and Tieran was her best option for that. Along with being her safest option—especially with Lord Shepton somewhere on the roads.

Liv's eyes trailed from Tieran's face down to his gloved hands, one on the reins, one balled, riding on his thigh. From nowhere, the vision of his naked chest pressing against her in the Roman bath chamber snuck into her mind, swallowing her thoughts. Under those gloves were the hands that had stroked her skin, shattered her into a thousand pieces, and then sheltered her as she fell back into her body.

Stop. Thoughts such as those did her sanity no favors.

Her face turning hot, she averted her eyes, staring at the glossy brown mane of her mare. What *did* Tieran think of her presence? She imagined she was a burr in his side that he was anxious to rid himself of. Too bad basic decency prevented him from flicking her off to the side.

And that was Tieran. Decent. Honest. Kind. Honorable.

She knew not everyone saw those traits in him—most were far too timid in his shadow to see beyond his height and muscle. And the frown he consistently wore did little to sway the casual observer to look deeper.

But she had always seen it in him. Seen who he truly was.

And he still, to the day in front of her, remained those things. Decent. Honest. Kind. Honorable.

Which was why he had been right to leave her at Mortell Abbey—she could not fault him at all for that. She possessed none of those qualities—not anymore, and no man would forgive what Tieran had walked in on. She hadn't intended for him to witness the scene with Lord Shepton, but before she could control the situation, Tieran had appeared.

Liv had made him leave her—as sure as if she had screamed at him that she hated him.

"Are you cold? The chill appears to have set into your face, Liv—your cheeks are pink."

She looked up at him, attempting to drain the flush—and the memory from whence it was born—from her head. "No, I am warm enough. It is much more bearable now that the bitter wind has died."

He nodded.

"Do you still think we will make it to your friend's estate before nightfall?"

"I do." Tieran pointed forward with his free hand. "It is just a few more miles before his lands, and then the manor is five miles inward. There will only be a few servants present, but Lord Luhaunt keeps enough staff on hand when he's not in residence that we shall eat well enough and have warm beds tonight."

"And you will not feel the imperious need to sleep in a chair to protect me from the many blackguards haunting the coaching inns?"

He looked over at her, eyebrows drawn together, ready to argue, but then his frown flipped when he saw her grinning. Teasing him had always been fun. Making his frown flip.

"They are indeed, a plague on this land, those curs," he said.

"Most assuredly, they are. I have never been so afraid. I was lucky to have you to" —she cleared her throat with a flourish— "attend to me."

A slight blush ran across his hard cheekbones as he averted his eyes far away from her. "You were."

She leaned forward on her horse, angling to look at him straight on while trying to stifle her laughter. "Has the chill gotten you, Tieran? Your cheeks look rosy."

His blue eyes shifted to her, the edges crinkling, striving for a glare, but not achieving it.

"You walk upon very thin ice, Liv."

"I would argue that last night it was you upon that thin ice when you were *helping* me from my shift."

"Should I have let you freeze in the cold bath?"

She sat straight in her sidesaddle, looking over the crest of the upcoming hill. Sheep walked alongside the road, their path clearer of snow than the road proper. "No. I appreciate your assistance. And I trust you kept your hands on the right side of honor."

"They did not stray."

She looked at him. "I never thought it of you."

He watched her for a moment, his eyes searching her face, his head bobbing with his horse's stride. So long and so quiet that Liv had to look away, suddenly on guard about what he searched for.

She knew there could be nothing between them, not after what he witnessed. But the way his eyes raked over her, it made her long to erase the last day—to at least be more cunning in how she had trapped Lord Shepton. If Tieran had never seen...

She coughed, shaking herself. What was done was done.

"Tell me, Liv," Tieran said, breaking the rhythmic sound of their horse's hooves crunching through the snow and ice. "Why do you still wear black? I wondered it last night when I hung your dress. I have seen you in nothing but widow's weeds, no matter the occasion. Lord Canton died more than three years past."

"Have you embraced color yet?" She glanced at him, wrapping another tight loop of the reins around her hand. "Your wife died nearly two years ago."

"Well, no, but my marriage with Rachel was..." His words dropped off.

She looked sharply to him. "A real marriage? A marriage where there was love? Grand passion? Was that what you were about to say?"

He shrugged. "Not in so many words, but yes."

"There was love in my marriage, Tieran." She exhaled, the warm puff crystallizing in the cold air in front of her nose. "Just a very different sort than the love poets create great sonnets about. It was a love born of mutual respect and kindness. Lord Canton had already had the great love of his life with his first wife. Just as I had with you. Neither of us needed passion—both of our loves were gone—his from death and mine from circumstance."

Her gaze went forward, unable to look at Tieran with the admission. "But we both still needed a sustaining love—someone to depend upon. I know the gossipmongers didn't account for our marriage being anything more than a title-hungry charlatan marrying a lecherous old fool. But I knew the truth of our marriage—I still do, and that has sustained me through the years of snide cuts and whispers amongst the *ton*. I honored that love we had for a long time with my clothing."

"And now?"

She looked to Tieran. An acute glint had surfaced in his blue eyes, both intent on understanding her—she recognized that part of the look—and with a hint of anger. Anger at what, she did not know.

She shrugged, the center of her bottom lip jutting upward. "And I still wear it now because it is easy. People are more forgiving of a widow. I do it as a constant reminder to the gossips, a whisper in the back of their heads that they were wrong about me. Plus, it frustrates the busybodies that had placed bets in polite drawing rooms about how soon I would appear in full red regalia, declaring my skirts open for trysts with married men."

A chuckle escaped Tieran.

A small smile touched her lips as her gaze went forward. "Most importantly, the black keeps all but the most obnoxiously bold men away from me. I have no interest in what they offer. I know you think me a coquette, but it is always on my terms, on my approach, and only when I have a purpose."

"Such as the list?"

"Yes, the list." Her eyelids lowered, her look whipping to Tieran. "I tell you again, do not think to press me for details about it, Tieran."

His hand flew up, calming against her ire. "I will not. I will drop the matter in deference to the truce."

The gloved forefinger of his hand turned into a point. "It is here that we turn. If we take to the fields, we will be faster."

Liv nodded, following Tieran's lead as his horse stepped ahead, silent as her mind slipped, quicksand out-of-control, into thoughts of the past.

She always tried to guard against it—stop herself before she became consumed with a past that never should have been. It was cruelty she heaped upon herself each and every time she let her mind do this. The injustice of it, of being stolen from her home and thrown into a whorehouse—when by all rights, she should have been safely ensconced in Tieran's home as his wife, waiting patiently for him to return from war.

Uncontrollable, her anger welled.

Cease. Cease before it consumes and exhausts.

She attempted to rein in her thoughts, hating when she wallowed. But the anger spun, wicked tentacles reaching out to tense every part of her body.

She looked up from the frozen ground, catching the easy swing of Tieran's body on his horse. It was so easy for him. Always so easy. Freedom to do as he pleased. Go to war. Marry another. Use her body and then abandon her.

"You could have married me before you left." The words blurted, uncontrolled from her mouth before she could contain what she knew was a childish whine.

Tieran visibly jolted on his horse, his look whipping back to her. For a long moment he stared at her, his eyes narrowed. Liv expected him to turn forward and continue across the field without a word.

Instead he slowed his stallion so they were directly side by side again and he met her eyes, his words slow, careful. "You were not yet eighteen, Liv. I swore I would not touch you until then."

She stared at him, her teeth running along her tongue. She should stop this now. Do not go into the past. Not when she was angry. But she had never been able to ask him and now she had just inadvertently started. She opened her mouth.

"I was two months shy, Tieran. Two months. Your honor could not sacrifice two months?"

His head fell backward, his look going to the sky as if to ask for either divine intervention or a lightning bolt to hit him. His chin dropped, his blue eyes locking into her gaze. "The truth of it?"

The four words chilled her to the bone. Yet she had started this.

She nodded.

"I wanted you to choose me as an adult, Liv—not as the besotted chit I met in the shadows of those stairs many years ago. As an adult. Do you not realize how beautiful you were—a spark of the highest order? You were magnificent. And I could not go through life—could not make you go through life—always wondering if I stole you away too soon, if you could have made a better match than me. I could not live with the threat that your eye would eventually wander."

Her head cocked backward with his admission. "When did I ever give you reason not to trust me?"

"Never." His head shook. "I did not trust life, Liv. I already knew I would spend my life staring down every man that looked at you with lust in his eyes—and I was fine with that—I welcomed that. But I could not trust that a choice you made as a child would carry you for a lifetime."

"And that decision would have magically become more resolute in those two months?" Her hand flew up, flabbergasted. "You thought I wouldn't choose you? I loved you, Tieran. Loved you more than anything. It would not have changed in two months—two years—twenty—fifty. Never. You were my heart, Tieran."

"Do you not think I regretted it—regretted it every single day?" His words bit out through clenched teeth. "That it has gnawed away at my soul since I left you for the war?"

He looked away from her, his jaw twitching, the whole of him palpitating raw energy—a storm brewing.

She would not let it be so easy.

Not when he was the one that could not bring himself to trust her. Not when he was the one that had left her. "But if you had regretted it, Tieran—you would have made it right—you would have come for me directly after the war. You would not have disappeared for a year without word. If you had just—"

His head whipped to her. "I was broken, Liv." His scream thundered across the snow-laden fields, rolling over the land to disappear into the far-off forest.

Their horses stopped on instinct.

Her eyes wide, her stare piercing him, Liv blinked, trying to jar her mind into working. "Broken?"

"Yes, dammit. Broken." His horse took a nervous step and he yanked on the reins, stilling it. He looked at her, his blue eyes tormented. "My hands did not stop shaking for months after I finally was able to step back onto English soil. They shook so violently on the way to your parents' home that I could not hold the reins. I almost turned back—almost could not come for you. But even with the tremors—even though I was broken—I only needed one thing. You."

She gasped. "You…you came for me? When?"

"Three weeks after you had married. You were the one thing I knew that could pull me back from the dead—pull me back from the things I did."

Her head swung back and forth haltingly, her world slowing, spinning about her. "But no—mother, father, they never told me."

"I don't imagine they would have. You were married. I was clearly not sane. If I had a daughter, I would not have let a man in my state near her either."

Her heart crushing at the pain in his eyes, still to this day, she inhaled, needing to ask the question, but not wanting to know the answer. "Why were you broken, Tieran?"

His look seared into her for a moment before he cleared his throat, looking away to a far-off crest. He nudged his horse forward, and Liv's mare followed suit.

Just when she thought he was not going to answer her, his voice interrupted the silence between them, low, each word spoken as if it was being dragged from the bowels of hell. "The war. Too many of my men died. Died with my hands cradling their heads. Died begging me to bring them back to their loved ones. Simple men. Complicated men. All of them died wanting one thing—to be near the ones they loved. They died one after another with only my hands holding them from the bitter cold ground. Died in pain, without mercy. It changed me. Each one just a little bit more. Hardened my soul until I did not recognize myself."

He fell silent, his eyes closing for a long moment. Several long breaths lifted his chest as he struggled for control.

Liv watched his profile, her chest in pain, struggling for her own breath. "And I was not there for you when you returned."

"No. No, you weren't, Liv."

Without looking at her, he clicked his horse onward, speeding its gait across the field.

Leaving Liv to stare at his back once more.

CHAPTER 14

Crack.

The sound, a sudden explosion of wood splintering, tore Liv from her sleep. She flew upright in the bed, frantic eyes searching the foreign room.

Crack.

The fire had died down to low embers, shedding little light in the room. It took a long second for her to pull her mind from dreams and remember she was in the estate of one of Tieran's friend's—Lord Luhaunt.

Her feet swung out of bed in the next second as she realized Tieran was in the room next to hers, and that was exactly where she had heard the crash coming from.

Crack.

She grabbed the borrowed robe the servants had procured for her and slung it over her shoulders, running to the door.

Pausing in the hallway at Tieran's door, her fingers curled around the doorknob.

It had gone silent in his room.

She considered knocking for one short moment, then disregarded caution and turned the knob, barging into his room.

Tieran stood next to the bed. His back to her, naked, heaving, the light from his fireplace glistened off the sweat covering his back.

He spun around at the sound. His muscles tight, twitching, his hands clenched into fists. But it was his face that made Liv jump. Wrath raged across his brow, turning his blue eyes darkly violent, while his lips had parted, seething dangerous breaths in and out. The whole of him had turned pure savage.

Fear—not of him, but of whatever had possessed him, darted down her spine. "Tieran?"

Her eyes flickered down his body, stopping before they dipped below his waist as she caught sight of the table next to his bed. It sat in a heaping mess, cracked, splintered into ragged pieces, shards of wood scattered about the floor.

"Leave, Liv." The strain in his voice made the words barely recognizable.

She took another step into the room, closing the door behind her. "No, Tieran." She scanned the room. Nothing but the table appeared to be destroyed.

"I said leave, Liv."

She shook her head, spying a brandy decanter on a small sideboard next to the fireplace. She went over to it, splashing brandy almost to the rim of a cut-glass tumbler.

Turning back to him, she found him wrapping a sheet from the bed around his waist, knotting it on the side. His breathing looked more akin to normal, though his brow still furrowed, the savagery not fully quelled.

"You need to leave, Liv."

"Yes, I probably do. And I will exit in a moment." She pointed to the wing chair by the fireplace. "But not until you sit and I am assured that whatever just happened in here has passed and you are not about to destroy more furniture."

"I'm awake, Liv. I have control."

Her head cocked to the side. "Do you? Your body is still taut—almost to shaking, Tieran. Sit, if only to soothe my silly worries."

He heaved a sigh that vibrated through the room and then ambled to the chair, plopping down, his fingers raking through his dark blond hair. His glare, centered on her while he moved, was unmistakable, but it also wasn't about to frighten her away.

Liv moved in front of him, using her bare toes to pull the footstool close to his knees so she could sit directly before him. She held out the tumbler of brandy. Another sigh, but he did thrust his hand out to take it. Their fingers met around the glass and she realized his hand was still trembling.

Positioning herself between his long, outstretched legs, she sat on the footstool, balancing her arms along the length of her thighs as she leaned forward, waiting for him as he emptied half the glass in one long swallow.

Before she could speak, Tieran pinned her, warning in his blue eyes. "Where I was in my dreams, you want no business of, Liv."

"Do I not get to decide that?"

His voice dropped to a growl. "Do you want to hear how I hated you? Hated you with such a passion it nearly destroyed everything around me?"

A slight gasp escaped her. Her lips ajar, her tongue slid to the side, running along her teeth, clamping back at rising to his baited words. "No. But I also do not want to see you in this state—in the state I just saw you."

"Then you shouldn't have opened the door, Liv."

She nodded. "But I did. Was that what was in your dreams—hate?"

"Amongst other things."

She exhaled with a silent nod, standing, then paused for a moment before leaning forward to take the glass from his hand. "Then it appears as though I have stumbled upon a moment of reckoning."

With a quick backward tilt of her head, she drained the rest of the glass, the fire burning a path down her throat. Going to the sideboard, she slowly refilled it, watching the quiver in her own fingers.

Before she turned around to Tieran, she forced a deep breath into her lungs, bracing herself. Steadied, she returned to him, handing him the tumbler as she reclaimed her seat on the footstool. She met his gaze. "You hated me because I failed you. I was not there for you after the war to help you escape the hell it put you in."

He set the glass on the end of his left knee, his fingers moving to hold it by the rim before meeting her eyes. "I hated you because you did not wait for me."

She fortified herself against the words, against the pain palpitating through his words. Of course he had hated her—she had hated herself. But she had also long since accepted the necessity of what she had done. "As much as I wish your forgiveness, Tieran, I cannot defend against what I chose to do. I had been ripped from my home. I thought you were dead. I was on the brink of ruin, of being disowned—I could only imagine the worst of what my life would become. Marrying Lord Canton was the only security I could find."

"I know, Liv. I know that now." His right hand ran through his hair again. "But back then…back then I hated you for a very long time. Knowing the reason now does not remove the hate I once felt. I still lived it, breathed it, unjustified though I now know it was."

A frown on her face, she nodded. She could do nothing but accept the fact.

His head fell back, his eyes going to the elaborate ornamental motifs on the ceiling. "So when you asked why I was broken, I did not want to speak of the hate. I did not want to put that upon you."

"But it was real. It happened."

"Yes. And when I came for you, I carried with me each and every dream of the men that had died on foreign soil— their dreams to return to their loved ones. I was returning to you—my love—not just for me—for all of us. Only once I came for you, you were gone."

"Married to another."

His look dropped to her, agony in his blue eyes. "And there, in that moment, I realized what their pain was in their dying moments—the horror, deep in their souls, that they would never see, hear, or touch their loved ones again. Bury their faces in the sweet smell of their wives' hair. Hold their children, clutching them to their chest. They knew dying in that muck they would never have that again."

Her hand went to his right knee, gently setting her fingers atop it. "Only death released them from those thoughts—whereas you had to live with that pain." Through the sheet covering his leg she could feel him twitch at her touch.

"Yes." He looked down to her hand on his knee and then shook his head, staring at it. "What I would have given for the merest touch from your hand during that time."

He lifted the tumbler, taking a long swallow. "But I managed to do the impossible—I managed to put myself back together, Liv. Put myself back together enough to walk, to talk, to eat. And I learned how to smile again."

Her hand slipped off the edge of his knee, curling back into her lap. "With Lady Rachel?"

His head slanted to the side, his blue eyes taking measure of her. "Yes, with Rachel. She was small and delicate and soft."

"Everything I am not."

Tieran's look swept her face, her hair, moving down her body and back up again. "I could not be around anything you were, Liv—anything that reminded me of you."

Liv nodded. She didn't want to understand, didn't want Tieran to have found another love.

But he had.

And she did understand.

"You loved her?" Her voice cracked.

"I did. Deeply." He took the last swallow of the brandy, looking away from Liv. His gaze landed on the wrecked table. "But I never did learn how to sleep again. Not properly."

Liv followed his gaze to the table, and then she glanced down to his knuckles to see if there was any blood. How he had destroyed the table so completely, in such a short amount of time, bewildered her. She looked to him. "I know you led men and they died, but what exactly did you do in the war, Tieran?"

He flinched, his look snapping to her. "I…"

"Yes?"

"No…no one has ever asked me that before."

"Not Rachel?"

"No." His head shook slowly. "She knew…knew I was damaged, but I could never tell her why. And she never asked. I know she didn't want me to dredge up pain that was best forgotten."

Liv stared at him. His breathing had quickened, his bare chest stretching tight with each inhale. His look went to the fire, to the mantel, darting from one thing to the next, looking for a haven. He was fighting against memories—she recognized it because she had done it herself a thousand times. "Just because it is best forgotten does not mean it does not fester within you, Tieran. Does not yearn for release."

He abruptly stood, shuffling past her legs and setting the tumbler down on the sideboard as he moved across the room. Stopping at the windows, he pulled the heavy velvet draperies back and stared out.

Silent moments stretched long, suffocating the room as she stared at Tieran's back. He wasn't going to speak. Not without encouragement. There was a time when she would have planted herself in front of him, demanding, nose-to-nose, that he bare all to her. And he would have.

But they were not those people anymore, and she didn't know how far she could push him without getting stung.

Liv stood and moved across the room, stopping several steps behind him. She looked past his bare arm, out the window to the vast land of snow covering the lawns and trees, the whiteness a sea of sparkles under the reflection of the three-quarters moon.

"What did you do in the war, Tieran?" Her voice soft, she shuffled closer to set her fingers lightly along a hardened muscle of his bicep. "Whatever it was, I can only imagine you did what you had to in order to survive. That is what I have been told about war."

Her breath held, she waited, her fingers frozen along the smooth skin of his arm.

And waited.

And waited.

Her fingers ached to move, to push him further, but she held still in silence, refusing to back away.

"It is survival." His voice crept out towards the window in the softest murmur. "War was survival." His head, his shoulders shuddered, and Liv could see his jawline tighten at the exact moment his muscle went impossibly hard under her fingers. "But then at some point—at some random and brutal moment in time—survival becomes irrelevant, and the only thing one is left with is the need for punishment."

"Punishment?" Her fingers wrapped around his upper arm, tugging him to face her.

Tieran inhaled, the breath lifting his chest high before he turned slightly, his blue eyes meeting her gaze. "It becomes the important thing—the only thing. Punishment for those that killed my men, men I considered my brothers."

"Punishment?" Liv repeated the word in a whisper, watching torment take over his eyes.

"Not just punishment, Liv. I needed to find all of the killers, and there was only one way." He stared at her.

"What does that mean, not just punishment?" Her head slanted, staring, searching for answers in his eyes. "No...not just punishment...torture?"

He turned from her, a tremble running the course of his body, vibrating her fingers with the force of it. The quaking didn't cease.

His head had dropped, his eyes closed as his voice cracked. "I became the monster everyone always saw in me. The monster everyone always knew was within me. And not a man stopped me. They wanted it as well. I was ordered to do it. But it was me, Liv. Me. My hands. My monstrosity."

He gasped a swallowed breath, his body shaking with increasing violence. Violence that wouldn't stop.

Liv swallowed hard. Swallowed back the rage in her throat. The injustice. The outrage.

That Tieran—her love—had ever, for even one second in his life—believed he was a monster. The sheer perversion of that blasphemy swelled in her chest, the infuriation burning, speeding her heartbeat.

She bit back a scream—a scream that would only rant at the heavens, at ghosts, at men that demanded power and greed be satisfied by the deaths of thousands. By the death of Tieran's spirit.

Tieran had once known he was an honorable man. But now—now she could see he questioned it in every step he took, every move he made, every word he uttered. It made her heart ache.

Her hands fighting tremors of their own, she settled both of her palms along his bare back, moving them up along his shoulders before they drifted downward, slipping around his waist to encircle him, her cheek nuzzling into the crook along his spine. His heat flooded her face.

"Tell me what I can do, Tieran." Her voice dropped to a cracked whisper. "Anything. I will do anything."

A soul-shattering quake rolled through his body, every muscle shuddering. She could feel the tears racking his body, but his sudden grip on her forearms at his belly told her he didn't want her to see. Nor was she about to force herself around him to witness them.

"Tieran?"

"Don't let go, Liv."

"That is all?"

A deep breath shook into his chest. "Don't let go."

She turned her head, her lips wispy along the skin of his spine. "I won't. I swear. I won't."

{ CHAPTER 15 }

Liv stepped gingerly down the expansive hallway in the center of Tieran's townhouse—gingerly because of her thigh muscles that had been strained and stretched to the limits earlier in the day at the last coaching inn.

She had not chosen a small man to love. And the rawness burning the inside of her thighs was, apparently, the price she would have to pay.

She grinned to herself. Not that she minded in the slightest. A tingle ran through her core at the very thought of what Tieran had done to her body hours ago. Her leg stretched high on his chest, his teeth raking along her calf. Her grin widened. She would pay the price of a few sore muscles a thousand times over to finally have Tieran as hers.

Tieran slowed his gait to match hers—just as he always had—and the heels of her boots clunked on the polished wood floors in tandem with his stride. Arriving on London streets hours after darkness, he had offered to deliver her to her townhouse and let her rest.

An honorable offer, but they both knew he didn't mean a word of it.

He wanted her by his side, and that was exactly where she wanted to be.

So they had continued on to his townhouse, entering quickly by way of the mews under the cloak of darkness.

Halfway down the hallway, Tieran's palm went to the small of her back, ushering her to the right at an open set of double doors.

Liv knew she was in a sitting room even before Tieran lit several lamps—it had a sense about it—a sense of comfort, of being enveloped in relaxation and warmth, even though the air was chilly without a fire in the hearth.

His staff had not known he was to arrive back in London so soon, so had not prepared the house for his arrival, nor had he wanted to alert them to his sudden presence so late in the evening, especially with Liv accompanying him.

One sconce and two lamps lit, Tieran closed the double doors and moved to stand behind Liv, his hands going down the length of her arms as he bent, his warm cheek heating her cool one.

"Sit, relax, Liv. I will start a fire."

Liv nodded, even though she had no intention of sitting. It felt so good to stand after the days of riding that she guessed it would be at least an hour before she could even think about sitting again.

Tieran went to the fireplace and Liv's gaze left him, moving about the room, studying her surroundings. This was a sitting room, but not a public one—not by far. It was much too cozy, far too personal to be shared with mere acquaintances.

Her feet threaded her about the room. Plush wing chairs upholstered in striped yellow silk damask were angled for both conversation and to the hearth centering the room. A pianoforte sat next to a harp. And side table after side table held needles in every size for knitting—from beautiful ivory needles, to functional wood needles that had been worn to a shine from years of use.

Stopping beside a delicate Sheraton cane-backed armchair, Liv's fingers rubbed along the rosewood inlay along the back rail as her eyes scanned the room. A woman's hand had touched the whole of the room—it was not ostentatious—truly done in very restrained, quality taste. Very few knickknacks cluttered the room of soft yellows and browns that fit a man, but were delicate enough for a woman.

Liv went over to the sideboard with the amber-speckled granite top, picking up a jade sculpture of a tusked elephant with its trunk raised in trumpet. The accompanying sculpture was of a mother elephant with a calf tucked around its hind legs.

She studied them for a moment, flipping the bull over in her hands. "These are beautiful. Where did you get them?"

Sitting on his heels as he balanced on his toes, Tieran looked up from the fire that was just starting to flame. His eyebrows drew together when he spotted what was in her hands. "The jade—I did not know those were there."

"You did not? But this is your house."

Tieran shrugged, his attention going back to the fire. He poked at the coals below the split log on the grate. "I don't spend much time in here. Any, to be precise."

Liv glanced fully about the room once more, her look landing on Tieran's shoulders. "Why not?"

He continued to poke at the coals. "I couldn't change anything about the room—touch what Rachel had created." He sighed. "Nor can I bear to look around at it, even when I happen my way in here."

"Why are we in here, then?"

He glanced at her, then looked back to the flames. "I do not know. It is comfortable—and I wanted you to be so. I did not think on it."

Her lips drew in, her breath landing heavy in her chest. She gently set the jade sculpture onto the sideboard. "You truly did love her, didn't you?"

His hand holding the iron poker stilled, his head dropping slightly. An agonizing moment passed, and he hung the poker along the fireplace, standing.

Tieran didn't speak until his look centered on her. Yet she couldn't read anything in the blue of his eyes—they were guarded, his words careful. "Yes, I did love Rachel, Liv. You doubted it?"

Her gaze flickered about the room, and she realized she was standing in the middle of a shrine to Tieran's dead wife. Her hand went out to land on the top of a chair, steadying herself as her fingernails dug into the silk. "If I am honest, I had hoped it was not possible. Not possible that you could love anyone but me."

His head cocked slightly, the guarded look in his eyes solidifying.

"But I very well realize how selfish that is of me— especially if she made you happy, Tieran." Her free hand went to her chest. "I made the choice to marry Lord Canton. I made the choice when I thought it was the only thing to do—and I stood by that choice—by him. I never approached you in those years because I had to respect my marriage—and your marriage. I couldn't have you, but I still wanted happiness for you, Tieran. As much as it stung that it wasn't with me. It just hurts my heart now to see how you had to suffer her death, when she meant…everything to you."

His eyes left Liv, landing on the jade elephant she had placed on the sideboard. "She did mean everything to me. For a brief time. She did."

A shiver twisted down Liv's spine.

She gave a slight shake of her head. "I thought I could, but…I do not think I can stay here in this home with you, Tieran."

His look instantly flew to her, pinning her. "I will leave it."

"No, I cannot ask you—"

"No. You are not asking, Liv—I want to come with you." His hand swung around him. "This. Everything here, I can no longer be around it. I knew it the second I stepped foot into this room. It pulls me into the past—into death, into the place where I do not want to live life. And I don't want that anymore. I don't want to burden you with it. I no longer want to be burdened by it."

She swayed slightly, wanting to believe his words but afraid to do so. The two of them being together while traveling, at coaching inns, at Mortell Abbey, was a very different thing than her and Tieran being together here in London. Here where the past would meet them at every turn.

"But this is your home."

"It is brick and mortar, Liv. Nothing more."

She swallowed hard. "You are decided?"

"I am. I want you, Liv. I want today, tomorrow with you. And that is better done at your home, or at the dower house, or at a home I will buy for us—anywhere but here."

She exhaled, the tiniest hope she had harbored since Tieran appeared before her at Mortell Abbey blowing into a real, true flame. A real chance at a future—no matter how convoluted—with him.

Tieran crossed the room to her, grabbing her hand. "Come. Come with me now."

She nodded, and within moments she had her cloak back about her shoulders and was pulling tight her gloves as they wound their way through the back garden to the mews.

After going into the stable to rouse the stable boy to ready their horses, Tieran stepped in front of Liv as she stood waiting in the open air. Slipping his hands along her hips, he drove her backward until her shoulder blades bumped into the outside wall of the stables.

He stared down at her, his blue eyes darkened by the shadows, but the heat in them was unmistakable. His look was unguarded for the first time since he had stood from the fireplace. The hunger she recognized, but there was something even more interesting sparking in his eyes, almost as if he had been freed from something weighing upon his soul.

His hands tightened around her waist, claiming her for the moment until the horses were ready.

She couldn't resist the smile that stretched across her face, taking over her entire being.

A grin flipped the corners of Tieran's mouth upward in response. "That smile. That is the smile I remember from years ago, but have not seen. What is it for? I thought you had lost it."

She leaned forward, kissing his chest through his clothes. "This. You holding me, hiding me from the world."

"Yes?"

She craned her neck, leaning away so she could meet his eyes. "It makes me happy. And I forgot what a moment of pure happiness felt like."

The frown came back to his face. "You have not known happiness in the last eight years, Liv?"

"Not since the day you left for war—even on that day, even with all the worry—I still had snippets of happiness. When you teased me about my inability to tie my bonnet properly."

"It was right after I kissed you by the cliff."

"Yes. And my hands were shaking. And you took an inordinate amount of pride in the fact that you made me tremble so."

He chuckled

She poked his chest. "You think too highly of your ability to make me quiver."

"Do I? Has there been another who could make your fingers tremble with a mere kiss?"

"No. Which is part of the problem with your arrogance—it is well earned in that matter, which makes it entirely more aggravating. So I dislike encouraging it."

Another rumble came from deep in Tieran's chest, shaking her body with his mirth.

"Your ego aside, you did tie it for me with those large hands of yours," Liv said. "That moment—in that moment I was happy. Happiness that was untinged—it held only the joy of the moment. It was the last one I remember."

Tieran pulled her into his chest, his right hand lifting, his fingers digging into the base of her hair. "I swear, Liv, I will give you those moments again. Married or not."

"By teasing me?"

"If that's what it takes." He tilted her head up to him, his mouth going to her lips, brushing against her skin with his words. "Or by kissing you. Or by sliding my hand along your boots, up your inner thigh in the exact way I have discovered you like. Or by taking your earlobe between my teeth, tugging, searching for the spot that makes you hum."

She swallowed, a lump growing in her throat. "Or what else?"

"My lips on your neck, moving downward. My tongue tracing a line along the slope of your breasts, stalking your nipple. Moving to the valley between your breasts, dipping downward, past your navel."

Her hips went forward, pressing into him through her skirts and his clothes, swaying against him with the need pooling between her legs, her core throbbing with every word he spoke.

Another chuckle, low and lascivious escaped into her ear.

"I know I just said married or not, Liv, but I would prefer married. I would prefer to be able to maul you in public like this without thought to propriety."

"It's not proper to maul your wife in public either, Tieran. Probably less so."

"Marry me, Liv."

Her hands went up, pressing slightly on his chest.

She had to distance herself from him, at least her hips, or she would start agreeing to anything and everything he asked of her.

Everything she wasn't about to give up.

She gasped a breath, attempting to control the blood pounding in her ears. "I know what you would ask of me, Tieran. So I cannot. I made an oath to myself to never marry again. To never let another control me. And were we to marry, you would want to control me—you already do."

"So? Your body loves it when I control you."

A short chuckle escaped her lips in spite of herself. "You know very well I do not speak of how my body enjoys your control, Tieran. I speak of everything that happens outside of what transpires when our bodies are bared to each other."

"So we will stay in a bedroom and never leave."

Her lips pursed. "An impossible dream. You know that. You also know there are things I must do that you cannot control. And with that, the actions I will take would taint you. Taint your title. I will not do that to you."

His voice dropped to a growl. "Give up the list, Liv. Give up whatever you are determined to accomplish with that damn thing."

Her eyes narrowed. "You know the list is none of your concern."

"No. But you are. And part of you right now is consumed with this list."

"So then take the part of me that I am offering."

"What part is that?"

"The part that has always been yours—needed to be yours. The part of me that loves you—will love you until my last breath—that wants nothing more than to marry you and be your wife and bear your children. And maybe someday…"

Her head shook. "But right now there is the other part of me I cannot deny—the part that demands vengeance and will not free me until it's accomplished. That is the part of me that cannot marry you. The part that was created in me after you left for war—it is real in me and I cannot deny it exists."

Tieran inhaled a long breath.

She could see he wanted to seethe, wanted to say so much more—to rail at her. Instead, his voice was even, calm as he exhaled. "Why is this damn list so important to you, Liv? Revenge for deeds done against Lord Canton?"

She went rigid. "You said at Mortell Abbey you would ask no more on it, Tieran."

"I did not realize at that time the extent to which this list holds you hostage, Liv. Hostage from me."

Her chin jutted out. "Take what I can offer, Tieran. Please. Do not press for more."

He stared down at her, the distrust in his eyes delving into her, trying to read her soul, her intentions. She couldn't blame him.

After the longest moment, he gave a slight nod.

"It's you, Liv. So whatever part of you I can have, I will take it, willingly, happily, gratefully." His hand went to her cheek, his palm cradling her jawline. "But do not expect this to be my surrender. Do not expect me not to demand at every turn for the whole of you. I do believe you forgot what a patient man I am."

Liv's cheek lifted in a half-smile. "I remember. I remember it too well. And I am depending on it."

{ CHAPTER 16 }

Contrary to Liv's insistence that they could do no such thing, she and Tieran had spent the first three days in London locked in the master bedroom of the empty Reggard dower house. The townhouse, nestled a street away from Berkeley Square, was spacious, but cozy, and most importantly, vacant.

Tieran had a few servants brought over from his main residence—his valet, cook, and a maid for Liv—and to a one, they were the utmost in discretion and only seen when called upon. Beyond that, they were alone. Blissfully alone.

It wasn't until late in the evening of the third day that the seclusion came to an abrupt end.

Papers and correspondence strewn across the four-post bed, Tieran lounged in the middle of the mess, his legs stretched long under the papers, his back against the headboard as he rustled through stacks.

Liv sat by the fire with her own correspondence that had been delivered from her townhouse. Her fingers flipping through the pile of calling cards, the reality of what life consisted of before leaving for Mortell Abbey was quickly starting to weigh upon her shoulders.

Beyond the list of social calls she would have to attend to, there were a dozen investments in her settlement that she would need to inquire into. She still kept careful watch on all of her investments—and the men involved—just as Lord Canton had taught her. That vigilance alone had not only kept her wealth secure, but it had also increased it by half.

Plus, the many connections through her investments had helped innumerable times as she had approached her dealings with the list.

The list.

She glanced up at Tieran. His brow furrowed, his eyes flipped down the length of the paper in his hand, concentration evident.

She would need to visit Viola soon. She was near to bursting wanting to share the news of her and Tieran with her friend. To share her happiness.

Aside from the fact that Viola had to be entirely anxious about what happened at Mortell Abbey. Liv had already seen evidence in the scandal sheets of Lord Shepton's great and wondrous fall. And he had only been back in London two days. It would only get worse for him from here onward.

Tieran cleared his throat, setting the paper down and picking up the next envelope in the stack by his leg. A red envelope, he unfolded the note card and quickly flipped it closed, discarding it to the pile on the other side of his leg. Two more pieces of correspondence he went through before he looked up at her, his eye catching hers.

"Anything of interest in your piles?" he asked, pointing at the papers in her lap.

"Nothing beyond the usual. Although, this is a much more relaxing way to go through the drudgery than to do so at my desk. You and a cozy fire are ideal." She nodded with her head at the bed covered with papers. "Anything interesting in yours? I never knew you were so disorderly."

Tieran grinned, looking down at the haphazard stacks. "I have to create a mess before cleaning it up. It's inherent in how I work."

"Indeed." Her eyebrow lifted in a pointed tease. "Well, before I crawl naked back into that bed, there had better be room for me."

"I can set fire to every scrap if that's the fastest way to get you back in here." He glanced down at the pile of letters he had just gone through, the grin disappearing from his face. "Except…"

"Except what?"

"It will have to be delayed for a time tonight." He started to tidy the many papers strewn about his legs, piling them crosswise as he stacked the distinct sets. "It seems I have some urgent business that does need tending to this evening."

"This evening? It is already late." Liv groaned. "Can it not wait until the morn?"

"Unfortunately, no." He shuffled the last of the papers into a partially neat mess. "I may be rather late, but I will be back as soon as possible."

Liv looked to the gold clock sitting atop the bureau by the side window—nine in the eve. She could visit Viola and return before Tieran finished his business.

Looking to her, he stood from the bed. "You will be here?"

For a second, she considered not telling Tieran that she would also be going out, but she didn't want him to worry if he arrived back to the house before her. "Yes. But I will take this opportunity to visit a friend."

"What friend?"

"My friend Viola. I mentioned her to you days ago."

"The one with the apple trick?"

"Yes."

"Is it not too late for a social call?"

She could feel his eyes on her turn to scrutiny. Looking down, she started to tidy her own correspondence, regretting her honesty. "It does not concern you, Tieran."

"There is only one reason you would say that, Liv." He walked over to stand before her. "Does this have to do with your blasted list?"

For all that he had resisted mentioning the list again in the past days, he suddenly did not hesitate to jump upon the topic.

She craned her neck to look up and meet his eyes. "It is not your business, Tieran. You will note I am not peppering you with questions on whatever it is you plan to attend to."

"No, but I have never given you reason to question my activities."

She stood, gathering her papers into her arms. "You told me you would leave it be, Tieran. Please just respect that."

"I do respect that it is not my business—until you go after one of my best friends. Then it is my business."

"You are referring to my actions with Lord Lockston at Wellfork Castle?"

"Yes."

Clutching her papers to her chest, she started to move around him. "Then I can only say to you, perhaps you should take better care when choosing your friends, Tieran."

He stepped in front of her, blocking her path. "Liv, whatever you are thinking, whatever you are plotting, I beg you to reconsider."

Her glare pierced into him. "I am seeing a friend, nothing more, Tieran. I have no nefarious plots afoot. Not tonight." She moved around him, yanking the bell pull for her maid before stepping into the adjoining dressing chambers and closing the door on him.

By the time she was dressed and had stepped back into the bedroom, Tieran was gone, his stack of papers from the bed now towering on the walnut writing desk by the window.

A carriage awaited her per Tieran's orders, and Liv took the gesture as both thoughtful and a clever way to monitor her movement. He didn't have time to follow her, but he also was clearly intent on finding out where she went from the coachman. Mr. Niles had still not arrived in London with her carriage from Mortell Abbey—she had seen herself how poor the roads had been along the way—so unless she wanted to use a hack, she had little choice but to use the carriage Tieran arranged for her.

As late as it was, Liv knew Viola would still be awake and at home, unless it was a rare occasion that Viola had convinced Lord Jearson to attend a function. Pulling up to the baron's townhouse, Liv was relieved to see dim lights shining from the interior.

Minutes and several hugs from her friend later, Liv stepped into Lord Jearson's drawing room as Viola pulled the heavy oak door closed. The room was hollow—very sparse with no rugs, no tapestries or portraits to soften the walls—only a few stark pieces of furniture dotted the room as Lord Jearson was impossibly cheap with his coin.

Door secured, Viola squealed and rushed across the room to Liv before she could sit and hugged her one more time.

Her ribs squeezed hard by Viola's iron grip, Liv laughed
at her friend's enthusiasm.

"It is utterly fantastic, Livia." Viola released Liv, taking
a step to the side to sit on the settee. "Every day debtors
have been calling on Lord Shepton—lining his front door.
The public humiliation is glorious—beyond anything I
could have imagined. I had hoped you could accomplish
his ruin—although I wasn't positive you could do it—but
it was masterful in how you have ruined him. You must
tell me every detail of what happened at Mortell Abbey.
No one knows how or what transpired—only that Lord
Shepton's brother-in-law has cut his finances to nothing
and has alerted all of Shepton's creditors he is now destitute.
The ambiguity of it all is even better for the gossips, as
they are in a furor and have been concocting the wildest
imaginations on what transpired."

Viola tugged Liv's arm, pulling her to sit next to her on
the hard settee. Upholstered in a brown lumpy cotton, the
settee held little stuffing to soften the wood.

"It has been delicious." Viola's bright green eyes glowed
in mirth. "Lord Shepton has been in town two days now.
He apparently thought he was quick enough to London to
head off Lord Mortell's demands his debts be called in. And
in those two days, all his staff has abandoned him. He has
been seen answering his own door—can you imagine?"

Liv had to stifle a chuckle at that statement—she could
imagine much, much worse than having to answer one's
own door, but she let Viola revel in her satisfaction. Because
of Lord Jearson, Viola had to live all of their victories
through Liv, and Liv didn't want to steal the joy from the
moment. "I can. I am just happy my business with Lord
Shepton is at an end."

Viola's hand went to her throat. "You say that almost as if you regret his demise."

"I don't—but I do regret parts of how it had to be done."

"Such as?"

Liv held her tongue for a breath. Viola didn't always care for the details on how destruction was doled out—just that it was. She frowned. "For one, his wife was devastated to find me half-naked with Lord Shepton."

"Half-naked? Delicious, Livia." Viola giggled. "And why should we care on his wife? The woman married the snake. If she held him in any esteem, it is better now that she knows his character, than to live a fool's life. Her brother will take care of her. If these first few days are any indication, Lord Mortell intends to make Shepton pay dearly and for the rest of his life. Shepton has been cut direct so many times in the last few days he will never recover in society, no matter what happens with his finances."

Liv nodded, attempting to share in her friend's glee. Where she had never felt it before, this particular victory seemed hollow—she had had to destroy an innocent bystander, Lady Shepton. The look on the woman's face when she saw her husband fondling Liv still hung heavy in Liv's mind. She imagined it always would.

Viola grabbed the top of her hand. "So where have you been? Were you delayed in the travel as well? I understand an uncommonly brutal snow held the land hostage for a while."

"It was a deep snow." Liv nodded. "I had to travel by horseback to London. Mr. Niles still has not returned with the carriage."

"He hasn't?" Viola's head cocked to the side. "He did not accompany you? That is not safe, Livia. Then I assume Charles was with you?"

"I actually have news, Viola." Liv looked down as her hand flipped over under Viola's, and she squeezed her fingers. "Lord Reggard was at Mortell Abbey. He accompanied me back to London."

Liv's gaze lifted to her friend. She could see Viola run through names in her mind, and the exact moment when she recognized Tieran's name.

"Lord Reggard? Your Lord Reggard? Tieran? The one that left you before the war and never came back for you?"

Liv nodded, her smile wide, near to bursting with wanting to tell Viola every detail of every minute she and Tieran had been together.

Viola's hand ripped from Liv's grasp, flying up, her palm to Liv. "Wait, before you say another word. Please do not dare to tell me you allowed anything to transpire between the two of you."

Liv's enthusiasm tempered. "I…well…yes—"

"That is the man that left you, Livia. He left you and he never came back for you after the war. He had a year and you were not important enough for him. And then he suddenly reappears in your life and you fall to him like a lovesick debutante?"

Liv's head snapped back at Viola's instant deprecation. "You haven't even given me a chance to explain what happened, Viola."

Viola's green eyes blinked hard at Liv's snapped words. A breath passed, and her face softened. "Of course. Please, tell me."

"There were valid reasons Tieran didn't return immediately after the war, and by the time he returned—and he did come for me—I had already been stolen for the brothel and had married Lord Canton. Then he married, and I never dared to even think on the possibility of our paths entwining again. But they have. And I am happy for it." Liv's mouth clamped shut. For all she had wanted moments ago to tell her friend everything, she now wanted to be done with the conversation.

"Truly?" Viola asked.

"Yes."

Viola patted her hand. "Then I am happy for you, my friend."

Liv exhaled. Viola appeared genuine in her support, but the sudden heavy pit in Liv's stomach didn't ease with her friend's words. She gave Viola a slight nod. "Thank you."

Clapping her hands together, a bright smile returned to Viola's face. "Let us move onto another topic. You have succeeded so well with Lord Shepton that I have hurried our Bow Street runner onto investigating Sir Bishman from the list. I have arranged a meeting with him a week from now. You will be available?"

Happy to see the smile on Viola's face once more, Liv nodded. "Yes, of course."

"Excellent. Though we still have Lord Lockston within our scope as I know you made some progress with him before leaving for Mortell Abbey. Do you think you can handle two of the names at the same time?"

The pit in Liv's stomach widened.

Lord Lockston.

He was on the list, and he was also the one that could drive an impenetrable wedge between her and Tieran.

She looked to Viola, taking in her friend's beaming smile.

No. She couldn't approach those particular concerns with Viola quite yet.

She would.

But not yet.

{ CHAPTER 17 }

The thrashing woke her up.

She had gone to sleep alone, curled on the side of the bed she and Tieran had shared since they had been back in London.

Liv had thought for one brief moment of returning to her own townhouse for the night after leaving Viola, but then disregarded the notion.

If Tieran did decide to return to the dowager house as well, she wasn't going to leave a cold bed to greet him. No. She would be in his bed, warm and naked and willing.

If she couldn't give him everything he needed from her, at least she could give him that.

But late into the night, she had fallen asleep while waiting for him.

In the throes of a deep sleep, the thrashing scared her, melding with a half-conscious dream for a long stretch of time. Her heart thumping hard in her chest, she roused herself, pulling away from the nightmare that she couldn't describe, only feel—feel terror ripping through her body, the sense of losing everything, of not being able to save herself.

It was another moment before she realized the thrashing on the other side of the bed was what had turned her dream into a nightmare.

Disbelief held fast in her grogginess for long seconds. Tieran was a perfectly still sleeper. Even in the mornings, he escaped from the bed without waking her. And he was always up early, in the study long before her brain even entertained thoughts of awaking.

But who else would be in her bed thrashing about?

Just as her eyes adjusted to the low light from the coals in the fireplace, he was on her.

Violent, his body landed on top of her—his hands searching through the tangle of the sheets, his body shaking with the thrashing, his legs kicking into the bed.

Fingers meeting flesh, he found her right arm to latch onto, the grip vicious. A growl, and his other hand caught her throat.

Just before his fingers wrapped around her neck, cutting her air, Liv managed a scream. "Tieran."

It was enough to stop the growl—an instant switch— and his mouth came down on her, kissing her with a harsh ferocity that channeled all the rage in his body.

His head moved down, his teeth raking against her neck as his hands mauled her body, squeezing, twisting flesh.

Confusion took over from the terror of her dream. Tieran continued his attack, his body, hot with sweat, pressing down on her, his hands flailing about her flesh, finding a spot to attack, paw, and then releasing and searching for more.

She could feel his shaft, rock-hard and expanding against her thighs with every ragged breath he took. But he didn't seek entrance to her body. Not yet.

His left fingers found her breast, grabbing the full of it, turning, tugging. Pain shot through her. Her eyes wide, she searched for his face.

It was then she realized he wasn't awake. Asleep and in the deep throes of a dream. A dream that had pulled him so far under he couldn't escape.

"Tieran."

She reached up to grab his face. His twisting body made it impossible to catch him.

Her left hand caught a hold of the side of his head, her fingers burying into his hair, holding on as his thrashing intensified.

"Tieran." She screamed his name.

Another growl and he shoved his hand under the small of her back, jerking her up from the bed.

She held on, pulling his hair, her right hand swinging upward to slap his face. "Tieran."

The sting on her hand stung, but it worked.

Tieran dropped her, both of his hands instantly abandoning her body. He lurched backward, sitting onto his heels, his knees still straddling her legs.

Perfectly still, Liv lay under him, silent, not moving, barely breathing. Her heart pounding, she stared up at him, waiting. Waiting for what, she wasn't sure.

His hands fell to rest on the top of his thighs as his chest heaved with every breath. It took long moments for him to open his eyes to her.

His look horrified, his eyes ran up and down her naked body, his face paling as his eyes stopped at every red mark on her skin. He swallowed so hard she could see the lump moving down his throat. "Liv—hell—I hurt you—the devil take me—I hurt you, Liv." He scrambled, trying to unsnarl himself from the sheets to move off of her legs.

Liv sat up, quickly grabbing his left arm before he could escape her. "No. Stop, Tieran. Stop. You didn't hurt me—not truly—but you did scare me—"

He yanked his arm from her grasp and tried to free his legs from the tangle they were in. She snatched his forearm with both hands, clamping down, not letting him pull away from her.

"Stop, Tieran. Stop and listen to me."

His motions jerked to a halt and his look, still repulsed at his own actions, lifted to her.

"I was not scared for my own safety—you scared me because I was terrified for you. Wherever you were in your mind. What sort of hell were you dreaming about?"

His look shifted from her to land on the pillow on his side of the bed.

Her fingers dug into the muscles in his arm, pulling, demanding.

"War." His mouth opened, the one word a cracked whisper. His free hand ran across his face, rubbing. "I needed something to bring me back from the torture, and then I knew it was your body under me and I...I needed you to bring me back."

Where his face had gone ashen moments ago, a red flush started to creep up his neck, inflaming his cheeks.

"Dammit to hell, Liv. I feared this. I am sorry...your body...I hurt you...I would never..." His head shook, his eyes going upward to the bed canopy. "I fell asleep at the moment I usually leave the bed. It was my mistake alone. I understand if you prefer separate chambers from here on."

Her forehead scrunched. "Wait. What do you mean you leave the bed?"

He shrugged. "I leave the bed every night before I fall asleep. I sleep in the study. I thought you realized that."

She shook her head. "No. I just thought you were an early riser."

"It is safer for me to sleep alone."

She dropped his arm from her iron clamp, her left hand going lightly to his knee. His muscles under her fingertips were stretched into rigid cords. "And on what level of madness do you think I would accept separate chambers from you? I am here to be with you, Tieran—you—not an empty bed."

"But now you will not be able to sleep soundly."

Her shoulders lifted. "Apparently, I can sleep through much if you were sneaking out of our bed every night without me aware."

"No. I cannot have you lying next to me, scared that at any moment I may attack you, Liv."

Her eyes narrowed at him. "Why do you presume to know I will be scared?"

"I…"

"What?"

His hand ran over his face again, his fingers simultaneously rubbing both of his eyes. He exhaled, meeting Liv's stare. "Rachel. The dream—it happened once—only once with her—I frightened her so badly…"

"That what?" Liv's fingers curled upward on his knee, brushing onto his thigh. He nearly jerked away at the movement, and it appeared to take great effort for him to keep his leg still under her hand.

"We never slept in the same bed again. I could not put her through that more than once. It is my burden—the dreams—the men I have killed, what I have done. How it distorts. In my dreams I am searching."

"Searching for what?"

"Something to pull me away from there—from what I did. To pull me into the present." His head shook, his look going downward along Liv's torso. "And your body was there, next to me. Warm and alive and where I want to be. But there is still all the rage of the dream and I cannot control it. Not in that state."

Liv nodded. "And you never told Rachel what happened to you in the war. She wouldn't have known what you battled."

"No." Tieran's entire body convulsed and he jerked away from Liv's hand, turning to get out of the bed.

She could see his body still warred with itself. His mind knew he was awake, a lifetime away from his sins, but his body still raged, still in the dream.

She scampered across the bed after him, jumping off and rushing between him and the door just as his hand reached the knob.

Grabbing his face between her hands, she had to force his head downward so he would meet her eyes. "You were not hurting me, Tieran. I am strong and I am not afraid of you."

"You should be."

Her fingers along his cheekbones, her thumbs dropped, lining his clenched jawline. "You would never, even in the worst hells of your dreams, hurt me."

He blinked hard, his head shaking under her hands. "You don't know that, Liv."

"I do."

He stared down at her, his look searing, disbelief creasing the edges of his blue eyes.

"You don't believe me?"

"I don't know what to believe with you, Liv."

She winced. His words a brutal punch to the gut. That she deserved his honesty didn't lessen the blow.

"Then believe this." Her hands along his face slid downward, curling around his neck as she lifted first her right thigh up and around his waist, and then her left.

Wedging her thighs on top of his hip bones, she wrapped her legs around his back, her calves going downward to lock along his thighs. Lifted to eye level, only a breath between them, she focused on his downward gaze. "I am not afraid of your body, Tieran. I have never been afraid of your strength. And I never will be."

His blue eyes lifted to meet hers.

"I will pull you back, Tieran. If my body can do that, then it is yours. Use it. However you need to. I will always be here—without fear—to pull you back."

Her words unleashed a brutal growl from the depths of his belly. The tip of his shaft still hard and already at her entrance, he stepped forward, her back ramming against the door.

His mouth captured hers in that breath, taking her exhale as he crashed up into her. Taking what he had denied himself in bed. Taking her essence, the promise of absolution, for at least that moment in time.

His hands went under her backside, spreading along the bottom of her thighs, holding her high against the onslaught of his shaft driving into her again and again.

No quarter, no reprieve, his body met hers, drawing out just long enough with each stroke to drive deeper with the next.

Her body tested, pushed to the line between pain and pleasure with every thrust plunging up into her, Liv gripped his neck, holding him to her—holding his breath, his mouth, his air tight onto her body.

It broke free, pleasure winning the battle over pain, and her body started to shudder, the waves building. With every exhale, a rasping moan escaped from her lips. Tieran answered her every breath with a new blow, demanding she release, demanding she give everything she possessed in order to pull him back.

A final stroke reached the depth of her core, and she gave it.

Everything.

Everything her body could offer. Everything her heart could offer. Her soul.

Her body clenched in spasm after spasm as he rocked under her, violent, his growl turning into a guttural roar. The explosion that shook his body shifted the earth, her very being, taking all air from the room.

She felt her body sliding down the door before she realized Tieran had dropped to his knees. He spun, gasping, crumbling against the door but not releasing her. He crushed her to his chest, his head curled over her shoulder as she straddled him, and she heard him fighting for breath, just the same as she was.

They sat for minutes, silent, until Tieran suddenly grabbed her shoulders and pushed her away, his eyes frantically searching what he could see of her body. "Damn me, Liv. I did hurt you. I can feel the hot spots on your body. I can see the red on your skin—your arm, your breast."

"I am unharmed, Tieran." She pushed forward in an attempt to curl onto his body again.

He wouldn't allow it. "Do not try and hide it from me, Liv."

She exhaled a sigh, flipping her hand palm up between them. "The sting on my hand from slapping you hurt worse than anything you did. Everything else is minor in comparison."

His head shook, his jawline tightening. "I cannot do this to you, Liv—sleep in a bed with you."

"You can."

"No. I cannot trust myself."

Her hand dropped to his chest, her palm flattening on his skin. "It is no matter what you trust, Tieran. I trust you. That is what matters."

His frown deepened, creasing the sides of his face. "How can you possibly believe that, Liv? You know what I could do to you."

She nodded, her head tipping to the side, considering. "You are right. I know your size, your strength. I know you could crush my neck with one squeeze. I know you could snap my wrist in half with a twitch. I know you could smother me in seconds."

He stared at her, each word she said making him wince, silent blows.

Her free hand went to the side of his face, her thumb tracing the line of the frown. "But you won't. Because I also know that just now, even in your darkest dreams—the purgatory you were engulfed in—even then you were not hurting me. You could not do it. You knew it was me. Harsh, yes, but it was nothing I could not handle."

His fingers lifted to cover the back of her hand on his face. "And if it becomes more than you can handle, Liv? That is what I fear."

"Then I will slap you and wake you and bring you back to me."

Her fingers curled on his chest. "I am not afraid, Tieran," she said, each word distinct, bearing the weight of everything she needed him to believe. "I have never been afraid of you, and I do not intend to start now."

She held his stare for long seconds, unflinching under his scrutiny for what he needed to find in her eyes. He needed belief. He needed her trust. She had both of those things unequivocally.

He nodded, an exhale coming from the bottom of his chest. "Then let us go to bed, my love."

Liv grinned. "Love?"

"Love." He said the word again, the promise, the future of that one word echoing in the room.

She leaned forward, kissing him.

All she had ever wanted.

{ CHAPTER 18 }

"You have us here, Reggard." Lord Lockston's hand on her back to guide her downward, Aunt Penelope sat on the settee in Lockston's library with a grunt. She lifted her cane, pointing at Tieran as he turned from closing the door and walked toward them. "Tell me there is good reason for pulling me from my game of whist. Lady Newdale is my partner, and she is particularly canny—I always win with her, so this had best be of the utmost importance."

Tieran's gait slowed as he walked across the library. When he had heard Aunt Penelope was to be at Lockston's townhouse for a small dinner party, he had thought it the perfect opportunity to speak with both of them at the same time. But now that he had Aunt Penelope and Lockston sequestered, he was suddenly at a loss of how to start this particular conversation.

The clunk of his boots on the floor came to a stop in front of Rachel's relatives, and he looked down at them. Rachel's brother had sat next to his aunt and had leaned back on the maroon damasked settee, his arm casual along the top carving of the furniture. Aunt Penelope sat as stiff as ever on the edge of the cushion, her hands curled over the gold pigeon topping her cane—prim even though time had taken much of the straightness from her back.

Aunt Penelope's cane pounded onto the floor. "Out with it. I can see your tongue has forgotten how to move."

Tieran looked to Lockston. He could only offer Tieran the slightest shrug.

Kicking himself for even bringing the two of them together in privacy, Tieran took a deep breath. Best to just blurt it out at this point. "Lady Canton and I have become reacquainted in the past months."

"Reacquainted with Lady Canton? What does that mean, Reggard?" Lockston asked, his eyebrows slanting.

Tieran's head tilted slightly to the side. "We have spent an exceptional amount of time together."

"So she's your mistress now?" Lockston's eyes went to slits. "You know what she schemed to do to me—to Talia at Wellfork Castle."

Tieran nodded. "I do. I spoke with her about it. It was a mistake on her part."

"And all is forgiven?" Lockston snapped his fingers. "Just like that?"

"No. I do not expect that of you."

"What do you expect?" Lockston asked. "For that matter, why exactly are you telling us?"

"Hush, Fletcher." Aunt Penelope's head swiveled so fast to Lockston, her pink turban went askew and she had to tuck it back into place. "You of all people have made mistakes in your life." She looked up at Tieran. "You are asking us for our blessing to move forward with Lady Canton?"

Tieran held her gaze as his head bowed. "Possibly."

"You are afraid I'll be upset?"

"Yes."

Aunt Penelope nodded, her tongue clucking on the roof of her mouth. Her look jumped to Lockston next to her and then returned to Tieran. "Have you forgotten Rachel, Reggard?"

"No." Tieran's answer was immediate, no thought needed.

"I did not think so." Her head shook. "I do not think you ever will. Rachel is a part of you. She always will be."

"Yes."

Her eyes pinned him. "Yet that does not mean there is not room for another."

Tieran nodded. "I believe that is the case, yes."

Next to Aunt Penelope, Lockston gave an audible sigh, almost a groan.

Aunt Penelope's hand whipped up in front of Lockston's nose, stopping the sound as she focused on Tieran. "Lady Canton does have a reputation, Reggard."

"Yes. That fact has not escaped me."

"Yet you wish to move forth." She leaned forward slightly, her hands tightening around the top of her cane as her eyes went shrewd. "Or are you asking us so that someone will caution you against her?"

The question took Tieran aback. *Was he?* He paused, his look drifting from Rachel's aunt and brother to the window behind them as he considered the question.

That couldn't possibly be what he was doing—looking for a reason to break from Liv—was it? Yet…there were things in the past that he couldn't deny—things he didn't want to acknowledge.

Liv had been the one thing that had sustained him during the war—he would have done anything for her— anything to keep her world safe. All of that. All of his sins. Only she had destroyed him when he had returned to English soil and learned she had married another.

Broken, devastated, it had been a hell like no other.

And now he was facing that very same thing again—if he allowed it of himself—for he knew he would do anything for Liv, no matter what it cost him.

No matter that it could very well cost him his peace.

The smack of the cane on the floor drew Tieran's look downward.

"You are pondering the thought—that is good," Aunt Penelope said. "As well you should for the trail of destruction Lady Canton leaves. Caution is paramount."

The instant need to defend Liv bubbled into Tieran's chest. "There is more to Lady Canton than you would know of, Aunt Penelope."

"Of course there is, Reggard." Her hand flipped into the air. "I recognize that. She is an unusual choice, but I understand you have history with her, and I also recognize you are not an idiot. Or at least I never thought so."

A guffaw slipped out of Lockston.

Aunt Penelope glared at Lockston out of the corner of her eye. "You, on the opposite, Fletcher, have been an idiot time and again, so you do not get to chortle upon it."

"Point taken, Aunt." Lockston looked up at Tieran. "Why do you even feel the need to ask for our blessing, Reggard?"

"You two were Rachel's family—and now you are the only family I have."

Lockston nodded, his look going hard as his arm dropped from the back of the settee and he leaned forward. "And if you don't get our blessing?"

Tieran drew a breath, his lungs expanding as the undeniable answer filled his chest. "I choose Liv regardless."

"Then why ask for it?"

Tieran's tongue thrust into the side of his cheek as he gave a slight shake of his head. "Just because I don't need it, doesn't mean I don't want it, Lockston."

Aunt Penelope's cane flew up, thwacking Lockston's shins. "Of course we give it, Reggard."

Lockston's look flew to his aunt. "We do?"

She thwapped him again with her cane. "Yes, we do."

His head shaking, Lockston leaned down, rubbing the front of his shin through his dark trousers.

For a long moment, the room was silent until Lockston straightened, looking up at Tieran. "I was graced with a second life myself, Reggard." He stopped, giving a slight sigh. "I do not see how I can hold you back from the same, if that is what you wish."

"It is. She is."

Lockston gave him one curt nod. "Then you have our blessing."

~ ~ ~

Liv stared at the latest stack of correspondence balancing high on the edge of her desk, chiding herself for her complete lack of enthusiasm for her work.

The papers and the tasks had been building up for a week in her study, untouched, and happily so. Every thought had been consumed with Tieran during the past week, and she wouldn't trade away a moment of it to deal with the drudgery that now sat before her.

"You are positive he has not even one vice? Impossible. What are we paying you for, sir? I want results." Viola's voice had gone hard, pressing the Bow Street runner, Mr. Tillman, Liv had hired years ago for their work on the list.

Having just ignored most of the conversation going on in front of her, Liv glanced up from her papers, giving Viola a sharp look. She was not in the mood to have to rein Viola in from her fits of impatience. Liv wanted this meeting done and over so she could make her way back to the Reggard dower house.

It was amazing how quickly her own house no longer felt like home. It had only felt cold and lonely walking into it, knowing that her heart was waiting for her fourteen blocks away.

"No, my lady. There be no vices," Mr. Tillman said, hiding his exasperation over Viola's tone as he looked to Liv across the desk. "And I have had three of my best working to uncover the slightest desire of Sir Bishman, but there is not a one. No drink, no gambling, no debts, no wife, no lover. Investments in only the safest trades. The only thing he even appears to care about is his daughter—dotes on her, even. They call her 'the crystal doll' in their circles. She is fifteen now. Beautiful and untouchable. And the man makes sure it remains that way. Scares off any suitor sniffin' 'bout her."

Viola shook her head, her finger tapping on the edge of the desk in front of Mr. Tillman. "Well, that is interesting, but not valuable. Keep looking at him, Mr. Tillman. He is one of the original names on the list, and deserves to be destroyed in the worst possible way."

Mr. Tillman nodded, his hands rubbing along the top of his dark trousers. "I will, my lady."

"And have you discovered anything more on Lord Lockston?" Viola asked.

Liv's ears perked up.

She hadn't confessed to Viola that she had mentally erased Lord Lockston from any intentions she had on vengeance. Yes, his name was on the list. But going after Lockston put her at direct odds with Tieran.

And she wasn't going to jeopardize their relationship over it.

Besides, she could put off Lord Lockston for some time—there were plenty of other names to pursue on the list.

"If you wanted to start again on Lord Lockston since his illness has had him resigned to his house, he reportedly is well enough to be at the Jacobson ball tonight. It is expected to be a crush, but as you know, the bigger the platform, the bigger the gossip." Mr. Tillman looked to Liv.

She could only offer a weak half-smile.

"Excellent." Viola clapped her hands together. "Thank you, Mr. Tillman. You will excuse us?"

Mr. Tillman stood with a slight bow of his head. "Good eve, my ladies."

Viola watched him exit the room, her smile beaming as she turned back to Liv. "This is perfect. You are already here and can attend the ball tonight. We should go up and choose a gown right away. What color was it again that Lord Lockston was partial to?"

"Blue." Liv's eyes fell down to the stack of papers.

"You do have that blue gown Lord Canton gave you a month before he died. It is the prettiest blue and still fashionable enough. Plus, it looked exquisite on you the one time I saw it."

"You know I only wear black, Viola."

"Yes, but I thought with your new liaison with Lord Reggard, you would finally be willing to let color back into your wardrobe. It can only help our cause, Livia. The black does age you beyond your years."

Liv looked to her friend, dread building in the pit of her stomach. Viola was going to hate what Liv had to tell her.

She took a bracing breath. "I believe I need to avoid Lord Lockston and focus my attentions on another one from the list, Viola."

Viola's eyebrows shot up, her eyes going to slits. "Not Lord Lockston? Why in the blazes not?"

Liv shook her head. "Please understand, Viola—I cannot approach the man. He is a dear friend of Tieran's and I cannot do that to him. Is there not another on the list that we can concentrate on while we wait for news on Sir Bishman?"

Viola jumped to her feet, her hands pounding down onto the desk. "Livia, tell me you are not choosing this… this…this fool that once discarded you over the list? Tell me the man doesn't have you so besotted that you have lost all your wits."

The hairs on the back of Liv's neck spiked, her own ire sparked. "I am choosing to be respectful of Tieran's world. That is all. Beyond this one friend, I wish for no other modifications to the list. I adhere to all that we have planned."

"Do you?" Viola's voice went low, dangerous. Her hands shoved off from the top of the rosewood desk and she stalked over to the settee before the fire. She picked up the leather portfolio on it that contained her notes.

Flipping open the top flap, Viola rustled through the papers, her head shaking, her mouth drawing tight. Liv could feel the fury spinning in a tornado around her.

Yanking a folded sheet of vellum from the bag, Viola straightened, stomping back over to the desk. "I also have something to share with you, Livia. Something you are not going to like—or even believe, I fear. But know before I even show you this, that it is true. It has been verified."

A shiver ran down Liv's spine, her instantly wary look going up to Viola. "What are you talking about, Viola?"

"I have an updated list." She slammed the piece of paper down on the desk in front of Liv.

Liv looked from the paper up to Viola. "And?"

Viola's lip snarled. "Your Lord Reggard is on it."

Liv sprang to her feet. "What? No. Impossible." She ripped the paper from the desk, tearing it as she unfolded it.

Flattening it on the desk, Liv leaned over it, scanning the names—names she had read a hundred times over. Three new ones were at the bottom, as they periodically appeared after Mr. Tillman delivered it.

Lord Reggard.

The second to last name, written in a scrawl with an ink splotch on the circle of the "d."

No.

She flung the paper at Viola. "It is wrong. Wrong. There has been a mistake. A similar name mistaken for his. A misspelling. It is not Tieran."

"I did not believe it either, Livia." Viola bent to pick up the paper from where it had fluttered to the floor. "That was my very first thought as well upon seeing it on the list. A mistake. Especially after what you just told me a week ago." Viola paused, taking care in folding the vellum in half as her words went calm. "So I verified it. It is true. It is your Lord Reggard."

Liv rushed around the desk. "No. Absolutely not. You are a thousand times mistaken, Viola."

Viola's hands went to her hips, a hard edge creeping into her voice. "I verified it, Livia. It is him. There is no mistake."

Liv grabbed her reticule from the hook by the door. "No. I refuse to believe you. I refuse to believe you verified it—how could you? It is not Tieran on that list."

"Where are you going, Livia?"

Her hand on the doorknob, she looked at Viola over her shoulder. "To find Tieran—to ask him how his name could possibly end up on a list like that. This is just some horrible mistake and I mean to find out why."

Cat-like, Viola pounced across the room, catching Liv's forearm before she could fully open the door. "Livia, no. You cannot go to him—not now."

Liv's eyes narrowed at her friend. "Why not?"

"He is there, Livia. There right now. Mr. Tillman told me before you arrived."

A gust of bitter cold snaked through Liv, turning every muscle in her body to jelly, the air in her lungs vanishing as though she had just been punched.

Viola grabbed a wooden chair from the wall, slipping it behind Liv at the moment she would have fallen to the floor.

Liv could barely comprehend her surroundings—unable to see anything in the room around her.

Viola's fingers dug into the muscles of Liv's forearm. "He is there right now, Livia. That is how it is verified."

Liv's head shook. Shook against the blasphemy her friend spoke. "No. No. He was going to a party tonight. That ball at Baron Jacobson's townhouse…he…he asked me to go with. That is where he is right now."

"No, dove, no." Viola set her hands on Liv's shoulders, squeezing. "I am so saddened to have to make you face this. He is not at the Jacobson residence. He is there at the brothel, the Jolly Vassal."

"Shut your mouth, Viola. A lie." Liv's look whipped up to her friend. "I will never believe you on this."

Viola sighed, her voice softening. "I understand the resistance, Livia. But will you ride in the carriage with me? Please? I am your only friend that understands all of you, and I would never want to hurt you with this. I hate to see you so distressed—yet I also do not want you to be duped. Above all, I do not want you to have to discover the truth alone."

Liv shook her head.

"Please, Liv. Just a carriage ride. I pray that I will be proved wrong." She squeezed Liv's shoulders tight, almost to pinching. "Just a carriage ride. I will alert Mr. Niles."

Her muscles still jelly, Liv stood.

Denial screamed in her head, yet she had to consider for one tiny moment that Viola could be correct.

Her head shook again. No. Not Tieran. Not the one
man that she knew was capable of nothing but honor
and good and generosity and respect and benevolence to
everyone he had ever met. He was a defender of the weak.
Especially women.

But…

But he had admitted it to her himself.

He had been a monster in the war.

A true monster.

And if he had monster in him, what else was he capable
of doing?

Her heart curdling with the tiniest possibility she was
wrong about her belief in him, she gave one nod, relenting
to Viola, her head betraying all that was in her heart—all
she knew to be true. Not Tieran.

Viola had to be wrong.

~ ~ ~

Viola sat across from Liv in the carriage, a whirlwind of
anxiety—picking at her skirts, her gloves, the rolled edging
of the carriage cushions. Her foot tapped incessantly, only
interrupted with the sound of her clearing her throat every
thirty seconds.

In contrast, Liv had sat perfectly still for the past hour,
staring at nothing but the front door of the brothel she had
once been sold in. She had no nervous habits to indulge in.
Not a pinky twitch. Not a grind of her teeth. Not a jittery
hum.

Perfectly still. Her breath in. Her breath out. Still.
Waiting.

And then it happened.

Out of the corner of her eye, to the left of the brothel, she noticed a tall, wide man dressed entirely in black—a long black overcoat, a black top hat obscuring his head—appear at the edge of the alley. She leaned forward, searching for a better angle to spy out the carriage window.

The man in black paused at the edge of the sidewalk, looking up and down the street. His face turned towards Liv's carriage.

Tieran.

No. No. No.

He stepped into the street, dragging a girl behind him. A girl in a scant shift with nothing to cover her bare arms and bare feet from the cold. A girl bound at the wrists with a sack over her head.

Not one passerby even glanced in Tieran's direction as he pulled the girl along the street. The girl stumbled, falling to her knees. He didn't stop his stride, he merely yanked her upright, her bare feet slipping sideways on the frozen cobblestones with every step. They disappeared around the corner of a building at the end of the block.

Liv stared at the spot where he vanished, willing him to reappear, willing her eyes to have mistaken what she had just witnessed.

Willing herself to not remember that was what had happened to her, to Viola, to countless other girls. Virgin meat, sold to the highest bidder and dragged out into the night.

The silence in the carriage stretched long, her world slipping into a vast, empty abyss.

Viola broke the hush, broke through the dark veil of numbness that had just enveloped Liv. "You are convinced?"

Liv could only nod.

"Excellent. Then shall we go to the Jacobson's ball? As we know, Lord Lockston will be attending, and I imagine you now hold no reservations about scratching him off the list."

Liv couldn't nod, couldn't agree, couldn't speak.

Viola flipped the trap door in the roof of the carriage, murmuring to Mr. Niles.

The carriage jerked forward. It did nothing to jar Liv from her shock. From her heartbreak.

She had thought she knew what heartbreak was. Thought she had experienced it those many years ago when she was sold in a brothel and then married Lord Canton, only to discover Tieran was alive.

But that had been a mere wrinkle for her heart to suffer.

For this time, it was not just heartbreak alone, it was a complete loss of her faith in humanity—the loss of faith in the one man she had believed to be above all others. The one man she had ever dared to love.

And he was a monster.

CHAPTER 19

Liv looked down, the swish of the blue skirt at her waist unsettling her.

It was foreign—color set upon her own body. But what did it matter now? The color, the cleavage, the drape of the dress over her hips could only help her objective this evening.

She had known changing into the blue dress would be beneficial—verified when she heard the gossips go into a whirl as she entered the main ballroom. Perfect. She wanted every last gossipmonger here talking about her tonight. Talking about the scandal she was about to unleash.

Tonight, she would deal with Lord Lockston.

Tomorrow, Tieran.

She had been to the Jacobson's townhouse many times before. The family threw a ball every few weeks during the season—and at least every month during the rest of the year. Men from the list had been analyzed here—flirtations started. And Liv had committed the floorplan to memory for that very purpose.

She edged out into the hallway she was poised next to. This was the corridor that led to the billiard room, along with several smaller rooms for individuals or small groups to retire to. She had hovered near the corridor for hours, easily lost in the mass of the crush, waiting for one of the smaller rooms to clear and for Lord Lockston to move into the billiard room.

Miraculously, both happened within minutes of each other.

After letting an appropriate amount of time pass, enough for Lord Lockston to have a tumbler of brandy and perchance a game of billiards, Liv moved into the empty side room halfway between the ballroom and the billiard room. She hovered by the doorway, leaning slightly out to keep watch on the billiard room.

Her patience was well rewarded when the door to the billiard room opened, and Lord Lockston exited, chatting with a man she didn't recognize.

With a swish of her skirts, she angled herself just beyond the partially ajar door to the side room. Giving wicked tugs on the opposite shoulders of her gown, she heard her sleeves rip free from the bodice. Angling her hands to her back, she quickly found the top ribbons holding her gown tight to her body, sewn into each side, and she yanked with all her might. Ribbons tore from fabric, and she threw the strips to the wooden floor behind the door.

The top of her dress dropped down about her waist, baring her as she wore no shift or stays for just this purpose. It fell perfectly. She quickly gathered a handful of the blue silk in front of her breasts, her forearm holding the fabric in place.

Footsteps approached, passing by the doorway to her room.

"Lord Lockston." Liv hid behind the door, her head popping out aside it. "Lord Lockston, please."

The two men stopped by the doorway, looking in at her. Lockston recognized her immediately, his head inclining toward her.

"Lady Canton." He made motion to move onward, and Liv jumped.

"Wait, Lord Lockston, please, don't leave. I have a slight problem and I have seen not a soul come by that I know."

Lockston's eyebrows arched as he assessed her, his eyes flickering to the door hiding her body. Suspicion laced his look. Well placed, for their last encounter at Wellfork Castle. At least the man had common sense.

His companion cleared his throat.

"Please, Lord Lockston," Liv pleaded in what she hoped was pathetic desperation. "I have seen no one I can trust and I am quite trapped in here. This will not take but a moment of your time."

Lockston gave a curt nod to his companion and the man moved off down the hallway. He turned to Liv, his feet planted in the corridor. "What is it that you need, Lady Canton?"

An embarrassed smiled crossed her face. "Has Tieran made mention of me?"

"He has."

She exhaled, relieved. "Thanks goodness. This would have been awkward if you did not know of our relationship." She nodded with her head toward the ballroom. "Can you find him for me? I seem to have had a rather disastrous mishap with my gown, and I was hoping for his jacket, at the very least, and then to sneak out."

"Oh. I…" Lockston fidgeted, looking to the ballroom. The bastard knew exactly where Tieran was. At a brothel buying a virgin. Worm.

He looked back to Liv. "Reggard was here, but I have not seen him in hours, perhaps he left. Would a maid not be appropriate? I can request one."

She bit her lower lip, horrified, as she let loose on a flood of words. "It is just…the gossips…this is the first time I have worn color in years and the gossips are already in a frenzy and they will skewer me if I cannot even keep a gown about my bosom properly and I have no one I can think of that will help me without word getting to the gossipmongers, and I so did not want to do that to Tieran once our names are linked in public." She attempted to squeeze out one drastic tear.

Lockston glanced back to the ballroom, and then sighed, looking at her. "Perhaps I can help? Is it truly that bad? Possibly a ribbon can be used?"

"Yes, perhaps, please, help me." She reached around the door, catching part of his sleeve and tugging him past the doorway.

He stepped in, moving to the center of the room. Holding the bodice of the dress tight over her breasts with her left arm, she turned her back to him, pushing the door near to, but not fully closed.

She heard laughter at the end of the hallway. Perfect. Exactly what she needed. A woman. Any woman to witness this scene. The gossipmongers would do the rest.

She awkwardly lifted her right arm, her forefinger pointing downward upon her exposed back to divert attention away from the door. "Do you see? I was pulling

a rogue thread and I yanked it and I do not know how it happened, but it unspooled the whole back."

She took a step to the side, waving her hand, positioning herself in front of the open crack of the door.

Lord Lockston moved to stand behind her, grabbing uselessly at the cloth just above her tailbone. "This is a mess. There are no eyelets. How was this together?" He pulled the fabric tight around her waist, attempting the use the few hanging threads to cobble the closing together. He cleared his throat. "Forgive me for saying so, Lady Canton, but no stays, no shift?"

She glanced over her shoulder at him, a blush filling her cheeks. Even if she was playing a part, and it was only her back, she still was not accustomed to anyone but Tieran seeing her naked flesh. She turned her face to the doorway, praying whoever was walking down the hall would walk a little faster. "I…well, we are adults, Lord Lockston…and I had assumed I would be going home with Tieran and he… well, it was a surprise for him."

"I understand." She could hear the smirk in his voice.

The footsteps got closer, and Liv could hear the woman talking. Only a few seconds more.

"Ouch." Liv shifted on her feet, tipping to the side, the top of her dress falling to her waist as she lost her balance, her arms flailing.

Lockston caught her at the exact moment the passing woman glanced into the room.

The woman disappeared past them.

Blast it.

A second passed as Lockston righted her on her feet, one hand on her arm, the other wrapped around her waist.

The door swung open.

"Livia?"

Liv blinked, looking at the woman, recognizing the face from long ago. "Ara?"

"Heaven's blazes, Livia, what are you doing?" Ara rushed into the room, her hands frantically reaching for the front of Liv's gown.

"Ara Detton?" The question sputtered from Liv's lips.

The man that had saved Liv years ago from the brothel had tossed her into a coach, and Ara Detton had been the woman waiting in that carriage to help her. Ara had taken Liv to a home on Baker Street—a house where girls such as she could live, build a new life after being stolen from their families and sold in the brothel.

Liv hadn't seen Ara in the six years since she had married, as Lord Canton had always demanded she cut any tie to her past with the Baker Street house. So while she had respected her husband's wishes to a point, Liv had always made sure large sums of money were donated to support the house and the girls.

Still fumbling with the front of Liv's dress and trying to cover her bared breasts, Ara looked up, her eyes going wide as they landed on the man behind Liv. The man with his hands all about Liv's naked flesh. "Fletch?"

At that moment, Liv saw the person Ara had been talking with in the hallway.

Tieran. Tieran standing in the doorway, heaving, his fists tight at his sides.

It stilled Liv. Froze her until she remembered.

Monster.

Ara yanked Liv sideways, ripping her out of Lockston's grasp as she attempted to cobble the hanging silk of Liv's dress up in front of her.

"Ara—how do you know Lord Lockston?" Liv asked, grabbing the fabric from Ara to cover her frontside.

Lockston advanced on Liv, his own fists clenched. "You little witch—you look to set me—"

In one swift motion, Tieran slammed the door closed and stepped in front of Liv, blocking Lockston's path.

Lockston sidestepped him, looking back and forth between the two women, his voice a growl. "Ara, how do you know Lady Canton?"

Tieran reached out, his hand flat on Lockston's chest, holding him in place. "Don't ask questions you shouldn't know the answer to, Lockston."

Lockston's glare left Liv, landing on Tieran. He stared at him for a long moment, then gave a curt nod as his fists unclenched.

Tieran spun to Liv. He wasn't about to let Lockston yell at her, but he held no restraint on his own tongue. "Bloody hell, Liv. I cannot believe you would do this. Not now. The idiocy—what the hell is it with this bloody list of yours?"

He moved forward, towering over her. "You damn well need to tell me this instant, Liv."

Liv glanced from Tieran to Ara to Lockston and back to Tieran.

No. Bloody well no.

The men were seething, judging, and Ara just had the most peculiar look on her face.

Liv stared up at Tieran, her heart shattering.

Monster.

She had to remember he was a monster. He bought virgins—stole their innocence. So no. She wasn't about to tell him anything. Her mouth pulled into a tight line.

"I have let this go on too damn long, Liv." His voice was strained to near breaking. "If you ever—for the smallest blasted moment in time—trusted me, then you will tell me this instant why you have this mad list of men and why you are determined to ruin life after life."

Ara gasped.

Liv's look swung to her.

"You have a list, Livia? A list of men?" Ara's eyes went shrewd. "It's the buyers, isn't it?"

Both men turned to Ara.

Having edged away when Tieran barreled in, Ara took a step toward Liv. "You have a list of the men who purchase the girls at the brothel and you mean to ruin all of them, don't you?"

All eyes landed back on Liv.

Hell. Ara didn't know Lockston and Tieran were on the list. Biting her tongue, Liv gave Ara a warning shake of her head. *No. Not in front of them. Not in front of the bastards that ruin innocents.* She willed Ara to be silent.

"What the hell are you talking about, Ara?" Tieran asked, his piercing look not shifting from Liv.

"Livia—heaven to hades—you have what I have always dreamed of having—a list of the men." Her words flying, Ara wedged herself between Liv and Tieran, her small hand going up to Tieran's chest to push him backward. Tieran let her. Ara glanced over her shoulder at Lockston, her look whipping back to Liv. "Blast it, Livia—Fletch is on the list, isn't he?"

"Bloody hell, *this* is what you wouldn't tell me?" Tieran stepped around Ara and seized Liv by the upper arms.

"Yes—and he deserves everything he gets, Tieran." Liv's lip snarled as she had to twist her hand awkwardly to keep her dress from falling from her chest. "As do you. I saw you tonight, Tieran. I saw you dragging that girl down the street, you bastard. You know exactly what happened to me and you still did that. So you need to get your bloody paws off of me, you *monster*."

The words lambasted him exactly as Liv intended—the one thing he feared above all about himself—he was a monster.

He deserved every emotion that skidded across his face.

The shock, the realization, the hurt, and then finally, the horrified expression that stuck in his eyes, unmoving. He now knew she recognized him for the monster he was. He couldn't hide it any longer.

For an instant, Tieran looked like he was going to strike her.

But before he could move, Ara pushed Tieran's left arm down and grabbed Liv's hand, yanking her away from him. She jumped between the two of them, standing sideways, one hand splayed on Tieran's chest to hold him away, the other gripping Liv's hand. "Livia, Fletch is on that list you have because he is saving the girls—the same as my husband saved you six years ago and delivered you to me—the same as Tieran did earlier tonight."

"What?" Liv's jaw dropped. "Who—who is your husband?"

"Lord Newdale."

Lord Newdale. Liv's head shook. Newdale had been on the list from the beginning. And Ara had married him? He had been the one to save her? "Are you positive? Lord Newdale was the one that saved me?"

"Yes. You were one of the first ones, Livia." Ara tugged on her hand. "My husband did it for years, and then he asked Fletch to help, and Fletch asked Tieran to help—they are saving them, Liv. Saving them."

Liv's legs shook, nearly giving out. She focused on Ara and Ara alone. Ara had saved her once. Ara she trusted. "Tieran?" The question croaked out.

"Yes, Livia. Tieran. He was there tonight—the girl he purchased is already safe at the Baker Street House."

Gasping for breath, her look slowly crept from Ara up to Tieran. "You?" She looked to Fletch. "You?"

Hell. Bloody hell.

The devil take her, she had been wrong—so horrifyingly wrong.

What other ones had she been wrong about? Viola had always procured the list and Liv had always trusted her, trusted what she said was on it, what Mr. Tillman verified, but…but…

Her look whipped back to Ara, her eyes frantic. "Who—who else?" She jerked Ara's hand shaking her arm. "Who else? Tell me."

"No one else, Livia. These two and my husband." Ara positioned herself fully in front of Liv, her fingers snaking a grip along Liv's forearm. "I tell you now, Livia, there is no one aside from these three."

Liv's eyelids fell shut, a sigh of relief sending a tremble through her body. She had been so close to a tragic mistake. If she had condemned an innocent man…

Her head shook, refusing to think on the possibility. On how close she had come to wreaking unjust havoc in Lord Lockston's life.

"Livia, this list." Ara jostled her arm again and Liv opened her eyes. "Do you have a copy, can I get—"

"No." Tieran's voice thundered, filling the room.

"Absolutely not, Ara," Lockston immediately echoed the sentiment, his voice stern.

Ara's grip on Liv's arm fell away as Lockston grabbed Ara by the shoulders, tugging her away from Liv. "But Fletch—"

"No." Lockston rounded Ara to force her to look at him, keeping one hand on her shoulder as he blocked her from Liv. "Your husband would kill me in a very long and painful fashion if he knew I let you get your hands on a list like that." He flicked his head toward Tieran. "And then he would kill Reggard." He looked over his shoulder to Liv. "And I do not believe he would afford Lady Canton any quarter either—woman or not."

Ara's arms crossed over her chest with a sigh. Her lower jaw shifted far to the side, but she nodded.

Liv watched with curiosity—it was obvious the depth of loyalty these three and Lord Newdale had for each other. And she suddenly felt not so much alone in her crusade to help the innocent girls in the brothel.

Ara glanced from Fletch to Tieran and her face went white.

Liv followed her gaze and she realized she no longer had Ara as a buffer directly in front of her.

No, now there was only air between her and Tieran.

And Tieran stood, heaving, clearly battling to keep his hands from throttling her.

{ CHAPTER 20 }

His fists clenching and unclenching repeatedly, the cords of muscles along Tieran's neck strained as he stared at her, deep fury whirling with horrified betrayal in his eyes.

Liv's mouth went dry, her heart stopping as she realized what she had said to him. *Called him.* "Oh, no…Tieran… Tieran…I…I am sorry—"

Her words jerked him into movement. Unleashed a beast she had never witnessed in him.

In one quick motion, he ripped off his jacket and whipped it around Liv's torso to cover her. Without a word, he grabbed her upper arm through the jacket, yanking her from the room and dragging her down the corridor toward the back of the house.

The height of his hand wrenched her shoulder up and she twisted, trying to slow him, but it only shot a blast of pain down her arm. "Tieran…"

His grip dug in, his fingers gouging into her muscle, the sound of his seething breath going rapid. He veered into a dark room, stalked across it, and pulled her out a back door of the townhouse and alongside the brick building to the street.

Ignoring the many people milling about, gawking at the pair of them, Tieran's stride didn't break until he stopped at his carriage at the end of the block.

"Tieran—"

His arm wrapped around her waist, landing hard on her belly and cutting her breath. He lifted her, opening the carriage door and tossing her into the coach.

Tieran's coat flew off of her body, and she scrambled after it, quickly shoving her arms into the sleeves and overlapping the front lapels across her chest as she righted herself on the cushioned bench.

He jumped into the carriage behind her, slamming the door closed as he sat opposite Liv.

"Tieran."

"No. Nothing. Not a word, Liv," he barked as he leaned forward, banging on the roof of the carriage. It jerked forward, the horses setting a brisk pace down the street.

Liv slumped back against the soft squabs, watching him. His focus on the slit between the curtains open to the window, his eyes avoided her, his chest rapidly lifting and receding, every breath fuming. And rightfully so.

The devil in hades, what had she done? Called him a monster. *A monster.*

Believed he was a monster.

Her fingers clutched the lapel edges of his jacket, drawing it tighter around her body.

She had been half naked with one of his best friends and had called him a monster.

There would be no recovery from this.

The carriage stopped, and Liv glanced past the curtain. Not her townhouse. The Reggard dower house.

She looked to Tieran, but he had already stood, ducking his head as he opened the carriage door and jumped to the street without waiting for the step. He turned, reaching back in to snatch her leg, pulling her along the bench. Before she could resist, he grabbed her about the waist, pulling her from the carriage and setting her on the street.

He snatched her arm again, dragging her up the walk and through the front door—setting all discreetness to the wind.

Not that she had any shred of propriety left. The scene of her being dragged away from the Jacobson's ball had surely taken care of that.

He didn't stop in the front foyer, instead pulling her up the stairs behind him. Her arm stretched to the limit, Liv attempted to keep up with his long strides, afraid to ask him to release her—afraid that he would if she did so.

Spinning her into the bedroom that had become theirs, he finally released her, leaving her standing in the middle of the room.

He turned from her, his movements slowing to a crawl as he clicked the door closed. He paused, his hand on the doorknob, not turning back to her.

Liv looked around the room—the room she had grown to adore—her eyes not finding a single spot, a single piece of furniture that they had not worshipped each other's bodies upon or against. Even the window offered no reprieve from the onslaught of memories this room held.

She looked down at the toes of her silk slippers. Memories would be the only thing she had after tonight.

An eternity of a minute passed in silence, and she managed to lift her chin to look at Tieran. He still stood with his back to her, and she stared at his wide shoulders, the muscles straining under his waistcoat and white linen shirt.

Now he couldn't even look at her.

She swallowed the lump in her throat, her arms wrapping around her waist, only the tips of her fingers reaching past the long sleeves of Tieran's jacket. "Tieran. I know. You do not need to speak. I will collect my clothes."

He spun around, his blue eyes blazing. "Why do you insist on the end of us every time I am furious with you, Liv?"

Her head snapped back, startled. "But what I did—"

"Why do you not think you are worth fighting for?" He took a long step toward her. "Why do you not think *I*— no, *we* are not worth fighting for?"

Dumbfounded, she dipped backward, her steps stumbling as her legs gave out. She landed on the wing chair by the fireplace just before falling.

"You…" She looked up to him. "You think I don't fight for you?"

"Do you?"

Her look fell from him, landing at the wooden floor by his feet. "I…I don't know."

"No—you do—you know."

Damn him. Damn him for always pushing her.

It took her long moments before she could lift her eyes to him. "I don't think I can trust happiness, Tieran. I can't trust being with you. That it is real and not just a dream slipping through my fingers. I had you once, and I was happy, and it was torn away. So how can I ever trust that again? How can I trust happiness when I know I am not worthy of it—when part of me is not worthy of you."

Her head dropped, the truth of her own words—never acknowledged before in her own mind—settling hard into her chest. "You want the girl I once was Tieran, not the woman I am now."

"What the hell are you talking about, Liv?"

Her head stayed bowed. "Tonight was a mistake, but there are things I still must do, Tieran. Things you do not approve of. Things that are not honorable. Things you cannot stand by and bear witness to."

His feet silent on the floor, he was next to her in an instant, his shin bumping into her knee. "No. Absolutely not, Liv. Do not even think it—you are stopping this insanity now—stopping this forever."

"No." She couldn't lift her face to him.

His hand curled into a fist, driving into the side of his thigh. "This list of men—it is madness, Liv—no matter the reason for it."

Her head still angled downward, she dared to lift her eyes, looking at him through her thick lashes. "There are you three on the list, mistakes, yes—but the rest of the list is still valid, Tieran. Men that need to pay. Men that need to be cut from ever buying another girl again."

"You have to stop this, Liv."

Her look pierced into him. "No. I have to do this."

He growled, frustration boiling. "You don't *have* to do anything, Liv. You can make a different decision."

She jumped to her feet, the toes of her slippers butting into the tips of his boots. She looked up at him, meeting his condemnation full force. "I cannot. I cannot stop this, Tieran. I know you do not understand, but I have tried—tried to stop this before. I have wanted to stop—but I cannot." Her hand flew up, thumping onto her chest. "I will make this same decision every time, and I cannot deny that. These men must pay. This is how I right what little I can."

His head shook, refusing her words. "This is not your revenge to enact, Liv."

She grabbed his arm. "No, it is. I was spared when so many innocent girls were not. This is how I repay fate for sparing me. What happens is an injustice of the cruelest kind—and it doesn't need to be—not when I can stop it—stop them."

"Liv, you are repaying a debt you never owed—you never had power over what happened to you in the first place."

Her hand dropped from his arm.

"Yes. But I have power now, don't I?" She took a step to the side, walking around him, her arm flying through the air as she paced. "So if not me, then who? Who will ensure these men pay for their lechery, for the destruction they cause? They ruin lives and then go about their business, never having to think on what they've done, on the lives they've destroyed. One night of vile fun to them equates to a lifetime of disgrace and anguish and shame and ruin for the girl."

She spun back to Tieran, her voice hard. "I am merely equalizing the consequences, Tieran. A ruined life, for a ruined life. And I can make no apology for it."

His hand whipped up to the side, palm to the ceiling. "This is not your vengeance to deliver, Liv. You cannot let this become you. You are so much better than this, better than only wanting to inflict pain upon others."

Her eyes narrowed at him. "I am not better than this, Tieran. I am not your perfect Rachel."

"Rachel?" His head cocked to the side, his brows arched. "This is about Rachel? You think I compare the two of you?"

"Do you?"

"No. Hell no." His fingers ran through his hair, his look suddenly wary on her. "But you hate her—hate who she was to me?"

"No. Goodness no, Tieran." Liv sighed, her eyes going to the coffered ceiling, tracing the white plaster lines. "I adore Rachel. I never met her, but I adore her. Respect her." Her gaze dropped to Tieran. "How could I not? I am beholden to her. She fixed you, cobbled you back together after the war. I could not have done that for you. But she did."

"You could not have done that—why not?"

Liv bit the inside of her cheek, not wanting to admit to the painful fact that she had not been the woman Tieran needed in those years. Not by far.

She knew she would have pushed him—demanded him—to be the same man as he had been before the war. And she would have driven him away in the process.

If she was ever going to make him face the truth about the person she was now, she would also have to speak to the truth about who she once was. Speak to her failings.

She swallowed the lump that had gathered in her throat. "I didn't know anything about life or death back then—I was still so young. I would not have been able to imagine the horrors you endured—not truly." Shrugging her shoulders, the movement disappeared in the oversized black jacket covering her. "But the years I spent with Lord Canton, it changed me, taught me of the frailty of the human body."

She shifted her hand upward, shaking it to clear it of the long jacket sleeve, and then rubbed her forehead, letting the memories of those years wash over her. "We are all at the mercy of time, at what our bodies can and cannot endure. In Lord Canton I watched the torture of a mind that was sharp, held hostage in a body that was crumbling. I watched a man fighting to keep his dignity. Fighting for what little happiness life had left for him. Fighting not to give up, when it was the only sensible option." She swiped a tear from the corner of her eye. "Humility, and patience, and resolve, and peace with what one has to accept only because it cannot change—Lord Canton taught me all of those things."

She took a deep breath. "But he also taught me about resolve—about the will to change the things one could. That was why he married me. That was why I took on the list. I can change this one part of the world, Tieran. I can fight for all of the innocent girls—all of them that will have the hand of the devil rip them from their innocent lives."

Taking a step toward him, she locked her eyes on his. "I was a child when you left, Tieran. I still don't want to accept it, and it kills me to speak it, but you were right to wait to marry me."

He moved to her, his head shaking as he set his hands on her shoulders. "No. I was wrong to leave you, Liv. I would change it a thousand times over if I could."

A sad smile crossed her lips, the sentiment squeezing her heart. "Just as you said you needed to leave for war to become the man that could be my husband, I had to go through what I did to become the woman you need. The woman you need today."

His hands slid inward, moving to slip underneath the collar of his jacket on her skin, his fingertips caressing the back of her neck. "What if I need you to stop this vengeance—this madness, Liv? What if that is what I need from you?"

Her hands lost in the sleeves of his jacket, she gripped his wrists, clutching him with all her might. "I cannot stop, Tieran. Please don't ask me to do so."

"I only ask it for your own safety, Liv. For your own sanity. I cannot bear to watch how this will eventually destroy your spirit."

Her head bowed as her heart contracted. "Please don't ask me to stop, Tieran. I will only lie to you and agree to do so because you speak reason—and then I will still make the same choice again and again." She lifted her eyes, tears brimming. "No matter what I lose—I will do this because I must, because it is who I am and know no other way to be, Tieran."

She ducked from his hands, turning away from him to stand at the foot of the bed as she tried to wipe away her tears with the end of his jacket sleeve.

His arm around her waist was instant, pulling her back into his chest as he set his lips next to her ear, brushing past the dark locks of hair that had escaped from her upsweep. "Then I will not ask you to stop again, Liv. I will walk by your side. No matter where it takes us. I will walk by your side, in front of you, behind you—anywhere you need me to be. Anywhere."

She doubled over, his words hitting her, shaking her to her core.

His forearm held her up, held her backside hard to him, his lips still by her ear. "I love you, Liv—all of you. The glowing debutante I remember. The exasperating, complicated, luminous woman that stands before me now. All of you."

"All of me?" The words escaped as a whisper for the lack of air in her lungs.

"Yes. All of you." His lips dipped to her neck, his fingers tugging down the jacket from her shoulder as his kisses moved along her collarbone. "The you that drives me to madness, yet is the very air I breathe. The you that is a warrior, determined to battle wrong, whether it is for a frozen bird in a snowbank, or for scores of innocent girls. The you that knows everything that I am, everything that I have done, and managed to never judge. The you that still finds the honor in me, looks at me as though I am her most favored champion."

"Never mistake that one, Tieran." His jacket already half tugged from her body, she let it slip off from her right shoulder. It dropped, along with the ripped silk of her dress as she lifted her right arm up, her fingers stretching behind her to wrap around the back of his neck. She held his mouth to her skin with every shred of strength she had. "I have only needed one champion in my life, and it always has been, and always will be, you."

Tieran's growl on her neck vibrated through her skin, into her chest. His hands glided along the naked skin of her belly, tearing, shoving down the remnants of her dress to the floor. The silk puddled around her ankles, twisting with his discarded jacket.

Before she could take a breath, his right hand descended, sliding between her naked thighs as his clothes dropped to join hers. Her core instantly alive, begging, her fingernails dug into his neck behind her, demanding.

His tongue slipped out to trace the dip along her shoulder as his fingers trailed up, slowly, torturously, moving into her folds, exploring, teasing as they circled her nubbin. Slow. Far too slow. Still clutching his neck, she bucked against his hand, the need for him staggering from only a few swipes of his fingers.

"Where do you need me right now, Liv?" His mouth moved next to her ear, his teeth clasping gently onto her earlobe. "Tell me. Wherever you need."

The words twisted her chest, her gut, her core, stealing her breath. She pushed sound out between the reckless pulsating of every nerve in her body. "Tieran—behind me." She exhaled raspy words. "Behind me. Hard."

A guttural groan escaped from his lips into her ear, ripping through the air. "Damn, Liv." He ventured no hesitation, his knee shifting between her thighs, spreading her legs, and in the next breath he drove up into her from behind, lifting her with the force.

Holding fast to him with her right hand, her left hand went forward to grip the post of the bed in front of her, holding hard against the wicked onslaught.

His fingers plied her with every thrust. Circled. Dipped alongside his cock as he withdrew. Every breath in her ear, ragged, straining. Drawing her higher and higher until her body pitched with savagery she hadn't known she possessed.

"Hell, Liv. Now." His voice a storm, his fingers sped, his shaft swelling into the depths of her. "Take it, Liv. Deeper now. All of you."

He withdrew, painfully slow. At her edge, a scream tore from her throat, pleading for heaven and hell and everything in-between.

Piercing, he buried himself far into her, his body ravishing every nerve. Higher. He pushed her higher. She shattered.

Fiercely, his body went taut, shuddering behind her. Wave after wave until he collapsed around her.

With monumental effort, he lifted the both of them over the low wooden footboard and they crumpled onto the bed, her tight to his bare chest.

Once proper breathing had returned, Liv tilted her head upward, opening her eyes only to find him staring at her. She searched the depths of his blue irises for any uncertainty, any lingering mistrust. There was none. Only love. "Ask me again."

"To what?"

"To marry you."

He inhaled, his eyes closing to her.

Slowly, he exhaled, the breath shaking his body and her with it.

Tieran opened his eyes, his look piercing her to her soul. "I want you in my bed, Liv. I want you in the morning smiling at me. I want you in the middle of the day chatting with me on the frivolities of the *ton,* or your thoughtful musings on politics, or your ponderings on investments. I want you in the evening, by the fire, curled up on top of me in a chair, staring at the blazes. I want your arm entwined with mine walking into the grandest ballrooms, without gossip, without shame, without hiding. Just simply my wife. I want you today. I want you when we are old and our bodies are mere shells. I want to be laid to rest next to you. I want you for eternity, Liv. From here until never."

His fingers lifted, cupping her cheek, the largeness of his hand swallowing her head, but the gentleness of the touch extraordinary. "Marry me, Liv."

She nodded, tears streaming down her face. She wanted every one of those moments. Every one. From here until never.

{ CHAPTER 21 }

Having just asked Mr. Niles to keep the horses and carriage readied for her, Liv looked up from the street at the light emanating from the sitting room on the second floor of her townhouse.

Viola was already waiting for her.

All Liv wanted at the moment was to be snuggled under Tieran's arm, warming her toes by the fire.

It was not to be. Just before Liv had left for the Jacobson's ball the previous night, she had promised Viola they would meet this eve to discuss the plan for continuing the ruin of Lord Lockston. Dependent, of course, on whether Viola could escape her husband for the evening.

But now that Liv knew the truth about Lord Lockston—and Tieran and Lord Newdale as well—that meant those three were off the list. The wrinkle was that she couldn't share the truth as to why with Viola—Liv needed to keep the secret of what the men were doing to save the innocent girls. Telling Viola could very well compromise their actions.

She exhaled, her breath puffing and mingling with the hanging fog in the cold night air.

Liv considered again telling Viola the truth. It would make explaining the situation about Lord Lockston so much easier. As it was, Viola would be infuriated that the three men were no longer targets. But as Viola didn't have the means to go about ruining the men on the list without

Liv, Liv hoped Tieran, Newdale, and Lockston would all be safe from Viola's wrath—at least for now.

Gnawing on the inside of her cheek, Liv stared at the upper window. Even though Liv had been absent from her townhouse, Viola—as she had always had free rein to do—had made herself comfortable in Liv's home. A fact that Liv could never disapprove of, for escaping her odious husband to Liv's house was one of the few freedoms Viola was granted in life.

Liv took a deep breath of the cool air, the chill seeping deep into her chest. It did nothing to remove the dread, steel her spine, or give her solace for the conversation ahead.

It just made her cold.

Viola would be furious. That was an understatement. There was no word for what Viola's reaction would be when Liv told her that she would never take action against Tieran, Lockston or Newdale.

And she was about to marry one of those men. A man on the list.

Horrified. Viola would be horrified down to the curling of her toes. There would be no understanding on her part. And Liv couldn't blame her.

Liv sighed as she walked up the front stairs of her townhouse. This conversation was impossible to prepare for, so she just needed to blurt it out and be done, consequences be what they may.

She straightened her spine, entering her house and smoothing the front of her black carriage dress as she moved up the curved staircase from the foyer. With one final deep breath, Liv opened the door and stepped into the sitting room.

Viola was standing by the front window, her face brightening as Liv stepped into the room and closed the door.

"Livia, I have the most wonderful surprise for you." Viola crossed the room, her fingers twitching in excitement.

"Viola, your cheek."

Viola's fingers went to her blackened cheekbone, running along the bruise as her look swept upward. "It is no bother, Livia. I thought I covered it well with the powder. But it was worth it for what I was able to accomplish today. What I have here."

It wasn't the first, or even the hundredth time that Viola had appeared with black marks on her face or neck or arms. But Viola's current enthusiasm overshadowed any pain the bruise may have been causing her.

The edges of Liv's lips turned up in a hesitant smile. "First, I have something I need to tell you, Viola."

"Oh," Viola's hand flipped through the air, "whatever it is it can wait, Livia. You must see immediately what I have brought. It is glorious."

Her friend needed this moment—whatever she was so excited about—much more than Liv needed to upset her. Liv let her smile reflect Viola's enthusiasm. "What is it that you have?"

In that moment, Liv noticed a rogue movement in the room as the top of a blond head popped out above the tall back of the wing chair by the fireplace. The hair was in a pretty upsweep, thick, light blond hair twisted and plaited in an intricate pattern. Wealthy hair. Only someone with a talented maid and lots of time could afford such a production.

"This." Viola bounced across the room, grabbing the chair and grunting with effort as she spun it around to Liv.

A girl sat in the chair, a strip of white linen cloth tied around her head, cutting back across her open mouth, gagging her. The girl was tied to the chair, both around the torso and at her legs. Her hands were bound together in front of her, brown rope biting into her wrists in a figure eight. Even with the tears soaking her face, the girl looked sweet and young—and terrified.

Horror welled into Liv's throat, crushing her breath. Confusion sent her forward, and she snatched Viola's arm, yanking her away from the girl.

"Have you gone insane, Viola? What is this—she's fifteen at best—who is she?"

The smile swallowing Viola's cherub face only got bigger. "No. Not at all. Not insanity. This is Sir Bishman's daughter." She giggled like a child just handed a sugared plum, her hand twisting around Liv's arm to grip her. "This is the one he dotes upon—the crystal doll. The whole reason for his existence—the one that is the most precious thing in the world to him."

Liv shoved Viola's hand off her arm, pushing past her friend to the girl. "You are not this demented, Viola." Liv dropped to her knees in front of the girl, her shaking fingers working the fat knot securing the girl's ankles to the chair.

"Don't do it, Livia."

Something cold hit the front of her neck.

Never in her wildest imaginations would Liv have considered what was truly at her throat. Not until the cold turned sharp. Long and sharp, digging into her skin, pressing against the long cords of her neck.

Hell.

Liv froze, not daring to move, not daring to turn her head to look up at Viola. "Tell me you don't have a dagger to my neck, Viola."

"One of my husband's finest. It's carved plenty of my skin."

A sob escaped from the girl through the cloth in her mouth.

Liv couldn't even swallow for fear of cutting her own throat. Her hands went weak, dropping from the knot. Slowly, so as to not dig the blade edge further into her neck, she leaned backward, turning her head to her friend, her look fierce. "You can cut me, kill me, Viola, but I am not letting you hurt this girl. She is an innocent."

"*We* were innocents, Livia."

"Yes. And now we have power, Viola—power that saves innocents, instead of condemning them to ruin. Do not abuse it."

"Do not abuse it? You have no concept of what power we truly have, Livia—none." Viola's upper lip sneered. "I am nothing but a piece of meat for my husband to torture—and you—even you—you are free of your husband, but all you have is an empty life—a cold bed. You are damaged just as I. Our chance for happiness—true happiness was ripped from us, Livia. And this is our opportunity to do something real to pay them all back—something beyond anything we have ever dreamt."

The blade at her neck shifted, and Liv could feel the warmth of fresh blood trickle down her skin. "I have never dreamt of stealing an innocent girl, Viola. And for what purpose—what could possibly be running through your mind? We need to free her and deliver her home—Mr. Niles is waiting with the carriage, we can—"

"We're not going anywhere with Mr. Niles, Livia."

"Please, Viola, it is not too late to reverse course on whatever you have planned. We can let her go. Go about our business as we always have. What we do is enough, Viola—we make those that should pay, pay. It is enough."

Viola's eyes went shrewd. "No, Livia, no. It's not enough and you are coming with us. I thought you would welcome this chance to finally do something real—real with paramount consequences. But you disappoint me. So I see I cannot let you leave—you will have to come with us."

Liv's eyes widened. "Come with you—to where?"

"I am not about to tell you."

"Then I am not coming." Liv's voice went hard. "Slice my neck, Viola, but I will not be a part of this."

"No?" Viola's glare skewered her, and then in a flash, she swung the blade from Liv's neck to the girl's creamy white throat. Viola moved to the side of the chair, out of range for Liv to shove her.

"You are coming with us, Livia. Or I slice her neck right here in your home."

Liv looked to the girl whimpering frantically, her wrists twisting in the rope, her eyes wide in fear as fresh tears spilled down her cheeks.

Liv's gaze moved from the silver blade to stare up at Viola, noting her crazed look. If she made a move to knock Viola's arm, it would only cut the girl. Her look flickered to the panic in the girl's eyes, then to Viola.

"Untie the crystal doll, Livia."

At a loss, Liv bent, yanking apart the knots at the girl's ankles, and then the knot at her belly that secured her to the chair. How had she never seen this in Viola? Seen that her friend had the capacity for this monstrosity within her?

Still trying to shove the disbelief from her mind at what her friend had done, she looked up at Viola.

"Where are we going to, Viola?"

"You will see. Back away from the chair, Livia."

On her knees and toes, Liv shuffled herself backward along the floor.

Viola watched her, only nodding once Liv was well out of reach. "Good. I have a carriage waiting for us in the mews. You will walk ahead of me—at least five steps."

"We can take my carriage, Viola—Mr. Niles has fresh horses waiting for us." Liv grasped at the only thing she could think of. "Anywhere you want to go, he will take us."

"No. I don't think so, Livia. Mr. Niles will just have to continue to wait."

Liv stood and they moved down the stairs and through the house, Viola pressing the blade securely into the girl's gut the entire time. Through the scant light shining through the fog in the mews, the three of them got into the carriage Viola had waiting behind Liv's townhouse.

A silent ride, Liv stared at what little she could see through the fog at the passing streets. She recognized Charing Cross as they passed it, and her stomach sank, hardening into an iron ball.

When the carriage finally stopped, Liv leaned forward to look out the window.

She wasn't surprised at what she saw.

{ CHAPTER 22 }

"The Jolly Vassal?" Liv's eyes stayed on the street, refusing to turn to Viola.

"Yes. Sir Bishman is so very good at destroying innocents. I have decided he should feel the pain of the same thing." Viola traced the side of the girl's face with the knuckle of her forefinger. "What it is like to have innocence stolen—he will feel that—he will lose his precious, precious, so very innocent daughter."

The girl whimpered, jerking back from Viola's touch on her face.

Liv's chest tightened, her words spitting out. "You mean to deliver the girl into there?"

"I do."

"So she can be sold?"

Viola smiled, one side of her face lifting high. She motioned with her forehead to the carriage door. "Out you go, Livia. Or shall I just gut the girl right here?"

A sob, muffled by the cloth cutting across her mouth, shook the girl as her eyes pleaded with Liv.

Liv glanced from Viola to the girl, her look dropping to the tip of the dagger digging into the girl's side. The yellow fabric of the girl's dress was already torn, flesh showing.

Liv swallowed, debating whether she would be fast enough to wrench the dagger from Viola. Or strong enough. Liv had height and long limbs on her side, but Viola had the weight behind her—along with a madman's mind.

Even if Liv did manage to get the dagger, they were sitting in a carriage Viola had secured with a driver Liv had never seen before—most likely a blackguard hired for this very purpose. Not to forget the fact that if Liv did manage to get the girl out of the carriage unharmed, they were in the middle of the East End on one of the most notoriously dangerous streets in London.

She might well get the girl out of the carriage, but getting the two of them out of the East End unscathed would be far more difficult.

For once in her life she needed to not react with haste. To think with caution about how to extract herself and the girl from this demented person that had possessed her friend.

Liv looked out the window at the fog moving past the front of the brothel. Maybe in there. Maybe inside, she could figure a way out of this without landing them stranded in the middle of the street.

Biding her time, Liv leaned to the door, turning the handle and pushing it open.

The driver was waiting, a burly man in a long black jacket. The scars cutting across his face indicated he would be of no help and was not one to trifle with.

The girl grunted, and Liv turned, catching her as Viola shoved her out of the carriage. It wasn't until Liv had the girl upright on her feet that she realized two other men, brutes, had appeared and flanked them on the street.

Viola smoothed her skirts after regally stepping down to the muck on the cobblestones. She flicked the end of the dagger toward the driver standing to her left. "Follow him,

Livia, and do not dare to think to run. I would hate to lose you as a friend."

Viola didn't bother to continue to point the dagger at the girl as the men closed in around them. She obviously knew who the brutes were, obviously expected them. With a smile, she neatly tucked her dagger tip-down into the reticule hanging from her wrist.

True, savage fear seized Liv at that moment.

This hadn't been a spontaneous kidnapping. This had been planned. Planned well.

Liv looked at Viola. Her friend gave the driver a radiant smile, quickly pinching her own cheeks to make them rosy. "Let us move inward, boys."

Everything she had ever known of her friend crashed about Liv. That Viola possessed this amount of cruelty dumfounded her entire perspective of the world—of what people were capable of doing.

Her feet like bricks, she moved with the group across the street to the brothel, her shoulders bumping in between the thugs. Every step they took, Liv's heart sank lower.

She had missed her chance.

If only she had wrenched the dagger away from Viola at her house or in the carriage, she could have grabbed the girl and they could have run. Could have had half of a chance.

But now.

Now they were surrounded. Surrounded by thugs that would do far worse to them than the damage Viola's dagger could have inflicted.

Liv could see little as they entered the brothel from the alley to the left of it—the same alley she had seen Tieran appear from the night before. The haze from pipes and cheroots hit her as they entered the brothel, the smell of whiskey and beer holding firm in the particles in the air.

Between the wide shoulders of the brutes, she could see a murmur sweep through the crowd in the large room. A slew of males turned, staring at them as they progressed, walking along a wall.

The distinct, sinking feeling of being promenaded like cattle washed over Liv, making her gag. She'd had a hood over her head when she had been sold years ago in this place, so she hadn't witnessed with her eyes this room— but the smell—this exact rancid smell hit her as the same. The whistles and rumblings from the crowd echoed from the past, the same as she had endured when she had been dragged onto a stage.

This time, though, she could see some of the men's faces. Rich, poor, drunk, sober, ugly, handsome—every walk of man sat in this room. Evil, apparently, had no standards.

Liv reached behind her to clutch the bound hands of the girl, hoping to give her a reassuring squeeze. Liv had endured this once before and knew the torment that had to be running through the girl's mind. The girl grasped Liv's hand between her fingers, holding on in desperation.

In front of her, the driver opened a door to the side, moving into a skinny area that led to stairs. They were ushered up the staircase to the brothel's second level, then pushed into a small room with ruby red draperies lining one wall, a bed shoved against the opposite wall, and a short dresser with a bowl of water and a mirror propped on top.

Liv tugged the girl to the bed, sitting her down onto the edge. She turned, attempting to position herself as much in front of the girl as she could without being obvious.

Just when Liv thought they were to be left in the room alone, a rotund man, half-a-head shorter than Liv, stepped past the brutes into the room. His jacket was of quality, or at least what sufficed as quality in this part of town, the bright blue fabric stretched tight over his belly. His double chin was greasy, as though he had just been stuffing bacon into his mouth and hadn't bothered to wipe the excess drippings away before vacating the table.

As instantly repulsed as Liv was, alarm also shot down her spine. His eyes were beady—canny beyond any of the brutes that had brought them up to the room.

He looked from the girl on the bed to Liv, and then his shrewd eyes pinned upon Viola. "Me lovey, you have arrived unscathed, I presume?"

Liv's jaw dropped as he rushed across the room to Viola, grabbing her upper arms as he looked her over. Viola didn't jerk away. Didn't show the slightest aversion to the man.

He lifted a hand to touch the black mark on Viola's cheek. "The bastard?"

Viola's eyes dropped as she nodded.

"No bother on that—he will get his due, me lovey." The man turned to Liv and the girl, slipping his arm behind Viola's waist as he pulled her as close to his side as his belly would allow. "And look at what you have brought me. This is the girl you spoke of?" He pointed to the girl. "The present I can sell?"

Viola smiled up at him. "It is, Bear."

"She is a delight, just as you described her, a crystal doll indeed. But you did not say you would bring me two." His squinty eyes landed on Liv, looking her up and down.

Viola glanced at Liv. "I did not—this is Livia, and she is not for auction."

"Then why bring her, me lovey?" He glanced down to Viola before looking to Liv. "I do think there may be fine options with this one."

"No, Bear." Viola's hand went to his chest. "She is my friend."

His face twisted as though he didn't understand the concept of "friend." A chuckle escaped his greasy lips. "You play with fire you know nothing about, me lovey, bringing her here."

He dropped his arm from around Viola's waist, starting toward Liv.

Viola grabbed his shoulder, stopping his motion. "Bear, no."

"Just inspecting what you have brought, me lovey." He shrugged off her hand and moved to Liv, pushing her aside to stand in front of the girl on the bed, assessing her as she cowered from him. "That crowd below be randy for the auction tonight, and this little one—the crystal doll, you say? Superb. She be ripe for a high price."

"I knew you would like her, Bear."

"Aye. You done well, me lovey." He glanced back to Viola, and then pulled a watch from his vest pocket, twirling the gold chain around his forefinger as he looked to the time. "As it is, I have to check to decide if the crowd below be ready for the auction—I had thought to just sell the virgin crystal doll tonight, but this one…"

He took a step to Liv, his hand snaking out to grasp her face between his thumb and forefinger, squeezing, tilting her head back and forth as he studied her. "This one caused a stir downstairs. And I am not one to pass up a stir. Virgin or not, there be plenty o' men that be wanting to fuck a proper lady like this—maybe I'll be selling up a line for her—five or six spots, top bidder goes first. How long cin ye keep yer legs spread, ducky?"

Bile hit Liv's throat. She tried to yank away.

His grip tightened on her face, squeezing to pain. "Yea, yer a pretty one, and will fetch a pretty coin, over and over, not just tonight."

"But not as pretty as me, Bear?" Viola set her hand upon his shoulder, the bottom lip of her heart-shaped mouth jutting out.

"Aye. I don't like the scrawn of her."

Viola rubbed his shoulder. "I did not bring Livia here to be sold, Bear—she stays off the stage."

He instantly dropped Liv's face, the back of his hand swinging out to smack Viola across the cheek. "Don't tell me what I can and can't be selling in me brothel, bitch."

Viola cowered, her head ducking down for a long moment.

"Don't hide from me, me lovey." He grabbed her chin, yanking it up. "Ye still be me favorite."

Viola blinked, her eyes crinkling in pain as she conjured a smile for him. Liv watched in fascination as, somehow, Viola's green eyes shifted to nearly glow at him.

He nodded toward the girl. "Try to clean up the doll while I'm gone. I be selling her without the hood if you can stop the tears. Leave the binder in her mouth, though—

don't want her bellowing down there." He glanced at Liv, his eyes raking her over. "Your friend there, she goes to the stage as well. But no hood on her—she don't look like she be shedding even a tear over this place, and her face be fetching me some extra coin."

He dropped his hand from Viola's chin, exiting the room.

Just as the door closed, Liv saw the three brutes line up outside the room.

No escape.

Liv waited a long second to be sure the man was gone before running across the room to the window, ripping wide the drapes. Ragged boards crisscrossed where glass should have been.

No escape.

Liv exhaled a bitter breath, turning back to Viola, fire in her eyes. "That man—he is how you got the list of buyers, isn't it? Tell me I am wrong, Viola. Tell me you haven't whored yourself out."

Viola shrugged. "I did what I needed to, to get that list, Livia. You never asked—you always thought the investigator produced it. You should never have assumed—if you had paid better attention, you might not be minutes away from being sold again."

Liv's hands flew up. "This is my fault? The devil, Viola, why are you doing this? Why is working through the list not enough for you—why go to this madness?"

Viola shook her head. "I thought the list would be enough, Livia, the revenge. And it was, for a time."

"But not now? Look at how many of those men we have stopped, Viola. This here tonight is nothing but cruelty you unleash."

"Cruelty? You know nothing of the cruelty I've endured." Viola bent, gathering up her grey wool skirt. "Look at this, Livia, look at it." She hiked her skirt high, past her tall boots, past her stockings, exposing her bare thighs. Scars, too many to count—some new, tinged red, some old, wrinkled lines of white—twisted haphazardly across her skin. From her stockings to the top of her thighs, a mangled mess. "This is cruelty, this is what I endure at the hands of my husband—years of it."

Her eyes wide, Liv stared at the horror. "Viola, I—"

"You escaped to a good marriage, Livia. I did not. Look at what he's done to me. And it doesn't stop—it never stops. I have been waiting years for the old bastard to die, years for him to at least pay me no mind. I whored myself out in marrying that odious man—but a prostitute with a title and money is still a prostitute." Viola let her skirts fall from her fingers, the fabric dropping to the rough wooden floor. "So being Bear's mistress is tolerable. He owns this place and as I was already accustomed to whoring myself out—it got us what we needed—the list."

The girl whimpered on the bed, crumbling into herself. She looked as though she just realized her fate was under control of a madwoman. Liv could only move to her and clutch the girl's shoulder, giving it a squeeze.

Liv inhaled, sucking in the stale air of the room. Of the thousand directions her mind flew—heartbreak for her friend, panic for her own safety, confusion on how her life had managed to, once again, be destroyed in a matter of minutes—getting this girl out of the brothel unhurt remained forefront.

Shoving everything except that one goal from her mind, Liv stepped to the side, putting herself between Viola and the girl again. She leveled her look at her friend, trying to gain a semblance of calm in her voice. "So let us go back to that, Viola, the list. We have so many more to stop—you do not have to do this. I swear we will find another way to destroy Sir Bishman—one that doesn't involve sacrificing an innocent girl."

"No. This is the way, Livia, this is how it needs to happen."

"But why, Viola? I am begging you, please, please, you can still get that man to let us go." She stepped toward her friend. "At least let the girl go—I will stay." Her words choked in her throat, but she forced them out. "I will do whatever he wishes. Whatever."

Viola's head tilted as she stared at Liv. "Admirable of you, Livia. I did not think you had that in you." She clasped her hands together. "No. We all stay."

"Viola…please."

Viola leaned towards Liv, a sudden smile on her face as her voice dropped to a whisper. "The base of the walls on the main floor, Livia. I had them soak it in oil—all of it, all of them are going up in flames tonight."

"What?" Liv moved to within inches of Viola, knowing she had not heard correctly.

"They don't even smell it, the fools." Viola's green eyes glowed. "Too drunk. Too lecherous. It is everywhere."

Her head shaking, the reality of Viola's words sank into Liv's mind. She had thought her friend had gone mad, but this—this was beyond all insanity. "Hell, Viola, what have you done?"

"The line of it goes all around the foundation." Viola clapped her hands. "Flames, Livia. Flames for everyone."

Liv reeled backward, dropping to the bed next to the girl, her body trembling. She stared at the tips of Viola's boots, having no basis for comprehending the horrors running through Viola's mind. "You planned this all."

She looked up at Viola, her voice stunned to a whisper. "You planned to take us all with it, didn't you, Viola? To kill us all."

Viola didn't answer, just looked at Liv, glee carving a wicked smile on her face.

{ CHAPTER 23 }

Liv sat in silence, staring at her friend for minutes, for an hour—she wasn't sure how long. She sat, unable to comfort the sobbing girl next to her, unable to lift even a pinky.

When had it all descended into so much torment—so much pain—for Viola, that this lunacy was all she had been left with? At what moment in time had the need for vengeance eaten away so much of Viola's soul that she cared no more for her own life? And how had Liv not recognized it—not stopped it?

The door swung open, the owner of the brothel stepping into the room again. He glanced about the room, his beady eyes pinning Viola. "Why is the crystal doll not readied? She looks like a drowned rat with all the tears." He stepped back to the open door, addressing one of the brutes standing guard. "Get a hood for her head—and be quick about it, the crowd is ready."

The shortest of the guards disappeared.

Shutting the door, the owner stepped back into the room, stopping in front of Liv. "Stand, ducky."

Liv tilted her head, her look travelling up the bright blue of his jacket, her eyes hurting at the garish shine of the threads. Past the greasy double chin. The fat nose. His beady eyes.

"Ye think to defy me, wench?" He sneered down at her.

"Bear, no." Viola jumped forward, pulling on her lover's shoulder. "She will go. She will do whatever you want. She told me she would."

He shook Viola off, leaning forward to grip Liv's arms, yanking her to standing. "Yer not ready for the stage, bitch."

Liv stared down at him, using her height for all it was worth. For once, she didn't mind being taller than a man.

He chuckled. "That bitter look will only feed the frenzy, ducky. Them boys below like a filly they cin break." He gripped the front edges of Liv's carriage dress, ripping it wide, the line of small jet buttons holding it closed popping from the wool fabric, scattering to the ground.

He smirked, taking in her bosom now only covered by her white shift and her stays. "There. That be what they be lookin' fer. Leave the jacket on yer arms—they be wanting to see the quality ye come with. But they be wanting to see more of yer diddeys."

He reached for her stays, yanking the binding fabric downward.

Liv's shocked stupor fell from her in waves, rage expanding in her belly, sending fire outward along her arms. She lifted her hand, gathering angle to strike him. Strike him with all her might, consequences be dammed.

His grubby fingers went to her shift, gripping, tearing wide the fine cloth. Her breasts spilled forth, her nipples bare to the air.

Liv swung, cuffing the side of the owner's head just as a crash on the other side of the door thundered into the room.

The owner staggered to the side from the blow, but it didn't topple him off his feet. "Bitch." He looked to Viola. "Give me your knife."

Her eyes wide, Viola shook her head.

The owner advanced on Viola. "Give me yer fuckin' dagger, me lovey, and ye'll be spared."

Viola gripped her reticule to her belly, the hilt of the dagger hanging from the opening of the bag. She stepped backward, her head swinging back and forth.

Another crash on the door, and the wood shook on its hinges. The girl screamed with the sound, scooting herself backward on the bed.

"Don't worry, me lovey, I would never hurt ye." Cornering Viola, the owner's hands went slowly forward toward the black hilt of the blade, a cat trying to catch a mouse.

Liv grasped her jacket, trying to cover herself with one hand while reaching downward to drag her stays back upward over her breasts.

With a grunt, the owner ripped the dagger from Viola's bag just as the door swung open, slamming into the wall.

"Liv."

Tieran filled the doorway, his face savage, fists bloody.

A warrior unleashed. A warrior with the blood of a hundred warriors before him pumping through his veins. A warrior determined to save what was his.

For one gasped breath, fear cut through her heart. Not fear at Tieran. Fear that he would think the worst of what she was doing here in a brothel. Fear that he would think she had willingly brought this girl here to be sold.

Fear that he would believe her vengeance was more important than him.

Tieran's blue eyes met hers, her dread vanishing in the next breath.

His eyes held no questions, no suspicion—just chilling rage that swirled with desperate relief as his eyes swept up and down her body. Satisfied she was unharmed, his blue eyes locked with hers. Only brutal determination to get her out of there remained, burning in his eyes.

He rushed into the room and Liv spotted a mess of limbs and inert bodies on the hallway floor behind him. He filled the space and reached for her with Lord Lockston on his heels and Mr. Niles stopping at the doorway.

Her legs going weak in relief, Liv exhaled a short cry. She didn't know how or why they had just appeared, but she would thank fate a thousand times over for not leaving her to the rabid wolves.

Viola screamed and Liv spun to her, watching in horror as the owner twisted Viola in front of him, the dagger at Viola's neck.

"Viola, don't move," Liv screamed.

A pistol appeared to her left, drawn and cocked. Liv looked up at Tieran, shocked that he had moved so quickly.

"No, Tieran, don't—you'll hit Viola."

"Does it matter, Liv?"

"Don't even think it, ye bastard." The owner spat the words out, hiding behind Viola's head. "Ye make a move and I slice her neck."

Liv turned her head, her voice a whisper as she went to her toes to reach Tieran's ear. "Tieran, no, we have to get out of here—I don't know where she put it."

"Put what?" he asked, his eyes trained on the owner.

"The oil." Liv had to fight to keep the screech out of her whisper. "Viola said it's everywhere. She's gone mad, Tieran—she means to torch the place. It could go with one dropped match."

He whispered out the side of his mouth to her, his eyes never leaving Viola and the owner. "We ripped this floor to shreds, Liv—not a man standing. Who is setting it off?"

"I don't know. Her? Someone she hired?"

"Hell, Liv," he muttered under his breath.

Liv dropped to her flat feet, looking behind Tieran's shoulders. "Mr. Niles—take this girl—get her out of here—get her out of the East End as fast as you can—she can tell you where she lives."

Mr. Niles stepped into the room, sliding behind Lockston, Tieran, and Liv to get to the girl on the bed. "Yes, my lady. But I should wait for you." He pulled free a knife, quickly sawing through the rope binding the girl's wrists together.

"No. Go. I have a carriage," Lockston said.

"You take the girl and I'll slit this one's neck, I will." The owner jerked Viola backward, tightening his grip around her.

"You will do no such thing, because the second she drops from you is the second I have a clear shot to your skull." Tieran's threat was laced with brutal efficiency. His eyes not veering from Viola and her captor, his voice dropped to a whisper. "Liv—tell Lockston what you just told me."

Liv scooted behind Tieran, moving to whisper into Lockston's ear. Tieran's friend had a bloody cut along his

cheek and his fists were dripping with smears of blood. Tieran clearly wasn't the only one that knew how to fight.

She quickly repeated the words. Lockston looked down at her, his eyes narrowing. He looked up at the back of Tieran's head. "Hell, Reggard."

"Exactly." Tieran didn't twitch, steadfast with his aim on the owner cowering behind Viola. "Clear the place, every floor, Lockston. Go."

Lockston didn't hesitate, turning and running out the door.

"Liv. Get yourself out of here," Tieran said, his voice steel. "Go downstairs and two blocks to the south. You'll see my horse by a coach with two guards at the back. Tell them who you are. They will get you out of here."

Her feet ached to twitch toward the door, wanting nothing more than to run from this place. Run as fast and as far as she could. But her heels dug in. "No. I'm not leaving without Viola." She wanted to grab Tieran's arm, but didn't want to jostle the pistol. "And I'm not leaving without you."

"Liv. Go." Growled, Tieran's two words shook the air around him.

The floor above them started to thump, feet running along the boards, rattling the building.

"What the hell is that?" The owner looked up, his slimy hand twisting the blade on Viola's neck.

Viola smiled, seemingly unaware that the dagger had drawn blood, two lines dripping down her neck. "They know, don't they? They are all running. Running like rats. They won't make it."

"What did you do, bitch?" The owner snarled the question in Viola's ear.

"Viola—no—don't say a word." Liv took a step toward her friend.

"Liv." Tieran reached out to grab her arm, yanking her to a stop.

Viola laughed. "The flames of hell are here for you, Bear. Here for all of you—all of us. They are going to light them—light them right now."

"Bitch." The owner screeched, an animal trapped.

He slit Viola's throat in one quick motion, the knife digging deep, separating skin.

Liv watched, horrified as her friend slid from the owner's grasp, dropping slowly to the ground, her eyes still glowing with madness.

Liv shoved Tieran's hand off her arm, moving toward Viola. Moving to catch her. To stop the blood.

A blast next to her ear. It stopped her, throwing her off balance to the side, falling, filling her head with nothing but an echo ringing in her ears.

Liv hit the wall, catching herself, and she realized that Tieran had fired the pistol. It hit the owner low in the shoulder, slamming him backward against the red drapes. He slipped down the wall, clutching the bullet hole, grasping at the crimson velvet surrounding him.

He opened his mouth, swearing, blood sputtering, gurgling out the sound.

In the next instant, Liv was lifted, flying through the air. Tieran had picked her up, carrying her along the skinny hallways.

She shoved at his chest, squirming. "Tieran—no—we have to get Viola."

He wrapped his arms tighter around her torso and legs, shoving the door open at the end of the hall with his shoulder.

"She's gone Liv. Gone."

He ran down the rickety stairs, moving through the main room of the brothel, now eerily empty. Yet the earlier haze still hung thick in the air.

Out the side door, Tieran carried Liv down the alley and moved across the street from the brothel, setting her down onto her wobbly feet.

Masses of people scurried madcap in all directions around them. Some clothed, some attempting to drag on clothing and boots as they ran. Prostitutes stuffed bills and coins and whatever was salvaged on the escape from the building into the bosoms of their dresses as they dodged through the people.

Dazed, Liv tried to drag her eyes from the scene but could not. "Tieran—"

"Stay here. Do not move a muscle. I need to find Lockston, make sure he is clear from the building."

Tieran left her side, a boulder moving with purpose through the crowd. She watched his progress, his head bobbing above the mass of people, and saw the moment that he found Lockston halfway down the block.

She exhaled. Tieran was safe. Lockston was safe. Mr. Niles was retuning the girl to her home. And Viola…Viola was dead.

It was all she needed to know.

Liv walked over to a random hack stuck in the middle of the scurrying bodies. Wedging her toe onto the stowed metal step, she jumped up on it, balancing long enough to steal the lantern that hung swinging next to the carriage door.

Lifting the lantern high, she moved through the thinning crowd, crossing the street.

Stopping by the front door to the brothel, she looked up at the building. Still fully lit from within, the wooden structure sat still, all people having moved far from it.

She looked down, kicking the toe of her boot through the muck at the foundation of the building. Bending over, she rubbed her fingers into the muck, then held them to her nose, sniffing. Oil.

"Liv—no. What the hell are you doing?" Tieran shouted from a distance, his footsteps thundering toward her.

"You need to get away from there, Liv." He skidded to a stop beside her, out of breath.

"No. I do not think I am done. Not yet." She looked from the building to him.

He looked ready to pounce, ready to drag her to safety. But he held himself back, resisting manhandling her—at least for the moment.

"What else do you need, Liv? Heaven to hell—what?"

She sucked in a deep breath, her eyes going to the building in front of her.

"Burn. I need it to burn to the ground."

He grabbed her chin, forcing her to turn to look up at him.

She stared at Tieran, letting him see every ounce of the torment still festering in her soul, refusing to let her go.

He exhaled a hard breath, his grip on her chin tightening. "Is this the thing that will release you?"

"Yes. I hope. I…" She shook her head, her chin knocking against his palm. "I don't want to become Viola, Tieran. I *can't* become her." Her eyelids closed, her body shaking with an inhale. She opened her eyes to him. "But I need it to burn."

Tieran leaned down, taking the handle of the lantern from her hand. He released her, turning to the building, holding the light of the lantern to the base of the wall.

After moments of searching, he grunted, standing straight and moving to the mess of advertisement bills stuck on the outside wall of the building. He ripped several down, twisting the paper into a long roll in his hands.

"Tieran—you can't." Lockston appeared out of the crowd in the street, stepping in front of Tieran, his hand on Tieran's chest. "You can't just burn down a building."

"Is everyone out?"

"Everyone but the owner—he was still alive when I passed him."

"Are the surrounding buildings brick?"

"Yes. But you can't, Reggard." Lockston's hand on Tieran's chest gave a slight shove.

For a second, Tieran looked as though he would strike his friend. Instead, he opened his mouth. "I stand by Liv, Lockston. This is what will happen—what needs to happen." Tieran's mouth clamped shut, and he stared at his friend. Stared at him, unflinching.

Seconds passed, and Lockston gave him one nod, his hand dropping to his side as he stepped away to the street.

Tieran moved to the front door of the brothel and opened the glass door of the lantern, lighting the end of the twisted roll of paper. Holding the paper torch high, away from the door, he set the lantern on the ground, snuffing the flame of it, and then picked it up, smashing it against the wooden door. Oil splashed everywhere.

"Tieran—wait." Liv grabbed his free hand, pulling it toward her belly.

He turned to her, his mouth a grim line as he held the flaming paper high and far from her.

"This is not you, Tieran. I refuse to have you compromise yourself, your integrity—who you are. Not again. And never for me—I cannot be the cause of it." She held out her hand, fingers bending, motioning for the lit torch that was quickly burning toward his fingers. "I will do it."

"And you can be sure as hell I am not going to burden you with it either, Liv." The frown of his lips softened, almost turning upright. His eyes met hers, the determination in them absolute.

"Tieran—"

"The point is, Liv, you don't have to do it. For you, my actions are never a compromise. You are the only one I do not question. So if you say it burns—it burns."

Before she could react, he tossed the paper torch at the door and grabbed her in one fluid motion.

He wrapped her in the cocoon of his chest, lifting her and rushing them from the building. She could hear

popping, hear flames bursting to life. A sudden burst of heat moved past them, crisping the edges of her hair.

Not until they were a block away, a safe distance from the building, did Tieran set her down. By the time she could look past him back to the brothel, the flames had engulfed the structure, licking ever higher through the fog into the sky.

She exhaled, her chest tightening in pain at what Tieran had just done for her. The compromise of his integrity.

He stepped in front of her, blocking her view of the flames. "Do not look back upon it, Liv. Do not wonder on the right or wrong of what we just did." He gently turned her, tucking her under his arm as he propelled her forward away from the brothel.

Liv exhaled, her feet numbly shuffling along the cobblestone, so slow Tieran had to rein his stride to tiny steps. Her mind as dazed as her feet, she attempted to order her thoughts.

Her look snapped to Tieran's face. "You came for me."

"I will always come for you, Liv." His arm tightened around her shoulders as he leaned down to kiss the top of her head. "Through the gates of hell, I will come for you."

"But how did you know what happened?"

"Mr. Niles. He said he was waiting for you at your townhouse, and then you abandoned him out your back door—oddly so—so he followed you when you got into that coach with people he didn't recognize. After he saw where you ended, he fetched me."

Her mouth drew, perturbed, to the side. "I both adore him for getting you and I am slightly miffed that he would do so."

A grin lifted the corners of Tieran's mouth. "Honestly, Liv, the man gets a healthy bonus from my coffers to act just as he did tonight."

She pushed off from his chest, not escaping his hold in the slightest. "What?"

He yanked her tight alongside his thick torso. "I mean to protect you always, Liv, whether you realize it or not. Making sure you are always accompanied with someone I trust is part of that. And it was just easier to utilize Mr. Niles for that purpose, since you already trust him, and I don't think I could have convinced you to give him up."

"Trust he has completely lost." She crossed her arms across her ribcage.

Tieran shook his head. "The man is more loyal to you than you would ever know. Let us just say he drove a hard bargain when it came to his agreement to alert me if you are ever in trouble."

"I hope he made you pay triple what I pay him."

"Ten times over, or so he says. It is probably more than that."

Liv chuckled. "Serves you right—and where did Lockston appear from?"

"Fletch was in the main room for the auction. He saw you as you were dragged in, but as he was alone, he was waiting to purchase you in the auction, should it have come to that. It is the safest way to extract a female from that place."

Liv looked up at him, her breath heavy in her chest for a moment. "You did not question what I was doing at the brothel—not even seeing that girl with her wrists bound—with what Mr. Niles would have seen and told you."

"For all I worry on your actions, Liv, I know you." He kissed the top of her forehead. "I know you would never hurt an innocent girl. Never."

Liv nodded, humbled to her core that Tieran still believed in the good in her—after all she had done—after what he had just done for her, setting flame to the building, sealing the fate of the owner, burning Viola's body.

He believed in her, yet she had not been strong enough to walk away—she had needed to see it all burn. Needed it in her soul.

Maybe she was not so far removed from the madness that had overtaken Viola.

Liv could not resist craning her neck backward to see the flames as she walked.

She had dealt in vengeance for some time, but she had never meant to take Tieran with her down that path. He didn't deserve it. He deserved only the best of her.

Her stride suddenly halted.

Tieran stopped with her, stepping in front of her, gently turning her face from the fire to him. He looked down at her, his eyes wary, remnants of the warrior that she had forced to the surface still etched along the lines of his face.

He waited until her eyes met his, her focus solely on him. "I can see what you are thinking, my love. But there is no higher ground here, Liv. Some things just need to be destroyed."

His words hit her—sank into her mind, sank into her belly, sank into her heart.

He was right.

And she was done.

{ CHAPTER 24 }

His knuckles soft on the door to Liv's chambers, Tieran peeked his head into her dressing room before anyone answered.

Her maid absent, Liv sat on a striped upholstered bench at the rosewood writing desk by the window. She stared down at a piece of vellum as she dipped her quill into the inkwell and then set the nib to paper. Her gown, a golden concoction, swept in a graceful fold across her back, dipping between her shoulder blades to highlight her long neck and the elaborate plaiting of her dark hair into her upsweep.

Tieran stepped into the room, closing the door quietly behind him. "You are ready?"

Her head bent, she nodded, her quill not stopping its scratching across the paper.

His fingers itching to trace the line of skin along the top of her gown, Tieran crossed the room to stand behind her, his knuckles gently brushing upward along her shoulder to her neck.

She softly purred, her head curling against his hand as her fingers stayed busy writing. Lifting the quill from the paper, she turned slightly to look up at him.

Tieran's breath caught in his throat. Liv looked an absolute treasure in the gown—a gentle gold, the fabric shimmered with interwoven strands of golden thread catching the light. The color of it pulled the gold in her brown eyes to the forefront, the twinkle of the dress reflected in her gaze as she looked up at him. Sweet and wanton.

She grinned.

Definitely wanton.

Tieran could feel himself hardening, and he clamped down on his wayward thoughts. It was not the time to be focused on removing the gown from her body.

He looked past her to the paper on the desk. "What are you writing?"

She sighed, the smile drifting from her face as she looked to the paper. "I am writing a list."

His eyes scanned the paper. A list of names.

Every one on the list, a male.

Tieran's gut hardened. "Is this a list of what I think it is?"

"Yes." She nodded, not looking up at him.

Tieran imperceptibly inhaled, stilling as he let his instant reaction quell. Control in hand, he set his hands about her waist, lifting her for a moment before he sat down on the bench and then settled her onto his lap. His voice neutral, his forehead tilted to the list. "Why?"

Her fingers went to the top left edge of the paper, rubbing the corner between her forefinger and thumb as she stared at it. "I do not want to lose it. Lose what Viola died for—how she got these names—what she sacrificed for them."

She looked at Tieran. "Do not mistake me, Viola went far, too far, stealing that girl. But before that, before she broke into madness, she was always steadfast in her need to stop the terror—stop what happens to those innocent girls that are stolen. She just lost her way at the end. Consumed."

Liv sighed. "And it seems such a waste to let the list go—it was what she fought so hard for, and I did not want to lose it. I needed to write them all down before I forgot—before I couldn't anymore."

The heavy weight in Tieran's gut expanded into a pit of fear and fury—Liv could not let this go—yet he willed himself not to react. Keeping his voice level, he watched her face carefully as he chose his words with caution. "And now that you have it, what are you to do with it?"

She inhaled, the creamy skin of her chest rising above the front cut of her gown. Looking down at the paper, it took her a long moment to answer, the rubbing of the paper between her fingers turning rapid. "I am at a loss. I do not know what to do with the list."

Her fingers stopped their motion, dropping the paper to the desk as she turned in Tieran's lap to fully face him. "What happened at the Jolly Vassal the other night—what happened after we escaped from it—all of that stripped me of everything. Everything I was, everything I have wanted in the past three years, everything that I have done. All of it was gone—and I was left with one thing—one thing alone."

"Which was?"

"You. I was left with you, Tieran, and I knew it without a doubt. You are the only thing that is important to me." Her hands lifted, clasping the sides of his face. "Our life together—it is what I always wanted—at my core—all that really mattered. I want us. Not vengeance. Not another's pain. Not imagining the worst in every man I encounter. I want none of it. Only you."

The pit in his gut dissolved, lifting to his heart, making it swell. Swell so wide his chest hurt. He was looking at the true Liv once more and his pride in her, his love, his gratefulness that she was right there, his to hold—filled him, choking his words.

His hands tightened around her waist. "You have me, my love."

She smiled, genuine, sparkling so bright she could light a million stars.

"So can I make a suggestion?" he asked.

Her dark eyebrows lifted. "Yes?"

"Give me the list."

Her eyes narrowed, instant suspicion crossing her face as her hands dropped from his face. "Why?"

"With your blessing, I would like to discuss the list with Lockston and Newdale. Will you allow it?"

"Yes, I can only presume you have good reason." Her words measured, she swiveled on his lap, grabbing the paper from the desk and handing it to him.

Tieran waited until her fingers dropped from the paper and it was firmly in his control. He quickly folded it. "Good, because I have already done so."

"What?" She swatted his chest. "A rat you are."

He laughed. "Yes, maybe I am. But a rat with your best interests at heart."

She poked at the folded piece of paper. "What do you intend to do with it?"

"We want the list so we can take care of it."

"Take care of it?" Her golden brown eyes bored into him. "What does that mean, Tieran?"

He shrugged. "It means it is no longer your concern."

"Not my concern—it's my list."

"Not anymore." Ignoring the indignation commandeering her face, Tieran leaned back to tuck the list into a pocket deep inside his jacket.

"Tieran—"

"Liv, you need to stop." He wrapped his hands around her waist and yanked her closer to his chest. "You need to pretend you never made the list, never handed it over to me."

Her bottom lip jutted out. "And you need to tell me more than that."

He sighed. He hadn't planned on telling her anything—didn't want to tell her anything. Yet the willfulness that had sparked to life in her eyes told him this day would not go quite as planned if he kept his mouth shut. "I offer you this—anything and everything that is done in regards to the list will be done with complete discretion. But it will be done."

"You, Lockston and Newdale—why the three of you?"

"We are men of action, Liv. We always will be." His hands tightened around the small of her back, the intensity of his words sending a tremor into his voice. "And there is no greater action than protecting our families—keeping our wives safe, making our world safer for our daughters. That is why."

Liv nodded, smiling, her head tilting to the side. "You think daughter?"

"I think daughters. And sons. So many I forget their names." His left hand moved from her back, squeezing between them to flatten along her belly. "But first, my love, it is time for a new oath. We need to go downstairs and get married. Everyone is waiting."

She blinked hard, appearing almost surprised they had still had that small matter of their wedding to attend to. "They are?"

"They are."

"I lost track of time." She scrambled off Tieran's lap, smoothing her gown as she stood, shaking the wrinkles from the silk of the golden skirt.

Tieran stood, unable to resist wrapping his arms around her once more, wrinkles be dammed. "I like this color on you. It matches your eyes."

"And it matches your heart."

He grinned. "Aunt Penelope will be pleased to see you in color. I believe she thinks my wooing of you has been a personal favor to her."

"Why would she care?" Her fingers ran lightly along the line of his jacket lapel.

"You don't even want to know, Liv."

"She will win some coin, by chance?"

Tieran shrugged.

Liv sighed, a grin cracking her face. "Was my dress at the Jacobson's ball not enough?"

His head slanted to the side with an exhale. "Apparently, there were too many conflicting reports about what was seen. If it's any consolation, I don't imagine she will actually accept the coin. Winning is more than enough for her. Forgive her."

"I do not intend to ever speak to her on the matter."

He smiled. "Magnanimous of you."

"I have much better things to focus on."

"Such as?"

Her chest lifted in a deep breath, her golden brown eyes looking up at him with nothing but love. "Kiss me before we go down?"

The chuckle stayed on his lips until he met her mouth, taking her, and he lost himself in her. Her soft lips gentle but demanding, matching his every motion, just as she always had since that very first kiss by the stairs. Kissing her was still a gift.

The surprises would always be there. The new layers to discover.

Yet now, the present was his.

Every moment, every day with Liv, the best gift.

{ EPILOGUE }

The unearthly scream ripped through the walls, tearing down the stairs to the library.

They weren't going to stop him.

Not this time.

Tieran set his head down, barreling toward the library door.

Just as his fingertips touched the doorknob, he was tackled from the side, his body slamming against the wall.

Intercepted, but not beaten. He shoved, twisting, struggling against the four hands pinning him against the mahogany paneling.

He gained one foot of space from the wall.

Only to be battered back against it.

A new breath and the scream from above exploded into the air once more.

"The scream—it isn't right. Not right." His shoulders locked in place against the wall, Tieran looked from Lockston on his right to Newdale on his left. Both of his friends strained, grimacing against his strength trying to fling them from his body. "Bloody well let me loose, you bastards."

Tieran heaved his chest outward, kicking off from the paneling. Their hands clamped against his shoulders, Lockston and Newdale shoved him back with a hard clunk onto the wall, the hanging painting near his head flinging out, almost falling from the force of the vibration.

"The scream is a scream, Reggard. Stop trying to break free," Newdale shouted in his ear. "Ara and Talia are up there—"

"As I should be." Tieran's snarl, his latest attempt to escape Lockston and Newdale, did nothing to alleviate the wildfire burning through every muscle, every nerve.

He had to make it to Liv.

"As you would be, if you hadn't tried to attack the midwife, Tieran," Lockston said. "Liv cannot birth a baby and control you at the same time. She will suffer this and she will make it through."

The scream hit a chilling height.

The rage in his veins bursting, Tieran tried to break both of their grips on his body. They scuffled until Lockston and Newdale managed to slam him against the wall again. This time the painting slipped from its hook, crashing to the floor.

"It's not right—the babe wailed a half hour ago, we all heard it cry—she should be done. Done. Not this. Not this screaming. I need to get up there." Tieran's voice had dropped from the growl to desperation. He looked at Newdale. "There's no reason for it—for her screams."

Newdale's grip on his shoulder tightened. "Ara will come down, Reggard. She swore she would, the moment you are needed—no matter what."

The next scream came in a blast, slipping to breathless shards.

Tieran's head swiveled to Lockston. "And I'm not needed for that? It's the same, Fletch. The same as before. She is slipping from me."

Lockston's mouth tightened, his head shaking. "It's not the same, Tieran. Not by far."

"It is."

"No." Lockston's voice went low, vehement. "I was there too. It's not the same. Not by far. Liv is not Rachel, Tieran. This is not happening again."

"You don't know that."

"I do." Lockston had to swallow, choking out his words. "Liv is strong. She is your match. And she will make it through this."

Tieran stared at him, wanting desperately to believe the resolve in Lockston's eyes—make the resolve a reality. But he was helpless.

A tiny whimper made it into the library.

The whimper grew louder as the door opened.

Talia appeared in the doorway clutching a wiggling, whimpering bundle of white cloth to her chest. She took in the scene quickly and stepped to the three men bunched against the wall. "Tieran, you need to meet your son."

She elbowed her husband's back. Lockston released his clamp on Tieran. Newdale followed suit. Lifting the white bundle to Tieran, she set it along his chest.

It took Tieran long seconds to lift his hands, taking the swaddling from Talia.

His breath held, he looked down. A tiny face. Red and splotchy and whimpering, his mouth smacking.

It took everything from him. All rage, all strength, all fear, all thought. The tiny face took everything he was, and demolished it.

Wonder. Wonder was what he was left with.

"And now you need to come upstairs with me," Talia said. "Ara is still upstairs with Liv."

His look whipped up to her. "She is...is..."

Talia smiled. "She is well, Tieran. And she needs to see you direct."

Clutching his son tight to his chest, he moved past Talia, finally free to see his wife again.

Tieran stepped into the bed chamber without knocking, desperate to see with his own eyes his wife alive and breathing. The only thing that had slowed his run was the small babe he was carrying.

The midwife bustled about the bed, removing blood-soaked sheets, and Ara stood by the head of the bed, her back to the door.

In the middle of the frenzy, Liv sat propped up in the bed, her dark hair a wet mess, sweat still glistening on her brow.

Liv looked from Ara to him, a weary smile instant on her lips. Her hand lifted, fingers motioning him to her.

Tieran strode across the room, moving to the opposite side of the bed from Ara. Sitting next to Liv's thigh, his hand went behind her head, clutching her, needing to feel in his skin that she was actually alive. Had not slipped from him. Had not left him for death.

He swallowed, all words lost to him.

Liv smiled at him, her golden eyes sparking through the weariness on her face. "You have not noticed."

He shook his head. "What?" The one word barely made it past the lump in his throat.

"What Ara is holding."

His eyebrows drawing together, Tieran looked from his wife to Ara standing across from him. She held a white bundle of cloth to her chest, much the same as the one cradled in his arm.

Newdale's wife grinned at him.

"What…" Tieran looked down at the bundle in his arms to assure himself he hadn't somehow set his son down without thought. Mouth still smacking, his son was secure in his arm.

He looked up at Ara once more, his eyes travelling to his wife.

"Two, Tieran," Liv said, her voice soft.

"Two?"

She nodded, her head tilting toward Ara. "And she is a girl."

Tieran's hold on the back of Liv's head tightened as his gaze went to the bundle in Ara's arms. Ara took a step forward, handing the babe—his girl—to Liv. She stepped out of the room with the midwife, leaving them alone.

The door clicked closed, and his world froze for a long breath, the reality setting into his mind, into his heart. His daughter in Liv's arms. His son in his arms. His wife sitting before him, breathing, alive, and beaming at him.

Her grin widened. "You had me carrying two of your babes, Tieran. That was extremely arduous."

The chuckle rumbled from deep in his chest, spurring from the mass of unspent energy of the last hours. It erupted, jarring his son and sending him into a wail.

Liv lifted her hand, slipping the tip of her pinky into the babe's mouth. He quieted.

"So I heard." His hand squeezed her neck. "I apologize for that."

"There is no need." The grin remained on her face. "Just promise me we will keep it to one at a time hence forth."

"I will make every effort to do so."

Her head shook in a half-hearted scold as her golden brown eyes met his. "Thank you—for you are not the smallest man to bear children with. And let it be known that I blame you for kissing me by those stairs so many years ago and making me fall in love with you."

"I will take the blame. Happily, my love." He leaned forward to kiss her brow. "I can claim that I knew from the start what a splendid match we are."

She laughed, a weary but heartfelt sound. "Then I take it back. It was me that made you fall to my charms."

"That I did, Liv. That I did." The wonder in his chest bloomed tenfold. His look went from the delicate face of his daughter peeking out from the blanket, to the tiny unfocused eyes of his son, to his wife's face, to her golden brown eyes. She had never been more beautiful.

The peace emanating from her wrapped around him—wrapped around all of them—and tears slipped down his face.

Always another layer.

Always another present.

~ About the Author ~

K.J. Jackson is the author of *The Hold Your Breath Series,*
The Lords of Fate Series, The Lords of Action Series,
and *The Flame Moon Series.*

She specializes in historical and paranormal romance,
loves to travel (road trips are the best!), and is a sucker for a
good story in any genre. She lives in Minnesota with
her husband, two children, and a dog who
has taken the sport of bed-hogging
to new heights.

Visit her at www.kjjackson.com

~ AUTHOR'S NOTE ~

Thank you for allowing my stories into your life
and time—it is an honor!

My next historical series will debut in spring 2017.

If you missed the *Hold Your Breath, Lords of Fate,*
or *Lords of Action* series, be sure to check out these historical
romances (each is a stand-alone story): **Stone Devil Duke,
Unmasking the Marquess, My Captain, My Earl,
Worth of a Duke, Earl of Destiny, Marquess of Fortune,
Vow,** and *Promise*.

Never miss a new release or sale!
Be sure to sign up for my VIP Email List at
www.KJJackson.com
(email addresses are precious, so out of respect,
you'll only hear from me when I actually have real news).

Interested in Paranormal Romance?
In the meantime, if you want to switch genres and check
out my Flame Moon paranormal romance series, **Flame
Moon #1**, the first book in the series, is currently free
(ebook) at all stores. **Flame Moon** is a stand-alone story, so
no worries on getting sucked into a cliffhanger. But number
two in the series, **Triple Infinity**, ends with a fun cliff, so be
forewarned. Number three in the series, **Flux Flame**, ties up
that portion of the series.

Connect with me!
www.KJJackson.com
https://www.facebook.com/kjjacksonauthor

Printed in Great Britain
by Amazon

35529590R00175